AUTOMATIC
WORLD

AUTOMATIC WORLD

STRUAN
SINCLAIR

DOUBLEDAY CANADA

Doubleday Canada and colophon are trademarks

Library and Archives of Canada Cataloguing in Publication
has been applied for

ISBN: 978-0-385-66470-7

This book is a work of fiction. Names, characters, places and incidents are
products of the author's imagination or are used fictitiously. Any resemblance
to actual events or locales or persons, living or dead, is entirely coincidental.

Book design: Kelly Hill
Printed and bound in the USA

Published in Canada by Doubleday Canada,
a division of Random House of Canada Limited

Visit Random House of Canada Limited's website: www.randomhouse.ca

10 9 8 7 6 5 4 3 2 1

For Victoria, Madoc,
Oscar and Holmes—not an automaton
among them.

THE TRAIN

The story you are thinking of begins with a train. This train will arrive; it will not arrive, everything follows from this. You have in your head an image, this image, and one or two facts: the train, a foot. Not invention, you remind yourself, but selection. So, the train, a steam train; and the foot, a mechanical foot. You will begin with what you know and more will come to you. The train, the foot, the aftermath. It begins with the train, with the temporal trick that means the train arrives in the town of far away Mither Harbour even as it leaves St. William's Arch. It is autumn, it is dusk. These are the details you must fill in. Was the night mild? Was the wait long? Did a station lamp flicker? Everything in this story begins with the train; with the brute fact of it, the sequence of it, the timing of it; time accounted for and time lost. It was autumn. It was dusk. It was mild. It had rained. The platform was busy. The station lamps were due for topping up. Were the signal lights in order? Were the brakemen drunk? In the aftermath, this will all matter. The stitching of events will be picked at and examined. Where. When. How. Why. So much causal netting to be carefully unsnarled.

You have learned the knack of splitting consciousness. You have the train before you and you distribute across it a set of figures: a girl, a bereft young man, an inventor and his drudge. To these figures you apportion stories: a mercy killing, a drawn-out suicide, exquisite machines. That these figures and these stories are connected you take for granted; you can point to theme, trajectory, origin point. You observe that these stories share a furniture and you give examples: blankets, sidekicks, wax, artificial limbs. There are resonances, echoes, things that come back. Characters recycled through different parts. An isthmus of shared plot. And yet—

And yet, it troubles you. The overall picture. The connections between connections. Provenance—it is a question of provenance, where the stories and their elements came from and how they fit.

You pause. Check your notes. You've gone over and over it. You'll get there.

So: the girl, the bereft young man, the inventor and his drudge. Mercy killing, suicide, exquisite machines. And you, of course. You. You have written down everything you ever knew or were told you knew waiting for something to strike you—and here something has struck you. In the train you have at last a socket for this story that contains within it all those stories you have listened to and learned. You have the main points and the fine detailing that will put flesh, as it were, on the bones. You have all this in working memory, and as you build it out loud you will add the repertoire of gestures you have practised which will signify passion, hope, fear, longing, attentiveness, shame, despair. In this performance you hope will set you free what is paramount is naturalness; you will be natural, you will be free. It is a performance, of course, they'll guess that straight off. It doesn't matter that they see you doing it, so long as they don't see how.

Difficult to manage all this, but possible. And by now you have experience. Here you are, speaking on request. It is a kind of homecoming for you and people are gathered and listening.

They are not spectators, not exactly. They, some of them, will decide where you are to end up. Among them are those who have told these stories or parts of these stories to you, and here you are returning the favour. A woman you cannot see clearly asks if you want water, a break—

I'm fine, you say, update your expression, narrow your focus to include only her. Sorry, I'm nervous, give me a sec—

Stop. Check your notes. The train—it's the basis, the fulcrum, stay with it.

You say:

It begins with the train—

And you're off, and they follow, those who can be bothered, and where things demand a little stretch you provide it, and where the action drags you hoop it along.

What are the elements? Trains, you say. This is a story of trains.

The characters, the themes. First, the characters: an inventor's dream of a folded world. The vengeful drudge. The girl with her misspent affections. A suicide father, his grieving son. Next, the themes. Storytelling. The long recuperation. Loss, yes; but also miracle constructions. Filial love and quack cookery. Grief and old prosthetics. Repetition, overlap, a pair of red gloves. Themes to organize, to structure and be satisfied. Themes, too, that diverge. Trains to link but also to sequester— four trains for four stories.

Why four? Why these four? You appreciate that this train is bound by certain laws: physical, temporal. But you see also that it is bound by narrative laws, story laws, with their distinctive causality and effect. You walk through this train but you cannot alter the fact that it is a train. You cannot change its route. You cannot make yourself, your wishes, understood to these characters, you cannot save them. And in the same way, the stories you have are the stories you have. You can cut a little, shift things about, yes. But their basic structure, their interleaving, the points at which they merge and disappear, their net effects; these are not negotiable.

Right, you say. I'm ready.

The train by now is a real train, the foot a real foot. You point out the plaque placed, unremarkably, by the freight entrance of the station that tells the story of the crash of 1855 in which as few as 197 and as many as 230 may have died, some of them children. You identify the location of the foot in a library that anyone with an interest in such medical curiosities may visit. There is the girl, a real girl, and the town, a real town you all might drive to if you liked. You—you're real enough, standing before them in your flat-seamed trousers, your Basque hat.

You. Between all of this and them—you. And you are— what? The elements, recurring images, expressions, motifs. *Red. He tries to tell them. September 7th. Three minutes. Grapple. Foot. Terrible terrible. I'm full up.* These words and elements are migratory. They will loop through your story like eyes on a line. The train, the foot, the aftermath. In and out, everywhere. This movement may seem haphazard; you find it difficult, even now, after all these interventions, to keep things straight. But maybe it doesn't matter that they be kept straight. In the story you are telling straight-keeping is not a virtue. Better modality, better eccentricity. And what you will make of this train and this foot will be modal, eccentric. Your challenge: to give them a story, a proper story. You have fixed upon this train, this foot.

You begin.

I

I AM BORN

In the beginning of September, sometime in the morning when the light is weak, I find myself emerging from an elongated dream. In the dream, only filaments of which I remember clearly, I perform a series of actions. I shudder, and seem to decide something. I raise my hands above my head. I open a door and step out. I fall. Each of these gestures has a rigged and artificial overtone, as if I were posing for a set of stills, a flicker-book that reads the same backwards and forwards. Shuddering. Raising my hands above my head. Opening a door, stepping out, falling. These actions, the word terrible spoken just to the left of my head.

From this dream to a still and whitewashed world. Pale rectangle, barely lit. Linen. A ticking, fragile and insistent as insects' wings. Something streaming in my mouth. Clutches of plastic in my wrist, throat, penis. Intravenous. Catheter. Mask and bag. I am in a hospital. Wall. Tube. Hurt. Cat-language, plant-language, the shock of something newly, dimly, aware of itself; I am awake, and I stay that way for long enough to realize that I am ill, well enough at last to know it.

—

I am thinking of this day as I stand in a station, waiting for a train. The train, due to arrive at 19:40 for an 8:00 p.m. departure, has been twice delayed. The backlit sign has erased and re-inscribed the arrival time as 19:48 and then 19:58 and finally slapped up the first three letters of the word "delayed," which happen also to be the first three letters of the word "delete," which appears to be what has happened to this train. Now the deleted train's passengers abandon the platform for the café and the waiting rooms papered with obscure coats of arms, the laconic heraldry of nostalgia tourism, to disseminate the crisis over sleek, new-generation phones. I find a seat that isn't stained or broken, watch the grass beat the wet tracks, and listen for the train I am waiting for, that is no longer about to come.

Down the platform a whiskered old gent with a limp reaches up for an overhanging lamp. A girl in a raincoat stands at the edge. A man holds his suitcase close by him. Say what you will about props in a fiction, there is honesty in their fixedness, their cinching of function to place. The station PA crackles and I wait for the word I know will come—*terrible*—flip the card from the stack in my head.

At some point, that first day becomes the last of the fifteen days that I have been asleep. This I am told by the nursing specialist assigned to me since I was brought here by helicopter. She introduces herself, pointing to her hands, shoes and a photo-tag she wears at waist level.

Eni. As in, Eni thing I can do for you?

For much of this early time Eni is with me. I know her by her scent.

Soap, fragrance-neutral, she tells me. Won't make you sneeze.

By her scent and her jelly-red fingernails, curved like canoes. I have trouble with faces. So Eni has her fingernails, others have accents, jewellery, birthmarks, tics. Sapphire Band is my neuro-specialist, Brown Moles my lead surgeon. Eni, Sapphire Band, Brown Moles. My team.

At this point I am bedbound. I am fed and voided intravenously and rinsed and barriered and measured and bled. I have no working glands above the neck. The insides of my cheeks are flushed and aspirated. Every four hours someone comes and lifts my goggles and droppers in an artificial tear. I learn to flex my fingers when I want attention, playing to the overhead CCTV. Sometimes I am read to.

My bed is equipped with an air compressor and I float a few inches above it so that the various grafts and fissures will heal. Periodically I am turned on my axis, checked and balmed, left to dry. The patient opposite has this system also and we spit and baste like two frankfurters, managing an odd unfocused smile when randomly on the quarter-turn we find ourselves face to face. I somersault from sleep to waking. White shoes flash. Encapsulated wheels of a suitcase. Candystriper pushing books on a cart; a train, a foot, the clatter.

I am able to attend to direct sensations and not much else. Gradually I become aware of my neck, then my torso, stomach, extremities. The nutrients I need are piped in and the wastes siphoned off and my organs are calibrated and driven by a series of white labelled boxes in fireproof vitrines. All of this dense mechanization to make my reassembled body lie still and from time to time generate ideas along the order of "yellow" and "sleep." All of it carried out with the good humour and can-do spirit befitting the crack medical unit that has done the impossible, brought a man in pieces back from the dead.

My neck and back are shingles and stitches, cracked yellow sores along the seam where my skin has erupted, allergic to its own healing. Scar laces do up both sides of my arms, scar coins lie spent across my shoulders. I am bald from nape to crown and I will stay that way, scalp turned in pink oyster-folds, until I arrange for a transplant, a patch of hair like a sod scrap borrowed from my thigh that takes root and dries up in the space of a month, leaving behind an imprint of itself around the edges. I wear a hat and then a series of cowboy handkerchiefs above thick-framed glasses through which, like slug quarters, bob my eyes. In the pictures they take to monitor my rate of healing I insist on three-quarter profile, like Claudette Colbert. My meals are served on covered hubcaps and plastic plates with rounded corners and for cutlery I have only spoons. My ration of pills is placed one by one on my tongue and I am watched as I swallow them.

Days are partitioned into fifteen-minute blocks: checks, meals, rounds, rehab, tests, meds. It is a perforated stupor, a sleepwakesleep. My blankets are changed, one soft breathable pastel in place of another like the leaves in a paint swatch from 1955, the blandness of the surroundings a counterpoint to the urgency of care.

On the ward we celebrate someone's birthday, a girl with leukaemia who asks for ice cream, only to puke it up gently, a brown-and-beige goatee, as they are taking her picture. I notice her teeth—squat, solid foundations—as if they'd been laid down and the face some time afterwards, built a little sloppily around those expensive, steadfast teeth. Not long after, she dies in the night in a room three down from my own. Several of the staff are in tears and although I am very thirsty I must wait hours for a drink. The girl was called Roberta; she leaves behind a cinnamon pony and a younger brother, Dex. A day passes before her bed is taken up, and there is the strangeness of mourning sincerely a death that was expected, her youth and courage—she had resolved to learn "Let It Be" on the piano and to turn sixteen. On the ward there is a chapel, a cupboard with some paraphernalia and a bench to pray on, and the nurses take turns to lay wreaths in a plastic basin by the door.

By now I am receiving phone calls. Because I cannot manipulate the receiver Eni passes on what is said, and I type out, on an adapted computer with oversized keys, whatever I want to say back.

thanks for the flowers. they are lovely and the card a real laugh. yes i am ver grateful and lucky. today I flexed my knee. great excitement. for supper, cutlet.

The calls and the books and the cards and the candy. I can't take the calls or open the cards or read the books or digest the candy.

Have 'em, I tell Eni. Go on.

These are fancy, they're European, she says. Are you completely sure?

She talks as she works on my back and lower limbs, pulsing with a square machine, stretching and twisting with gloved powdered hands. The farther down my body she travels the less I can feel her. I alert her at the point of numbness. It is my hips and then my thighs and then my knees. For several days it is my knees, and when it is my calves we are euphoric.

Still, I rarely leave my room. Even when I am given crutches, silver and twisted like cocktail forks with which I can manage a few feet before my armpits sting and my wrists go numb. Even after I am stronger, I only ever travel the length of the ward (and then in one direction), pretending all the while to be engaged in some fearsomely interesting and satisfying experiment in which I am designer, subject and control.

Eni, Brown Moles and Sapphire Band. Sapphire Band is impressed by my neural rebirth, the swift synaptic hand-to-hand by which world is converted to thought. My object recognition is improving and my vocabulary—I am lexically voracious, says Sapphire Band.

Brown Moles is delighted with the recovery of my motor skills. Amazing! she breathes, as I lift, over five excruciating minutes, my left arm one inch off the bed. Next I'll be playing

Grand Prix tennis. I'll be running, leaping, exercising my right to joy. When I manage to track a bouncing blob of light halfway across a head-mounted LCD screen, I fear for her heart.

Well *done*! she shouts.

When, assisted by a hydraulic lift and two rubber straps, I lever myself into a sit-up, she pounds her clipboard like a coach who is watching her team win a World Cup.

That's it! Brown Moles whispers, tensely. *Atta*boy!

Eni is strong as a horse. She says she was born cheerful. She has a bright sturdy voice, can curl her tongue from root to tip, has ankles shaped like water towers in black shoes and socks. Her father is a grocer and a brother is in the muffler business. A second brother builds computers and her little sister is pregnant—

Up the duff, Eni says, scathing and sad.

She frets about her sister without understanding her: says she's too young, too satisfied, she hasn't any ambition. Ambition is important to Eni. It has substance, like a medal or a suit of clothes, that advertises one's hunger and one's worth.

Why wouldn't you want to go places? she wonders of her sister. Families, she sighs. The big what-if.

I have plenty of attention from the staff. Groups of interns on their rounds are invited to read my chart and offer a diagnosis. My colander head, my deaf limbs—noticeable improvement. Can still more be done? My flapjack reflexes, milkshake blood.

Give us a leg lift? Left leg. That's it.

I listen in to learn what is wrong with me, but all I latch onto is that I am asymptomatic. Asymptomatic. The meaning of this seems to change with the audience; it is an excuse, challenge, point of pride. My wayward symptoms, free agents prone to aliases and trench coats, spreading neural sedition in the piss-soaked alleys of my temporal and limbic lobes. The genome for the old human orneriness expressed in my new-made, adminis-tered self.

Control pads let me raise and lower my bed and change the channels on the television I leave on to lessen the ward noise. On the wall beside the window is a painting of a window. Through the painted window is a nursery school scene of boats and ducks with white pastry wings and apricot beaks; the water is a sterile blue. Hand wash is red, painkillers almond. Sleeping pills are yellow and attention screens are brazen pink and painkillers a soft shoe brown. I come to see myself, my body's shapes and wastes and colours and textures, as pill or tube, round or long, tinted or translucent. The pills meant to reboot and repair and finally relaunch me, the tubes that regulate my functions in place of the functions themselves. The vertebrate bed rises until I can see the window, the boats in the harbour, the paddling pastry ducks, and I sew offcuts of conversation to have with Eni, which fray from the second they're made.

It'll come, Eni promises. Don't rush it. Learning a life is like learning a language.

Where am I? What do I remember? What do I see? When I first come to I find that others have become transparent. Dim sum dumplings. Jellyfish tribes. I can see their insides working, their organs, the pulse of blood around the body's grooves and funnels. The buzzing spiral brain. Emotions and thoughts plain to me. This is exciting and troubling at the same time.

Not so close, I tell people. I'm overloading.

All this time I have visitors. My mother but not my father. A student of prosthetics and a man of the cloth. Someone to whom, apparently, I have entrusted my keys. A cub reporter. Others, a few others. They tell me stories about myself that I am meant to recognize. They tell me stories about myself that I have no way of contesting and that I don't want to hear. They tell me stories that seem to span several lifetimes, that have me in two places at once.

So where am I? Who knows? During this phase I am only sporadically present to myself, can't follow even a simple conversation or track a tickle up an arm without being distracted or cut off. I inhabit something like a marsupial consciousness, narcoticized, good-natured, intermittently aware. The film footage taken of me at this time shows few expressions, ponderous motor movement, vocalizations unrelated to the activity at hand. Joy. Yes, the film shows joy. Stripped down to sapient fundamentals, what is left, surprisingly, is happiness. In one scene where the stimulus, off camera, cannot be glimpsed (teddy bear? torch? balloon?) I lay my head back and unscrew my mouth to fashion a lone long vowel: enormous uncomplicated soul-bottoming joy.

What else does the film show? It catalogues my slow-growing ability to do rather than just react to things in the world. I never have the same experience twice. I am attracted to certain image or sound or meaning patterns without knowing why. It interests me that there are trees among different trees. I am drawn to hospital carts, ball bearings, things that move and stop, to potentiality and interruption. To the name of the night nurse, Carmelita. There is a task involving a golf bag full of toys that I painstakingly remove and sort; I can do this for hours and still fail to develop a heuristic for grouping the toys by their properties. It interests me that some objects, like clocks and bodies, have working bits inside them and others, like stethoscopes and tables, do not, I shake and prod and try to skin the stethoscope, compare its textures to my throat. Simple movements, like tapping a disc with a mallet, are for me densely populated with all manner of tension and associations. All the senses blend. I keep a slice of pear on my table for its fine bell shape. I would not be surprised see a dolphin living in it, or an oak taking root on my brow.

There is a period of time where movement seems to be like rain and the people around me are rainpeople. They run with rain. Their faces gutter with it. Their bodies glisten with it, great stretched sloshing bodies, full of detritus, opaque except for odd deep wells of the most perfect transparency, as if they have been intubated with a long lens. It is a hard streaked world and I am relieved when it finally ebbs away.

Replacing it is a dream: I am in a large, soft house that gives the impression of being attached to nothing, of allowing nothing to attach to it. There are pots of light providing unexpected illumination, sometimes very focused and sometimes very broad. Every so often there is a pressure and a bit of myself is scooped away—surprising, but doing no harm. I have an idea that the house and I are of the same substance, merely tinted and refashioned and put to separate use. I feel that while I am being dangerously depleted, this work is necessary. Go on, I say. Take what you like.

Again and again the series of actions. I shudder, and seem to decide myself. I raise my hands above my head. I open a door and step out—

When I report these and other hallucinations I am told to relax, my brain is repairing itself. Certain areas and functions must be shut down or partitioned off for this vital work to be done. I should expect headaches and other referred pains, highly realistic delusions, temporary language loss. No portion of my inner life should surprise me. I am given a pebble on a string and a troll to carry. A black pebble and a pink troll on loops where my pockets would be. One smooth, one wrinkled and hairy and smashed—these are my touchstones. Why? They are simple objects whose shape and texture I can recognize without thinking. Should I find myself locked into a daydream or language pattern I must only reach for these touchstones and reality will return. Above all, I shouldn't worry. These psychic disturbances are in fact encouraging, proof of the reseating of neural filaments and pads. When in their thrall I reach for my belt-loop charms, breathe deeply, put the greatest possible pressure on my eyes and let the retina's weird iridescent backgammon play out across the scenes beneath. Two lucid thoughts out of five means progress, I am told. To thread these clean thoughts together, to link them to a plausible willed action, becomes the work of the next few months.

An oddity: during this first phase I cannot distinguish between what has actually happened to me and whatever else I have absorbed. Memories and anecdotes and books on tape have equal status. I believe myself to have been born a woman. Pinched and tiny, born with milk and menstruating. I remember that I was born a woman and when I turn seven I see this lovely smooth boy, Thomas Pitcher. I run to him and take his hands and as I kiss them he begins to cry. He is little and he cries like a seal.

I AM MOVED

By four months I am walking on crutches, and a few days later I give up my hospital bed for an apartment where I will live as an outpatient under close supervision. Eni is to check in, daily then weekly, and there is a helpful neighbour who has volunteered as my monitor and my meals-on-wheels. Round and fond of floral dresses, moves like a turnstile with even rotations of arms and legs, has pronounced views on marriage—nothing involving bank accounts ought to be unto death—and once as a schoolgirl declined to curtsey to the Queen. I meet her as I struggle after Eni from the taxi to the door.

This is Mrs. Damstra—

Polia. Poll is fine.

Poll. Good. Hello.

I wait in the yard while forms are signed. The front is grass and evergreens everywhere marked with ribbons indicating a want of horticultural attention. In the back I find flag-stones, a herb-garden-cum-anthill, twin trees splined by wired-on planks, their oval leaves dark with rot. A Falstaffian tabby cat with a vast apron ruff, all head no body, sits halfway through the fence.

G'way, says Poll to the cat, who does not. Sandcherry, she says, pointing out the trees. For three days each spring they're lovely.

I am shown around the apartment. It is small. Pains have been taken to make it friendly. The doors and walls are painted in yellows and light blues. Helpful signs are posted everywhere, rich in smileys and exclamation marks. There is a set of beads in a frame for meditating on and a painting of some pixellated bathers. Restrained, safe, welcoming. No harm can come to me here. The bedroom is a cork-edged night table and a low pallet with fireproof sheets. The living room has a couch and television, three monastic plants—no topsoil, no stones small enough to swallow. The kitchen and bathroom are without viable poisons, sharp edges or slippery floors. The bathtub has grips and a close-fitting door in the side, thermostatic faucets. The toilet features a grab bar and a raised, scooped seat. Above the sink, a rugged plastic mirror. In the kitchen the stove has been stripped of its fuses and wall sockets are fitted with locking plugs like storm shutters. The towels are made of ripstop. I learn to use the bath and toilet, to tune the radio and television set, to manipulate a fork and knife. I learn to take corners with my new hollow-frame walker, play at coping on my own.

My routine: an alarm I cannot shut off helps me to start my day by flashing a pattern-puzzle, the solving of which will stimulate my prefrontal cortex. I lie and watch the alarm keypad for the seven minutes required for it to give up on me. Then I exit the bed slowly, rolling into a kneeling position and from there to squatting and finally standing in the pen made by my walker. I wet my face. I eat the bland soft infant cereal that will nourish me but not unduly stress my freshly made jaw. I do the first half of my mental and other exercises. I am taken to my appointments. I am returned home. I have audio books, classics and best-sellers read badly by kindly volunteers that I listen to purely to rearrange the words in my head. I do a portion of my exercises. I fret. Whistle (inward whistle). Masturbate (spinal tension release). Sleep. Wake. Sleep.

I welcome visitors. Eni, of course, and the team from the burn unit, who bring balloons they take away again and a giant get-well cookie mined with Smarties. Loon Amulet, thin, grey, fidgety, with long bird feet, remembers some of the houses I have lived in, the landscaping and the interiors, where the windows were.

You were a great one for digging, she tells me. You had a wagon with rake and spade and a sieve you kept your worms in. It was soft earth, peaty.

She talks about the various complications arising from spruce trees too near a window. Needles piercing the bellies of new, expensive washing machines. Buildup of buds and gum that can prove catastrophic in house fires. She finishes with an eerie account of the passing of an aunt in Australia: the body had been in the ground for six months before they (the family) knew anything about it.

They held the funeral, the reception, everything. It was pre-paid, she says. Who came? Who knew? It is terrible, the things we must prepare for, that we must see coming, she says, reaches behind for the padded back of the chair she is sitting in, fingers like worn twine.

Each room of the apartment has a red-handled one-tug cord linked to hospital emergency, installed flush with the trim, a panelling of angels. They're designed to be comforting but I come to find them unwholesome, voyeuristic, waiting like Poe's black cat for their chance to erupt from the walls.

What an interesting story, I say, to Loon Amulet.

She closes her eyes and flutters her hands when I waggle my jaw in a kiss goodbye and her face suddenly is wet all over and I wonder why she comes here to tamp forcibly this version of me over whatever one she'd been living with before.

I'm sorry, I say. For what? For my condition.

No, please, no, she tells me. It's Thursday, that's all.

I am attuned to my surroundings, the rhythms of solitude:

bird sounds, refrigerator hum. The movement of dust, the gradual ripening of a banana, the way drying towels are folded on the rack, ceiling cracks. I note the colour composition of my meals, dried rinse on the juice tumblers, worrying sediments in the last bit of chamomile tea, the fluent sparkle on my urine. I am nervous about movement, too anxious and clumsy to travel very far. I still have trouble distinguishing images before me presently from images remembered. I look out the kitchen window above the yard and see a buffalo peering through a section in the fence. Suddenly curtains are waterfalls, sparkles spout from my nose in place of breath. When I am puzzled like this I am meant to close my eyes briefly and refocus until it is gone. I close my eyes and refocus maybe ten, fifteen times a day.

Poll arrives with my lunch and my supper, knocking at the door by way of being polite. Everything she cooks is cartoony: blocky meatloaf; chicken drumsticks; butter-tossed spinach; desserts with goblin hats of whipped topping from a tin; eggs whose whites loom from the plate like Fifties phantasms; apple drink in my untippable mug. Today it is cold cuts studded with olives and macaroni, sticky white bread.

When I was a kid I loved dragonflies, she says brightly. Thirty thousand pieces to each eye.

After eating I sit before the television. The chair goes up and down with a lever. On the television a man probes a car. Transmissions, he sighs. With a certain thrill, I know that I do not care about transmissions. I get in my walker, moving as I have been taught, step-drag, step-drag, gimp my way to the room with my bed, inevitably made.

I HAVE MY HEAD EXAMINED
In the second phase the team's focus shifts from my body to my brain. Its daily working. Its stutters, dropouts and fails. The guiding principles: everything slowly, everything in its place.

This is the point of routine. I must rise and eat and be dressed and take my medications and do my exercises and set myself however grimly to leisure and manage a short walk and converse with Poll or another volunteer and sign my name to various documents and retch my way through lunch and nap and read and be tested in various exhausting ways and perform a simple social task—a small basket of necessities at the local grocery—and have tea with other outpatient residents one of whom is at the point of neural disintegration and whose limbs alternately wander off on their own like enraptured tortoises and another from the burn ward with the telltale tarmac second skin down a third of his body, Jamey, motorcycle smash, who has a bouquet of tubes to feed from and favours books about climbers who will just about freeze to death; edge-of-hell fiction, he calls it—and then to the fitness suite to return the blank stares of the weight stacks and anticipate the moment when my turned-out feet will catch in the treadmill's gutters and stop it, dead, to the sound of an alarm that will bring the PT invariably running only to stop and hiss through her teeth before she bastes on the smile that is a cornerstone of the submedical professions and then it is suppertime and Poll's nephews who disappoint her, stoned on fertilizer (who knew?) and threatening to join the army every time a privilege is taken away, and a few pages of whatever large-print thriller has not yet been stolen from the hospice library and to bed but not before a rigorous emptying out of my head of all the disturbances of the day—centipedes in eardrums, a trombone that is a head on a neck that blares and blares and lengthens and lengthens and yes, why not, an experiment in prayer in which I close my eyes and pat my hands together—carefully, they no longer overlap exactly and can slip with too little pressure— and ask to be better and deliberately leave better open to interpretation, better in all its available ways. Better. Sleep, wake, sleep.

The rebuilding of my brain has three priorities:

1. Parallel processing (simultaneous events)
2. Narrative recognition and sequencing (story order, information transfer)
3. Cognitive renewal (short-term memory, empathy training, coping, learning)

The first and the third are ongoing. The second preoccupies Gold Medallions as the rare and vexing problem that his research has always been leading up to, even without his knowing. Not for the first time with my team, I am aware of medicine tying up with religiosity, with fate, the holiness of certain interventions, the weird symbiosis of patient with doctor, paired destinies, her heart his veins. It is a world of interconnection, of pigtailed lives.

Narrative recognition. Story sequencing. It is not my memory that is impaired but my interpretative and creative faculties. Somehow, it seems, I have lost my punditry. We strive, Medallions says, in a world of narrative. There is nothing outside story. Except, temporarily, me.

He hands me a plastic panel containing beads in tracks. Coloured beads, coloured tracks. The blue with the blue and the yellow with the yellow.

Imagine that the grooves are stories, he says. And each bead represents a story element. This is how our brain understands them. One thing followed by another followed by another. *Story logic*, he says. Now, he says, here's you.

He shakes the tray twice and I watch the slow miscegenation of the beads. The yellow with the blue with the red with the green. The odd disjointed tracks.

Imagine the time and the effort, he says, to fit all of these back in their place.

On another occasion we do an exercise in which I have a selection of picture cards with objects and actions I must turn into a story. Card of a sun, of a basket, a lawn, a boy and a girl. Under Gold Medallions' increasingly irritated scrutiny—no prompting no helping—I make blond Jimmy get a book from a library. I make him and his sister Jenny picnic at Old Man's Creek.

It takes me a long time. I'm perfectly able to sit the siblings down at their picnic but can't think what happens next. Perhaps they walk there. There's a hair across the belly of the sun—

Hang on, slow down; look at what you've done, says Medallions. It's disconnected. You're taking a pile of toothpicks and throwing them onto the floor, that's what you remember and in that order. Nothing fits.

I cannot follow the sequence or grasp the implications of people doing things for reasons. Character, setting, action, theme, prop. Everything happens at once for me, and merely *happens*. I cannot parse and evaluate. I cannot decide on good or bad. I cannot assess the weight of one person's actions. I cannot predict what will come to pass. I am in a constant present, and although I have not forgotten anything I cannot tell then from now or discern what made *then* then and what makes *now* now. I am shown a thick line transected by points in blue and red with balloons for events in time.

Let's plot this, he says. First, we'll list—

Part of what Gold Medallions means by "sense" is sequence. That a man cannot be in the shop that he then walks into. That a woman cannot drink from a glass she has not yet poured. Sense, here, has nothing to do with meaning. Meaning is the next, the untaken, step.

A long arcade of experiences. Facts in syrup, in a chill, set gel. I am collecting stories. Am I making sense? I do not match stories to bodies, to brains. I do not distinguish between fiction and fact. It is the same to me. Unicorns in dustbins, apoplectic harps.

I try to make things fit but nothing fits, I tell Medallions. Isn't that the way?

No, he says. He takes his hands and interlocks them, spread of knuckle and pinched skin. This is the way, he says. Later I will think about how he has forced his hands into this position, the compression he has exerted, the grip-force. *This* is the way, he says.

Cognitive renewal. I am not sleeping. Why do I not sleep? My insomnia is temporary, normal, apparently, a side effect of the brain's rewiring itself, all that surplus electricity shunted into cravings for lime juice and replaying the previous day. There are pills for it. I take pills designed to rein in or counteract effects of other pills I take. My brain and organs, my tissues and nerves, have become a kind of pharmaceutical arena and I think about swearing off medicines altogether and dumping the lot in a Devlin tray and watching them battle it out.

The new pills are the shape of a stylized eyelash, and they come with a questionnaire and a checklist and a follow-up plan, including online FAQ and exercises. Waking up at the same time every day is part of the checklist. Using my bed only for sleep or for sex is on the checklist—

For sleep, chuckles Half-Australian. We all behave here.

It is one of the myths of the chronic care hospital that illness, serious illness, trumps sex. In fact all these compressors, ICUs, fresh-air filters and piped-in Vivaldi merely take the edge off constant, scratching, low-grade masturbation.

Yes, sleep, I say. I am to tense and relax my muscles in sequence—the same sequence—and think of a shape in space.

What did you think about? asks Half-Australian.

Labyrinths, I tell her.

Ah, she says, brightly. Very restful, those.

I have a photo shoot at the OT, me in my patient's button-up whites, sat in a wheelchair, flanked by Sapphire Band and Brown Moles. I stare towards a distant sea. I give the thumbs-up. I smile the smile of the cured, the smile that looks towards a future that will never know the past, the smile that shows a willingness to come to grips with absolutely everything.

It's tremendously exciting, I say. I'd cry if I could.

Polly is distracted.

Her nerves are frayed, poor thing, she says of Manners, her square white hankie of a dog, whose abiding fear of any form of motion has reduced her to a life of permanent stasis between her doggie doughnut and the backyard. Manners's food is ferried to her, as are her amusements: rawhide barbell, Let's Go Sailing Trudie doll, a bit of burlap she tugs from the edge of the yard.

It's the low pressure, Poll says, looking up. Poor sausage. She smells rain.

Poll twice drops the cheese she is slicing for sandwiches. She mustards too heavily, scrapes off the extra with the back of the knife.

Through the window I see Manners at the back of the garden, scuffing at the earth. Something in that corner that attracts her. It's the first place she goes when she's here.

I shut my eyes, refocus. Again. Again. I ask Poll for the tomatoes.

Let me do that, I say.

I am given a video to watch. Facial expressions. Gestures. Getting about in the world. The shape on the screen raises her hand, oscillates it gently.

Hello, says the shape.

Goodbye, says the shape.

A subtitle: *Goodbye. Conclusion of Part 1: "Greetings."*

In weeks to come I will follow the shape as she answers the door and the telephone, deposits a cheque at the bank, manoeuvres a drive-through gas stop, attends an auction and a nice cocktail party.

Twenty-four, calls the shape, bidding on a boat bed.

How amusing! exclaims the shape, to a pink drink on her left.

Who is this person? Who writes her material?

Forget the material, advises Gold Medallions. Just watch her hands, and see how they agree with what she is saying, and how she looks.

The shape looks a little forced. This life she leads, merry-go-round of human interaction, from brunch to the races to the trading floor she apparently works at, hustling blue-chip stocks. The pets she takes to the veterinarian, that we never see again. The evening class she finds time to teach and the chartered sloop.

I'm watching, I'm fascinated, I say. Such a full life.

In the shower stall, a big broad meathook of a fixture, a caterpillar sticks like a furred, bitten-down pencil, poised above the drain. I'm alone in the apartment taking a shower without hot water, cleanser or soap. I've opened the taps a quarter turn until a trickle escapes the faucet and I let it solder itself to my forehead, my nose, my belly.

My new skin, hairless, grown in a lab in flat, shallow tanks translated as "skin graft trees." I can see where they have built up my right leg by the bolus of scar tissue, much darker the skin there than on its opposite number. The pelvic bones too are reinforced, and the ankles, and shin. My left elbow is not wholly my own, nor my shoulder blades, rotator cuffs, the back of my skull, whose manufacturer's stamp may still be seen where the weave begins. I am the result of modern engineering and good, old-fashioned kinderskool craft, back-of-the-comix invention. Hypoallergenic resins, aerospace foams. Danish austerity in the design of my heel. Only a very small percentage of my new body is responsive to pressure, to pain. I will for the rest of my life have to be careful near gas fires, scissors, playful teeth. I am sensitive to frequency; garage doors and baby monitors, certain musical notes that produce hum in my innards, Doppler rings like the old RKO beacons, travelling through the cushion of water between breastbone and artificial lung.

Global product. Radar man.

Brown Moles asks me to dance.

Come on get up put those things away, she says. Stand up, bud.

She has a cube that plays music. An egg on a stalk that takes very fast very clear pictures. The cube plays something swingy and Brown Moles has my hands on her hip and shoulder and we vacillate about the room to the whine of the camera, forwards, backwards, bumping corners, getting a belt loop trapped on a door, Brown Moles stepping and jutting, the camera screaming, and I think absolutely nothing, just dance as I am told.

As I rearrange my apartment I notice heavy indentations in the single stuffed chair, brown discoloration of the seat and back. I lower myself into it, lay my hands along the armrest, note the divergence between my shape and this one. Evidence of another person in this room. Before I got here? After? Why should that matter? I'm not fussed about the pubic hairs in the varnish on the bathroom floor or rugfuls of dormant infections. Odd however that as many times as I sit on this chair now, I cannot leave a lasting impression. I get up and sit down. I sit until it is painful and then I hobbleskip round the room to relax my muscles and take the chair again. Nothing. I unbuckle my trousers hold them under the tap till they're soaked through. Then I put them on and sit in the chair again and count and examine the ceiling quadrant by quadrant and decide whether I actually see or merely imagine that I see a reflection from the window behind. There. I have left a wet dark overlay in the chair that serves only to highlight the original outline, even broader now, more pronounced.

The photo frames made from formed wood, the radio tuned to a station other than the one I prefer. I have the sensation of movement all around me, a man reaching out for the telephone. Shouldering the door with sacks of groceries, the day's post between his teeth. In the kitchen slicing an onion, ladling from pot to bowl. He flicks over lampshades, slips about the newspaper, occupies the crease of an aspirin I am about to take. I close my eyes; refocus. I close my eyes.

C A L

Cal is practising a story. The story is one he has told over and over. But he has never gotten it right. He stands in the outer lobby of the Belmont Suites, a late-Sixties confection of splayed sofas and brown marble and a long low fish tank trimmed with a fine, square glitter that makes the fish seem expensive and the lobby cheap.

Seven times, says Cal.

He thinks he will begin with that, and see what happens. Seven times, he will say, and let things take their course. He watches a boy in a uniform leave the elevator. He watches a courier angle in with her saddlebag of flyers and samples and contests, press all of the buttons in freehand sweeps of five at a time, wait for the buzz and scatter a handful of promotions. Outside, someone fiddles with the light bulb. A girl smooths her dark column of a raincoat, waits to cross the street. From inside the lobby the scrape of a crutch.

Cal has a schedule and a fire-engine suitcase on wheels. The Traveller. The Traveller is wedge-shaped and double-walled and avid; its desire is strong. Everything about the Traveller—

advanced polymer frame, inline wheels, telescoping handle, shoebank feature—means business. At times Cal has to physically restrain the Traveller. He anchors himself, and holds on.

It is getting dark and Cal is still working, item by item, ticking off his schedule. His schedule, his plan, his list. He is making his house calls. Tannis. The pastor. Jay. Apartment 801. Then he will catch his train. This list is what sustains him. Its clarity, its endpoint. The list lies sheathed in plastic at the top of his elegant new organizer. Full-grained leather, hand-sewn sheets—a philatelic dream.

He has been to the train station, bought his ticket, checked all his bags but the Traveller. Inventory: bug spray, disposable camera, fold-up shovel, surveyor's tape. His list—he has kept to his list.

Hello, says the speakerlet.

He has been to see Tannis. He has been to see Jay. The pastor. Here.

Hello, says the speakerlet. Hello, this is 801.

Seven times, Cal whispers into the tenants-only speakerlet. Not quite a speaker but more than a hand cupped over one's mouth. A painted and countersunk hole in the wall upholstered in a perforated metal mesh he is starting to find hypnotic; recombinant tiny holes and, behind them, the ever-present possibility of sound. He waits politely for a meter reader and her electric notepad to buzz the concierge and clear the brushed-metal mailboxes and inner doors. The Traveller tenses its ABS wheels, high-impact nostrils flaring.

This is 801, says the voice again. Hello?

Hello, says Cal. He moves a little nearer. Hello, he says.

There are several things happening here, he thinks. The foot—the foot and the spine and Merle and me. Everything once was separate, he thinks. And then everything began to blend in. But to start—to start, there was Merle.

On the folder in his hand is written the number 4. His notes for the scribe of 801. Everything is in there, everything is written down. Better to have consistency, to have everyone on the same page. So: Merle dies. There were the rehearsals and then there was the thing itself, Cal has written. Seven rehearsals, then the thing itself. Seven times. Then—

Cal is leaving. Merle is dead.

This is 801, says the voice.

This is Cal, says Cal.

$$\oplus$$

Cal has tethered the Traveller to the C-shaped door handle, hooded it like a falcon with his coat. He stands beneath the compact floodlight the better to read his list.

I *used* to work there, 801 says. I don't any more.

You've moved on?

No one moves *on* from a local weekly, says 801.

Well it was your story, Cal says. Remember?

Whoa, correction, says 801. I just wrote it up.

You authorized it, says Cal.

This was the story, as Cal told it and 801 wrote it up:

Respected company man and solid local citizen Merle D., arriving home tired and itchy with hayfever, steps into the garage-door weights—old oil drums filled with cement, lifted and lowered by iron loops—and sustains a concussion. The car is on, engine warm, exhaust pumping. His son Cal, with whom he has recently reconciled (there's a story, a *hu*man story), who happens to be in the neighbourhood on business of his own, sees smoke filtering from beneath the door, manages to crack it open and slide underneath, performs first aid and telephones an ambulance. Merle, thank god, is all right.

Okay, says 801.

Okay? Listen, says Cal. Wake up—stay with me. It's all about paying attention, he says. The timing will bug you, and the plot, he says. Seven times I found him. You know what then? he says to the speakerlet. Don't get all caught up in what happened, Cal says. Forget content—focus on the elements, the groupings, the shape. It isn't straight lines we're looking at here, he says. This is unexpected, he says. It's odd, I know. But it was your story too. And your story, he says—sensing impatience on the line—your story isn't right. The timing, the whole, he says.

It's been a while, says 801.

Sure; it's old news, right? says Cal. I won't take up your time. I won't keep you, he says. But you *wrote* it. Does that not matter to you? I don't *blame* you, he says. I wasn't . . . accurate. For example—

For example: Merle is in Emergency. There is a rapid burlesque in which two doctors dispute the degree and even the fact of his death. Had he, conclusively, crossed the line and returned miraculously; or had he hovered just one side or the other? The printout will confirm it.

This broken line is your father, the tall doctor tells Cal, running a pen over the EEG.

And here, and here, says the short one.

I never told you about that, Cal says to 801. Even there, I took a liberty, he says. Right off the top. I smoothed a few corners. Left some things out.

It's human nature, says 801. It's fine.

Well actually no, it isn't, Cal says. It isn't honest.

Does that matter now? says 801.

Yes, it does, Cal says. You need the story as it was.

I had the story.

No, says Cal. No—listen.

The story—the story *isn't* a story any more, says 801. You know?

It's a story again, believe me, says Cal. He's dead, maybe you heard. I can read it—should I read it? It has a nice flow. That day, you came to the house and I walked you through it. My father wouldn't speak to you but I did. I did. Did you wonder at that? I thought it would help if I got it into the open, if I flushed him out. I thought, get it in print, get the word out, how much harder would that make it for him to go through with it? I thought that you would tell the story and he would read it and somehow, with all this telling, he'd have a fit of, I don't know, decorum. Decorum, he says. He would have the decency not to keep doing himself in.

But why are you telling *me*? asks 801.

Why shouldn't I tell you? This is your story. You took it on when you wrote it down. Why shouldn't I tell you? Why shouldn't you take responsibility for it? I'm leaving it with you, he says. I'm transferring custody.

Good, fine. So then just tell me, she says. Jesus H. Christopher; throw me a bone. Start.

Cal starts.

Cal brings Merle back from the dead. Merle is Cal's father. Cal is Merle's boy. There is something in this, from the point of view of 801 and the other journalists who pick up the story. For a few days, locally, Merle and Cal are talking points. Interviewing Cal back then—Merle is recovering, no time for the press—the scribe of 801 has some questions.

How did you know he was in trouble? Was there—a sign?

Yes, says Cal. A sign. A connection.

What went through your mind when you found him? Take us through it: you arrive; the doors are open—

And the taps—

And the taps are turned on; incidentally . . .

I don't know why, says Cal.

And you have, what, ten, twenty seconds—

About, says Cal.

And you find him, take his hand: he's weak, his hand shakes—

His hand, says Cal.

And in that instant you feel—what? An electricity? A . . . force?

Yes, Cal says. Something like that.

He takes her through it. Merle, arriving, the garage-door weight, the concussion. The car, the exhaust, sweet and nutty, the mess of him; the extreme unlovely mess.

And what did he say; you know, when it happened?

Say? In that situation there's a point at which . . . Cal says, shrugs, shimmies at infinity.

Ah, says 801. She writes: *The dying man said: "Hold on . . ."*

For a few days after the story breaks Cal has a mild celebrity. *"Glad to Have My Dad Back" Says Samaritan Son.* Something in the story—filial love, selfless rescue, possible telepathy—initially appeals. But Cal can see the strip where the goodwill ends, bold as highway markings. There is the down-home awkwardness of it. There are competing stories—toddler trapped in a skin of ice, dogs dialling emergency services. And there is from the start a subtle confusion surrounding events: the headshot of Merle in a clever shirt Cal does not remember him owning—glossy, striped—his eyes strung like charms along the stretch of his silvery, well-tended brow. Holes in the plot: if Merle was in the car, how had he injured his head? Why was the garage door shut anyway? Then there is Cal's mysterious triggering feeling. The phrase "bringing back," as if Cal had cast deep into the stuff of death and, hand over hand, reeled Merle in.

Felicities. Messages. Merle's stricken colleagues. His harelipped cousin from Detroit, mother to triplets with frizzy toy hair, squeezes Cal's hand, says she has spoken to just everyone about him and it must be marvellous to have seen the Other Side.

Well, I didn't see it, personally, Cal says. But that's what I hear.

He explains about the light and the fragrance and the beating of wings—

I don't like to use the word angel, he says; her ecstasy colours her like blush.

Several men seeing the story are moved to write to Cal of heart attacks and gunshot wounds, of dipping into death. *It was bright and humid, there was a beating of wings—*

No one is interested in Merle. At least, no one is interested in his life or thoughts or history except in relation to his return from the dead, as if the dead were not in fact a stuff at all, or even a state of being, but a place one bought an airline ticket to and got vaccinated for and visited and were cheated in and dutifully photographed and complained bitterly about the whole time one was there and then recalled, twenty years later, as the time of one's life. Like the Outback or the Florida Keys. Hundreds of times Cal is asked, on Merle's behalf:

What was it like, coming back from The Dead?

Fine, he wants to say. Great, had flu, shame about the crooks in the markets and all the snaps I took that never turned out.

It was difficult, he says. Difficult—and sweet.

For all his sometimes snide ambivalence, when this phase passes, Cal is wistful. Long after the journalists stop caring about him and his friends get back to their work, Cal finds himself regretting. How much more helpful he might have been to the scribes! How much more of an inspiration to the pastor of the Church of the Elucidated Soul who knew Merle and wanted Cal to get in touch.

Eventually—fine, it's late, he's been drinking—he does.

What did your dad hear, when he crossed over? the pastor wants to know.

He said there was a voice, a calling voice.

This voice—was it deep or shrill?

Deep. Very deep. Booming—like sonar.

Sonar is shrill. Peepy.

Like deep sonar. Deep in the underwater sense.

The pastor sighs. The voice, the light, the sonar. If I had a nickel . . . he says.

The truth is I hardly knew him.

Merle introduces himself when Cal is sixteen. Where have I been? asks Merle, opens his hands, smiles. In his suit he has a stem-like quality. They go to a film together, Kubrick's *2001*. I hope there's air conditioning. Is there air conditioning? Merle wants to know.

Afterwards he insists on walking Cal home and fidgets his address onto the glossy, hard-to-write-on back of a mining prospectus, the only bit of paper he can find. Then he writes it again on Cal's hand. The prospectus and the hand—artless, and yet the prospectus is folded to leave a blank space and the address fits Cal's hand exactly. Already Cal senses he is being configured, recruited. Merle, it seems, has plans.

When did he leave them anyway? Five? Eight? Eight. Merle leaves when Cal is eight and then there is a period of several months when Cal must first remember and then reinvent him. Merle on a ladder fitting storm windows. Merle sorting through odd lots of seafood (cuttlefish, prawns) only hours before company comes. In designing his memories Cal works backwards from some present quality of Merle's to the conditions under which he might have developed it. To explain Merle's charity, Cal imagines for him a plain, denuded childhood, homemade toys, charity shop clothing, paper routes and bottle deposits, out-houses, naphthalene. To cover Merle's absence he attributes illnesses, amnesias, espionage, missions to the East. There is no way for him to test these hypotheses. None but faith.

During the year and a bit between Merle's first and final attempts, Cal works for a pharmaceutical giant. Whenever he names the company whoever he is talking to instantly recognizes it, says: Oh, the pharmaceutical Giant, as though its very size defines it, and Cal falls into this habit, saying The Giant slumbers or The Giant strides forth when asked about what's happening at work. His office is a primary-coloured cubicle subdivided into other cubicles so that each cog, or teammate, inhabits a Rubik's Cube of her or his very own, and once a month in a grand approximation of a solution everyone moves one space left.

He is Blue Cal and Red Cal and Yellow Cal and Green Cal. Blue Cal is on the front lines, taking calls from potential customers who see a product advertised and want to know more. His immediate task is to take their name and other details and input these to a universal mailout exploited by the Giant for its own promotional agenda and then sold at a profit to other firms. How it works: you phone the Giant. You are intercepted at the front lines (Blue Cal). Your personal details are tapped into a database. You then receive, free of charge, pamphlets on the drug of your choice plus a subscription to the Giant's newsletter and missives from the carefully selected firms to whom the Giant has flogged your valuable mail slot. When you have a moment away from reading about cruise lines, diet revolutions and off-season HVAC specials you may learn about the diseases you suffer from—now, someday—and arrange a slot with your family physician, plucking her or him if necessary from the pocket of a lesser Giant, and demand drugs.

From his front-line foxhole, Blue Cal is required to be familiar with the Giant's infopaks, four-colour printed on pricey matte stock and featuring a diverse selection of couples whose drugged-up good health is evident in their bright colourful clothes, their white and round and even teeth like soda pellets, their perfect poreless skin. Within these lives lurks no cancer or angina or halitosis or heartburn or ague, but the promise of ordinary people taking complete charge of every decision, sebaceous or digestive or circulatory or reproductive, undertaken anywhere in their bodies or their minds.

Red Cal lasts three weeks as a telesales prompter and is bumped upstairs after a series of discreet, ruthless redundancies that no one is meant to ask about amounting to an exhibition of close-up magic on an absolutely massive scale.

People are disappearing, Red Cal says to a colleague, during a taxing copy job.

Throughput, she says.

Pardon?

The light, she says, and points to the undilated pupil on the front of the machine.

Right, he says, probes the thing's carbon gorge until he hears it reengage.

Anyway *shh* not *here* in the *op*en, she says, and that's that.

Yellow Cal is another character part. He is interned briefly in the health sciences library along with a practising vampire. The Vampire represents the undead in their archival capacity and Yellow Cal helps to install a series of tiny glass houses for early instruments of surgery from the Victorian Age, including a set of forceps including a mask for the dispersion of anaesthetic including a blade polisher (automatic) including a set of left-handed prosthetics: hand, arm, leg, foot. The foot: hollow straws of steel beaten into a smooth glow, each toe present and more than that, alive, flexing independently, pert as fresh-cut lawn.

It came with its blueprints, says the Vampire. But this was the only one made.

Can I try it?

You can visit it, the Vamp says. But you'd better book your slot.

When Yellow Cal trades in his jersey he checks in on the foot. The Vampire hands him a memento mori, a business card in the form of an anthropomorphic skull.

I'm giving guided tours, he explains. The Urban Sanguine.

I'm here to see the foot, says Cal.

It's there, repositioned slightly so that it appears to be walking, the slow kinetic crunch, led from the heel, the toes a kind of spreading afterthought. The mother-of-pearl of the nails.

Amazing, he says.

You think it's a child's but it isn't, says the Vampire. It's built for an adult, a male. Sometimes I sit and think of it moving, says the Vampire. And my heart just roars.

Later, as Green Cal, on the advice desk, he finds that patrons call him for advice, to talk. He can't really take these calls (it is forbidden for him and his colleagues, unlicensed as they are, and uninsured, to dispense medical advice) but he listens. They call him complaining about ulcers, pain like shattered windows in their guts. Food stalls in them, there is blood in their stool (no one is shy addressing the Giant over the phone). Blepharitis, cataracts, that margarine glaze; loss of colour vision. They are depressed, slivers in a pit; they no longer *know*-know themselves. Their hair is shedding in a fine, dry sleet. Their hearts, saturating migraines, flip-flop cocks.

There is hope, he tells them. Did I get your name?

Their bombed-out libido, no sniff of a fuck in months. Their sewer breath. Liver tight as a pond leech. Kidneys so packed with stones might as well be a quarry. Insomnia, active bladder, thoroughgoing ennui. Phobias, asthma—breath in a cage.

Spotlight on Prostate covers that, he tells them. *Understanding Stress.* Let's run through your details once more.

It doesn't do to be over-sympathetic. All conversations are monitored for quality control. Some callers are encouraged and want to open a chat account. One man, complaining of colitis, gets through every few days.

Twenty-two Pine Drive here, he says, to Cal's irritation. Just thought I'd check in.

I can re-send your package, should it not arrive, Cal says, sticking to the template.

Can't keep anything down. Broth, glucose syrup. Jell-O in squares.

How did you know it was me?

Phoned until I got you. Been on hold for hours today. Don't hang up. Not yet.

There is something thrilling in it. It is a kind of pain hormesis; stimulating in low doses, toxic in high. He listens to them and feels his chemistry changing.

They call and want to tell their stories. They call and want to talk.

What don't they tell him? This is the post-medical, the epidural conversation. Quibbles. He hears about quibbles. Anger. Contempt. He hears about casual infidelities, couch fucks and fitness room fucks and kitchen counter fucks—whoops, the Merlot—the studied eroticism, the toys and the visuals, the infernal geometry of fetish, the make-you-come phrases, the sniff of the fingers and the changing of the locks, the deletion of voice- and foot- and head-prints from all the varied surfaces of a life.

I'm listening, he says.

The fruitions and dissolutions of the flesh the spirit.

I have for eleven months pretended I was blind, says 1235. I hoped to develop fingers that see. Ten little periscopes—my god.

Take stock of things, he advises. Have a plan.

My partner is grainy, he is elusive, she says. Where are we going; where do any of us go? I've got needs, I want to be with someone I really fancy. I want to be in love again, she says. Sometimes I want this so bad I *thrum*.

Be good to yourself, he tells her. Do things for you.

The karmic avalanche, deed upon deed. The confines of duty and good, common sense. The exit strategies. Cal has a cold and his shoulders are twitching, the weight of all this sin.

There is less and less of me daily, says 0000000, unknown number, returning cancer, older woman somewhere out west.

What can you prescribe, is there anything? Anything, she says. There is less and less of me left.

You're in a good place, he says; platitudes, platitudes. Take things easy. Baby-steps.

He follows the Giant's script until he hears the rough click of the QC recorder timing out. Then he tells his callers what he feels they ought to hear.

He is making it up. Lying to them. Why should he not? Consolation is a bet you lay. Where is the truth in consolation? So he lies to them, makes it up, narrates the ad pictorials in the Giant's newsletter, gentle and uplifting stories of recuperation against a backdrop of white sands and boutique shopping, amusement parks and ensuite bedrooms where signature-shaped pills nestle alongside the Lalique.

The people in his stories are driven, active. They do not wait on death. They make deals, they tumble among Pacific combers, jitterbug along boardwalks, trawl for swordfish from the decks of expensively rented yachts. Not people but shapes of light, colourful arrangements of energy dressed in catalogue clothes; the atmosphere recollecting itself, twice a day, with water, after meals.

Take control, says this spirit of wellness. Organize your body with a decision you make for you.

They call—what can he do for them? How can he help them? He absorbs their illnesses. He eats their sins. Before long he is suffused with illnesses, beset by sin. His yellowing fingers, brittle counterpanes on the beds of his nails. He spends less and less time in his cubicle, eats his meals at his desk. A forest of suction cups on next door's window and Cal in the same stinking clothes making it up, lying to them, inventing new drugs and procedures, doodling a logo fit for the Giant: a coat of arms of a dove and crossed splints. And a motto: *Panton est teres.* Everything's fine.

—

And then Merle dies.

I'm so sorry, says 801.

Yes, Cal says. Note the timing, he says.

That day's events have no throughline. Cal picking up the message. Finding the body. Speed-dialling EMS. The two doctors.

At the hospital there are a number of forms Cal has to sign. The business of dying is protracted and severe, nothing is done lightly. The taller of the two doctors comes by to see him and is a little eager, then a little distant, as though Cal ought to have tipped him or shaken his hand.

Thanks for all you've done, says Cal.

Oh, we didn't do anything this time, says the doctor. I remembered your dad from the cookies. Just wanted to say how much we liked him round here.

He was something, says Cal.

He was remarkable. He was a whole-hogger, says the doctor. We all admired that.

Cal wonders, not for the first time, whether something important is being left out of this conversation, whether he has been confused for someone else.

Merle, he says.

Merle, says the taller doctor, a benediction, a paean.

I'm sorry, says 801.

The woman in 801 is trying. She finds she does remember the case but is unsure about this man and what he is saying. At first she listens to ascertain that he is not raving. Then for any suggestion that it's her he wants. *He isn't raving and it isn't me he wants*, she writes in her memo pad. As he talks she makes a few notes. *Father dead? Kd. of mission. Reproving substance?* She finds herself wishing he would just come up but doesn't want to be the one to initiate this. There are considerations. For instance, a brackish filth in the sink and three burnt-out light bulbs, backsliding hygiene and basic home repair since she—what? Moved in a year ago. Propriety. Strange guy—freak?—and her, alone, whatever, call her a prig. *Seven things I can see without moving my head require immediate attention*, she writes in her memo. *Says father "induced."*

Your father, he dies, I remember, I'm sorry, she says. I'm sorry for you both.

Would Cal say he was sorry? No. Not sorry, not even sad. He feels something but it is neophyte, undifferentiated. He waits for this feeling to play out in actions—weeping, laughing, kicking at a wall. He will feel and then he will act and he will know by his actions just what it is that he feels. But he does not act. And the feeling, all this feeling, lurking like Iago at the side of his thoughts.

Merle dies, and five days later the Giant hands Cal his pink slip and two weeks' pay.

In the wake of Merle's death Cal takes three days off, and then he is back in his cubicle and yet more reckless. For two hours he is locked into an absorbed stasis, strung along the hooks and eyes of office noise and office function. And then he begins his jag, his bender of helping others out. He prints a list of everyone he has ever called on behalf of the Giant, goes through it alphabetically, time zone to time zone, town to town, breaking only to use the bathroom and later to change shirts. He begins on Wednesday at 11:00 in the morning, and when they come for him on Friday night he is well into the Ms and he is on a roll, euphoric. He makes it up, he lies to them. He invents diseases. Spores released in drinking water that loosen cartilage until the limbs drop off in their skins. Modular diseases of the spine, a billion viral dremels hollowing out the discs. The buildup of electrical charge in the brain, fearful spoke lightning.

There is no precedent here, he tells them. We are on the bleeding edge.

Some hang up on him; it is 2:00 a.m. Others listen to him and are shocked. He takes all of the things he knows about Merle and distils it into a serum to be injected into everything he says. He gives them years of anger, he gives them reconciliation, he gives them this grief.

What isn't the government telling you? he asks.

He advocates the harshest, most powerful drugs. As prevention. As a pre-emptive strike. All the colours of the rainbow; every shape between circle and square. Once properly ingested, separated from their polish and filler and binding agents, their true chemical selves emerge and join forces to penetrate membranes and erect scaffoldings, descaling and widening and mending and finishing-touching like a billion on-schedule on-budget public works wheezes.

People begin to gather by his cubicle. Lucy brings him water and the Vampire takes a picture of him, lethal, beatific, head back in a beam of light.

It's hard to keep up. For every breakthrough malfunction appears a breakthrough cure, backed up by fail-safe clinical trials, only to be frustrated by hidebound government legislation, corporate greed, sheer microbial invention: cancers mentor other cancers; street-smart bacteria in Kevlar vests—

They come for him. A security man he remembers as Ed and a floor supervisor in a button-down blue shirt and flag trousers, dress-down Friday. Cal makes no trouble, but as he enters the great revolving door that is the thorax of the Giant, in which each tiny square of glass contains a stamped facsimile of one of their 1,383-and-counting patent drugs, he thinks he could have fed these to Merle. All of them. Sat Merle down and laced him up and A- and B-trialled him, double-blind tested him, peer-review published him, monitored him every which way.

Swallow, goddamn you! Heal!

Cal pauses, stretches his neck sore from nodding. The Traveller slumps in a corner.

The building super on her way back from the recycling lends Cal a chair in canvas with festive pimento stripes.

You can't stand all night.

Thank you, he says.

Keep your weight on the left side, she tells him. The seam is no good.

Cal remembers that early on when he thought Merle might simply be accident-prone he asked him what he thought about dying and Merle said he thought it might be interesting but that was all.

What part?

What part what?

What part of it is interesting?

The set-up, said Merle.

Cal is telling these things to 801 but he does not remember them. That is, he does not remember them in the way that he remembers the last time he swam—cold water, frisky weeds—but in the fuzzy, segmented way he is able to talk about news stories and bold developments in areas of technology he does not really understand.

Whoops—shoot—that's something burning, says 801.

Cal thinks there's a chance that Merle never said those things and never even sounded like this, never managed the tented melancholy that Cal is attributing to him. He thinks that some kinds of death make claims to profundity after the fact and that some do not, and some people—Cal?—step in and lever painfully simple deaths into complicated territory.

He thinks that Merle's quietness was not an attribute but an element, present and sharp, unaccompanied by some elaborate gestural vocabulary or alternate system of making a point. There are times when Merle's face ripples with a potent agony of not speaking, as though words roll like film credits a millimetre under the skin. There is no peace in this quietness, no beatitude. Merle's apartment is three high square rooms in a building called the Edelweiss, a residential hotel that spoons a courtyard with a Swiss clock that opens to a snowy Mont Blanc twice daily. At six o'clock Merle appears on his balcony in a green V-neck sweater.

Don't come up, I'll come down, he says.

He is asked to leave the Edelweiss—change of management, condo conversions, upscale—and buys a character flat aggressively tenanted by students living three to a room and a white witch with broad poetic sensibilities who makes subtle offerings of wreaths and ceramic crosses and lines from the Rosettis and Baudelaire. A gang of cats left to fend for themselves shit on the landings and striate the carpets with their claws. The floors are sprung and uninsulated. There are holes in the sun-porch screens. Constant random alarms that no one pays attention to. Cal is tense in the first five seconds.

I like it because no one else does, says Merle.

Cal wonders about the cleanliness of the apartment, bleached surfaces, dry counters, showpiece bed. Merle travels patterns made for a larger space; he misses corners and seems likely to walk right through walls. In all these years he has not adjusted to new surroundings. He still walks the routes he established in the house he shared with Tannis twenty years ago.

On Merle's birthday Cal comes by with a book.

Ersatz. It's won prizes, he says. You'll love it—are you there?

But the door is open and Merle is out. Cal walks to the bed and spends a few minutes arranging the book and the card symmetrically across the thin, stiff pillows until the gift looks as if it was not placed but born there, then notices that the key he dropped off has not been moved. It has been more than six weeks since he last came by and Merle has not slept on this bed. He has an image of his father coming home and dozing where he stands, rigid in a corner, propped upright by the fridge. Merle's scent at chin-height all over these walls.

So he takes the book and the card and stands them against

the wall outside. When he next visits two weeks later the wall has opened to receive them but they haven't moved an inch.

I'm back, says 801.

He thinks about Merle and his faint, faxed directions to places and about toasting socks, woollen croissants at 350 degrees Fahrenheit, crimped into foil.

I'm here, go on, says 801.

Back, yes. Forget timing, sequence, plausibility, coherence—focus on the elements, the groupings, the rhythms, Cal says.

The what?

The groupings, the rhythms. Then and now.

Whoa; stop. You're losing me, says 801.

You want to know why and it doesn't matter why, Cal says. It's the elements, the overlaps, the *rhythms*. The story—it's still moving, every which way at once.

Merle dies, you freak, various breakdowns, some crackpot apartment, the groupings, the rhythms, not the plot. What am I *doing* here; what is my *role*? asks 801.

You're my listener of record, Cal says. You're keeping track, he says.

EARLIER, TANNIS

Cal and the Traveller get to Tannis's house by taxi, at noon. The Traveller gets out first, tilted back, rearing. The trip has whetted its forty-litre appetite. It has the scent of the carousels and is wilful, impatient; a bonny red bronco lined with sateen. Cal leads it, lurching and kicking, by its integral halter to the door.

We're together, says Cal, of the Traveller.

Well come in. Round the back, Tannis says. It's filthy and I don't want tracks. Isn't it nice, the vestibule? Tempered glazed glass, ceiling to floor. That's Italian, she says. The flooring. It comes packed in a pastry tube.

Italian, Cal says. Nice. 12:12. He finds his list in its Velcro

— 44 —

pocket, guts the Traveller, eases out a folder marked with the number 1. His notes for Tannis.

Like pastry. Like pastry the kitchen puffs and cracks, peeling all the way back to the sink. Under such pressure even Italian flooring must give. Everything has elongated in the aftermath as if in dying Merle became adhesive, pulling this house along with him. Drooping blinds, varicose marble, stretched-out broadloom. The gravel drive oriented north.

You've got mail everywhere, she says. I had a box. A mailbox, she says. Where is it? Who the hell knows? Lost. Like everything. Is it you who loves lamb?

In the yard chestnuts are primed scattered mines. The toolshed door, hinge rusted open, hosts squirrels and centipedes and weird luminous beetles that push their belongings before them in huge wheels of dust like rubbies with their shopping carts. Broad-hipped ants, garter snakes. Everything here lives by rummaging.

Sunday was his birthday, did you mark it? she says. He'd be what—he'd be fifty-two. Seven in the morning. Long at birth. They could have swaddled him in a bun and sold him as a hot-dog, ha ha.

Though Cal came in the back she asks him to walk round and ring the doorbell.

Like you're taking me out, she says. Like it's something special.

When Tannis is ready, he walks round. Rings. Waits. From inside, her vague hustle. Clumps of mud and grass, a suite of headless garden tools in a rack.

That's not some garbage, it's landscaping, she says. Wipe your feet, she says. No shoes inside. Let's have your coat, she says. Hold your horses, she says, tilting up at his face, flirting. Jeepers—it's you!

$\oplus$

Tannis stands and peers into a group of boxes. The boxes have significance, associations. They have been places, carried things. She will stare at a group of them, set in a pattern reflecting some lunar mystery, some unseen pattern of the gods.

Hmm, she says critically.

While Tannis deliberates, Cal explores. The house she has chosen is a new sheen on an old plan. It has a vertical row of sash windows cross-hatched like the buttons on a duffel coat. There are flagstone paths and beds of colour-coded perennials even she will be unable to harm. While she decides upon the dimensions of the bespoke front deck the steps stand by themselves fifteen feet from the door. A single stack of steps, with railings, a wrought-iron atoll on the lawn.

Awaiting attachment, she says. Detachment. What's the difference? The jerk who's going to build it hands out tins of licorice mints.

Merle and Tannis. Tannis and Merle. Tannis and Merle played instruments. Tannis played the piano, badly enough to be thrilled by the effect of the sustain pedal. She whacked and eked and echoed her way through "Ode to Joy" and "Voodoo Chile" and "Four Strong Winds." Merle had bought the best guitar and the finest set of drums. His guitar lay in a felt coffin with gorgeous gem-like picks tamped beneath the strings. Merle set the metronome, strummed part of the chord into "Goodnight Irene."

A, says Tannis, persisting in the note. A—A—A—!

They went to workshops together to learn their animal totems and to conclude that they were the offspring of this or that concatenation of stars. Covertly, they ate magic mushrooms, over pasta, in a cream sauce. Tannis sold the jellies and jams she made with soft wax seals. Merle took to watching the news.

When does it happen, the dissolution of Merle from Tannis, of Tannis from Merle? What causes it? By the time Cal makes kindergarten—glue and pasta, Dixie cups of juice—tension is the soil he is expected to thrive in, riding between home and Mrs. Kidney's classroom pinched into the plastic bicycle seat, quick suppers, low intense arguing voices and who was it anyway who let who down?

Know? I don't know, she says. I can't understand you when you talk so fast. I don't have X-ray eyes.

Fine, says Cal.

Don't yell at me, she says. I'm old, and I can't bear it.

Once he saw them kiss, heads back, tongues sliding, both with their eyes shut. Tannis slimmed her fingers and pressed them down Merle's trousers, squeezed his bare ass. Tannis whispered, Merle laughed. Her mouth at his ear, chanting.

I'm looking for the thing the thing the *base*, says Tannis. It's silver and has a bird shape. There was a fish and a bear and a loon to match the jewellery I already have and to hold the salt. I thought, well obviously not the fish which was frankly curly and not the bear that used its paws. The loon was so pretty, its mouth was open, and somehow they've got separated, the two pieces. No, she says. Not that box, it's receipts.

Fine, says Cal. Let me know, he says. No rush, he says. This one? he asks.

Everything is in pieces because the movers were in a rush—

Well, I'm not in a rush, says Cal. This one? he asks, again.

—didn't bother with the lists and the labels that said what went with what. Who knows? she says. For three days I wore my neighbour's glasses. I took store coupons to the bank. Stop it, she says. What would you have done? How many weekends did I ever get away for? If he had done it in your house, would you have stayed put?

—

They rented a cottage on a cold lake. Merle in long trunks, grey as a snail in the sun. Triangle sandwiches and thermos juice, pale-green grapes, crumbly walnut cookies, damp books with curling pages and exciting covers: girls with flashlights in caves, New York brownstones. Adventures, conundrums; six thousand dimes in a jar. Three rooms with yellow-brown carpeting, alluvial sanctuary for woodlice and earwigs puzzling their way back to their homes in the walls.

It's small and it smells, says Tannis of the cottage by the lake. The size is a turn-off but the smell I can't stand. I can't bear it, she says, it's revolting.

Cal looks at his notes. Dad planned this, he says. He'd been planning it for years.

What? says Tannis. It's one o'clock, she says. If we're going we'd better scoot.

It was Tannis who went and arranged the cleanup team before she could put the house up for sale. Accidents. Misuse. Death remediation. Murder.

It's my responsibility, Cal says to Tannis. I'll do it myself, he says.

You will understand if I don't pay much attention to what you think.

Clean Scenes is the company. It dispatches teams and a range of promotional videos. Death remediation with a 100 percent satisfaction guarantee. All traces removed, all surfaces cleansed, disinfected, resurfaced. From grime to blood and hazards.

I'll talk you though it, says their liaison, Clean Scenes Customer Sales Rep Number 12. Alf. He is dressed in a sparkling bio suit with integral name tag and bar code. Everything about Alf is clean and reassuring. His voice would whiten coffee. His close shave and healthy chest, diamond in the buff. His clipped hair in the shape of a tonsil.

We're first of all gonna define the spill zone, says Alf. He smiles, and punches a few keys on his tablet. To do this we use visual marking and infrared. Then we seal and steal—separate the scene from the rest of its environment and get straight to work. We are not merely bleaching and fumigating here. We are using the highest possible technology in order to remove all traces of the event to be remediated.

But it will be clean? Tannis wants to know.

Ma'am, smiles Alf, I doubt you'd ever want to eat supper off these floors. But if you did, you could.

They arrive in a branded van, all wearing suits and helmets. Alf and four others with trunks of equipment and locking orange sacks for the disposal of waste. Sounds of vacuum and spraying, buzzing lights. Cal thinks about all the smoke ghosts of Merle, all the CO_2 stains on the walls, like cave paintings, the once-indelible images of death. Now even that can be neutralized, he thinks, made pine-fresh.

We know what happens when a trauma scene is released, says Alf. This and that removed as evidence and the rest left as is. Loved ones should not have to confront this, he says, sounds as if he really means it. Blood and body fluids, brains on the wall. Our task—our mission—is to remove painful reminders and ensure future safety. Our patented process, recognized by many leading law-and-order organizations, allows us to clean what our rivals cannot see. Pathogens and micro-organisms. Filial love. The laciest, palest lies.

Alf and his gang work steadily. Their respirators hum, and the fans in their goggles. They floodlight the garage. They spray enzymes from canisters mounted on silent, low-slung trolleys. They find the raised edge of good intentions, whisk them up and away. They funnel last chances dozens at a time. In six hours the building and its annexes have been secured.

Even the bill is a bit of class: a gatefold envelope, with before and after photographs professionally time- and date-stamped. All clear. Alf is very nice. His whole team come by for iced tea and sugar cookies. They wriggle free of their helmets and shake off their respirators, emanating tough-times comradeship like the boys of Apollo 13.

Thank you, they say. Homemade?

It's difficult. This marvellous cleanliness, this fine conscientious erasure of one spiky, disjointed moment. Tannis in a fanciful sweater and large stone earrings dishing out bought sugar cookies to a team of ghouls in their underthings, bright biohazard tape everywhere, the neighbours stopping and staring, the ozonic fresh smells. He thinks he might convert his memories of Merle—but where are they? where are they?—into stain agents, fast dyes splashed everywhere to soak into everything, unsightly and profane.

The windows have been done. The floors. The kitchen and the three scattered bathrooms. By done, Tannis means recuperated, scooped out and filled in and high-polished to her taste. Rosy stone, low fixtures, elbow-shaped taps, invisible appliances: the dishwasher sits in its own chest of drawers, the oven slides into a closet, a toaster is lodged in a wall.

It is a dream house, impractical by daylight. The cool floors are stripped, stained, pitted already, less than twenty days old. The dishwasher scours the plates and pots and glasses and cutlery during the wash cycle and while rinsing obligingly regurgitates the dirt. The toaster sears the right side of the thin bread it exclusively accepts, and leaves the left side raw. The blender and the mixer stall. The attractive new gem-cut windows, flush with the walls, develop hairline fractures in their grouting and admit moisture into the supposed vacuum between their three glazed layers, and fog up. Spiders lay eggs in the central heating ducts, and the brood balloon majestically down in their thousands. The dryer overheats and its elements are exhausted, and the resultant humidity entices burrowing beetles and mice the size of corks who feast upon cloth and plastics.

Enumerating these disasters, Tannis grows radiant.

And, after all that, would you believe, the part—the only part—is no longer manufactured. "Duct tape will hold it," he told me. Duct tape!

Here, Cal says. Is this it?

No, she says, a little weary. No—that's the base for the bear.

Cal asks for an autopsy. He wants to know how the thing was done. He wants to establish that Merle was free of disease, or perhaps that he wasn't, that all of this has had a specific, visible, organic cause: a lethal blast of leukocytes, a clot upon the brain.

No, says Tannis.

It's important.

No, what were you thinking?

Cut him open, says Cal.

No.

Cut him open—at the chest.

No.

At the ankles, run a zipper up his back—why not? asks Cal, reasonably. Incidentally, I'm the one of us who is considered next of kin. What does it matter to him? We'll know something, he says. How can that hurt?

Tannis runs her fists against him, abraded and pink like herring mouths—what has she done to her hands?—and swears decisively. She scatters and packs and scatters and packs her bag and stands outside his door crying to herself.

Cal thinks about Merle neatly nipped about his contours before an admiring crowd in one of the old operating theatres you can pay to tour or rent for a party, a circle ringed with hard seats, the surgeon under anamorphic light.

Here is the spot, says the surgeon, snips and extrudes something hot and quivery from Merle's nasal cavity. Here's the culprit, here.

Cal will stand close and study Merle from the inside out and if he prepares himself and is careful and thorough he will learn something conclusive.

Full of holes, says the surgeon. Organs like cribbage boards, chewed clean through.

Cal calls Tannis. I'm sorry, he says. You don't know. I wanted to find something I could use, he says. You have no idea.

It's done, says Tannis.

What's done?

I burned him, says Tannis. At Greenlawn, on Thursday. It's done.

She waits for Cal to speak.

It's too late for such cruelty, she says. You'd better think about that.

Cal thinks of the ovens, of the pulse at the back of the blaze.

No; you're too late, actually, he says. Whatever he had, I've got.

I'm going to lie down, Tannis says. I'm exhausted. I'm peaky, not enough sun. If it were east-facing, she says. Instead of locked in by alleys. It's like living in a spoon.

She is smaller than he remembers, more fly-away, all stray hair and roomy shoes, a cough could topple her. Merle's death, this move and its marathon renovation have nearly defeated her. That noise—a pounding and scraping at Tannis's roof, her neighbour at his infernal machinery in the oily mess of a pigeon roost.

It began as a stick, says Tannis. Now there's a scoop at the end. Yesterday the lever that operates the scoop. I see he's waxed the end, for what? For greater glide. He is now in a position, says Tannis, to pry the birds from the roof. You should see my shingles. Marks like teeth.

From next door the banging, the cunning work of the lever.

He's got one, Cal says.

He doesn't want one. It's the trying he loves. The refining.

— 52 —

—

Cal recalls a time—once, distant—when Merle is approachable, lying in his bed with a basic pocket television that broadcasts the medians of channels, summed noise and picture, swimmy and approximate. There are three to six channels at once or no channels whatsoever, two ways of looking at the world. Cal comes in at seven-thirty to watch the playoffs blended with a game show and a car chase and the news, reports on the apparent movements of the ghostly, fractured players so distorted by the scattered signal that they skate across several planes of space and time simultaneously and Merle tilts the antenna in minute increments and Cal thinks that what Merle, after all, is willing to share is his focus.

Sit down. Take it easy, Cal says to Tannis. We'll go when you're ready to go.

Merle and Tannis manage one another through things they remember, stories they tell. Merle's are about events, happenings. Tannis's concern states.

That's when—Merle says.

We were—says Tannis.

Merle in Tannis's stories is fractious and bemused, operating with a brisk irrationalism. He walks out of restaurants and won't go to restaurants and objects to new ideas and sits in the living room reading the newspaper holed by a toxic leak from the roof he refuses to have fixed because it was guaranteed for thirty years and there are eight years left. He loops around and around a ski lift he never bothered to learn to dismount safely. He drives them to a lodge in Vermont because he missed Quebec. This is Merle—blunt in his disasters, whittling in his needs.

Tannis in Merle's stories—the few Cal has heard—is brilliant and wilful and disgusted. She loses ancestral pearls at the school's parents' night. She takes lessons on the sly so that she can beat him at everything. She shaves her head to travel round Europe.

She has contested, asynchronous friendships with people she admires but cannot commit to getting on with because she knows they are bound to disappoint her.

Cal has no way of squaring these different versions of his parents; they will never add up. He knows nothing about Tannis that might lead her to pause in the middle of grading a paper on language and its discontents and know absolutely that while her world includes her husband and a son and a job with limits and a house set into a ravine like a larynx in the middle of a scream she can imagine herself with none of these things and might even prefer it. He knows nothing about Merle that could convince him to sit at a folding card table that was the temporary table in their pantry for twenty years and decide, once and for all, to destroy himself. Merle and Tannis. Tannis and Merle.

Near the end they had supper, the three of them, first time in years. Merle, shaky, finding it impossible to eat with a fork, said he'd bumped into a guy he'd grown up with, a lawyer now, who had ten brothers, enough to ice the first two lines of a hockey team.

You'd never get that now, Merle said. That *fecund*ity.

Don't swear, said Tannis.

What grows now? I mean left-alone grows? Nothing, Merle said. Not kids.

Oh please, said Tannis. Listen to him!

They weren't even Catholics, Merle said. Not even Catholics, he said.

Cal's Merle and Tannis's Merle. Cal and Tannis and the deep blue Merle between.

He was kind to me when my sister died, says Tannis. He sang—a real tenor.

This is the last time Cal and Tannis talk about Merle that he remembers. His kindness when they were twenty-one. His mild uncrafted tenor. A habit of collecting things to forget them, peony in his back pocket, chocolates in the glove of the car. The resin in his best ideas. And then, finally, seeing his way with unaccustomed clarity towards his one great deed.

Some people construct their lives in the direction of achievement, order, staying afloat. Merle built his towards pity. For Merle, pity was the thin wedge.

Hey, Cal says to Tannis.

He hands her the loon salver.

Oh! she says, all sleepy. Oh, where did you find it?

She is in bed with her feet up to rest her ankles. Then she will raise her head and neck to drain her lymph.

I tried, Cal says. I tried my best to save him. What could I do, long-term?

He didn't want you to save him, she says.

No, says Cal. To save him, no. He wanted me to find him, and in time. He wanted me to find him and generally I did. He hid but he advertised widely. He found me out, Cal says.

The inquest is held in a box room with a raised platform where the officials sit and punch busily into their computers and interpretation is available and translation is available and coffee and water and tea. Cal and Tannis, Tannis and Cal.

It's certainly far bigger than I thought it would be; it's a much larger room, Tannis says. Are those microphones? she wants to know. My one wool suit and it's covered in cat hair; how did that happen? she says.

A medical examiner with a runny nose discusses levels in the blood and seizure of the facial muscles and tinting of the skin. Everyone nods.

The presiding official clears her throat. We are all here, she says.

Tannis is itching and Cal is nauseous and he thinks that in the car on the way over Tannis sat holding her feet in the air above his all-season mats, and here she is in this rented theatre and her feet are firmly planted.

There is no doubt in anyone's mind and everyone is free to go and they do so with many feeling glances for Cal and Tannis and the horror of this is that they *are* genuinely feeling glances; it has come to this, so general and devalued is empathy that anyone has the right and the obligation to care about anyone else, and this collection of fourteen government appointees and their minions—every one a former valedictorian, every one a tither, every one a grinder of coffee and a layer-down of wine—can care, honestly care, about Cal and Tannis and even, perhaps, Merle. The empathy, the empathy, this grief.

On the way home Tannis is quiet and Cal wonders why she kept her feet off the mats and what this must have cost her, her ruined knees, thin calves.

Thank you, she says, after a while. Thank you for driving and . . . for driving.

He tries to tell her. There were the rehearsals and then there was the thing itself, he tells her. Seven rehearsals, then the thing itself. The car and the pills and the bridge and the traffic and the propane and the bag and the car and the cookies. Seven times, he says. You didn't know that. There's something else—

Tannis shivers, lets herself out.

There is a time when Cal thinks that there might be somewhere in the world a prosthetic through which Merle might yet be saved, his rusted-up basal ganglia swapped out for a new stiff synthetic will guaranteed immune to the body's trickery. No akrasia, no dystrophy; just good old lust for life.

Why do you do it?

Merle drives.

Why?

Merle by now has let everything go. Apartment reduced to a mat on a floor. His clothes stiff and shiny. His body slack as a glove.

You've given this some thought, Cal says.

Merle drives.

Cal thinks back to the Giant's gorgeous foot, whisked steel and wire and a high arch Merle could pack with Semtex. Beauty, love, blood-ties, threats—none of it will sway him now.

He takes Tannis out to lunch to a place someone she knows has recommended, compact booths, breadbaskets on the table, salt and pepper shakers like transparent rooks, serviettes folded to soft white swans, prints of Tuscan landscapes. Knotty green olive trees, deep hills. The waiter's pad is in triplicate, whatever he writes he writes thrice. Tannis twists her neck to the right and the left as if unscrewing and reseating it.

Those pigeons, I don't know if he could bear to kill one, she says. They keep him going. We grow older, we waste less. Your father, with you, was not frugal, she says.

No, says Cal.

It is the seventh of September and Merle has been dead one year.

My house, she says. Why did he have to do it in my house?

I don't know, Cal says. It was one place he remembered clearly. It was on his route.

Well, says Tannis. They are unpleasant, those birds. Dishevelling. I was brushing my teeth with the window open and one hopped in. I screamed and it jumped, and just hovered. Hovered, she says. Vitruvian bird.

He drives Tannis home, sees her to the door. She takes pleasure in all the wrong things, he used to think. Sophisticated wind chimes, traditions in paint hues, pendant lips, clothes worn by other women, tenderness. Tannis turns her key, turns to Cal and curtsies and straightens, curtsies and straightens; in the arch of the doorway, vitruvian, the dishevelling bird in the hand.

THE TRAIN

You begin.

You begin with the train and the great synchronizing of the clocks in September, 1855. Where was time before this? There was no agreement on a present, a now. Now might be noon in Brighton and 2:17 in Carlisle and between 12:04 and 12:51 across London, a city in which it was possible to take a short trip and arrive before you had left.

You have them. This is history, after all, just the kind of human knot that interests people, the slow precise dismantling of the screening between then and now. You have your watch—visual aid—you bring it up slowly to the space between your eyes, let it turn, turn, turn and—continue. Time, trains, the question of when now is.

Now. There is a signal, years in the making, the perfect hour wrought and polished and wrapped and sent from Greenwich, that will install a perfect rationalization of time. The hour like this story not merely arrived at but designed, constructed in its 3,600 one-second partitions and thoroughly inspected, walked around by men and twenty different makes of watches tweaked by tiny screwdrivers until it sheds less than a minute with each daily rotation, until it is an hour they can be proud of, an hour to be kept under glass.

In every railway station identical clocks made of cast-steel with a glass dome and arrows for indicators. Swiss movement, Welton manufacture, each with a key and twin indentations for minute and hour. Freshly wound today, at one minute past midnight; those clocks that lost more than a minute by seven this morning were retired and replaced. What a display of precision, of technology, of mankind harnessing the springs of the universe to the great project of travel, the free exchange of goods and bodies throughout these islands, a yoke upon the world.

With their seven hundred handsets and their seven hundred clocks the men and women listen and count and set, listen and count and set.

Twenty . . . twenty . . . twenty . . .

The hour and the minute hands already centred. Second hands poised in shallow divots. In this way the country will align itself with twenty-twenty, at the end of this glorious Fall day, in the hole left by twilight, in the sleek chromatic dusk.

It begins with the train. You know this. That is to say, you know a little about this train. Anyone might, if they had taken the time to look into it. You know that on the night of September 2 the families and friends and landladies and lovers of anywhere between 322 and 430 passengers expected the 16:10 from Cavern to Birkenhead, scheduled to arrive at 19:04. That it didn't arrive at 19:04, you know. You know, though the families and friends and landladies and lovers could not have, that this train would never arrive, that it lay stranded and smoking twenty-eight miles and seventy minutes southwest between stations at a town whose value to anyone who didn't live there (and even to many who did) was as a switching-point and a ten-mile shortcut and whose value as a shortcut was threatened by a recently tabled motion calling for new tracks to be laid through Crawley by the following March after the settling of outstanding claims.

Now the 16:10 special from Cavern to Birkenhead, scheduled to arrive at 19:04, sparks along a wet track, powdering twigs and stamping bottle-caps set carefully on the line by enterprising children into freshly minted coins. The train, fourteen carriages bolted trunk to tail, some of which are new and some of which are old and therefore lack the latest safety features, windows that lock from the inside and compartments of glass partitions instead of wooden panels—innovations intended to control the burglaries and occasional murders perpetrated on the main line and to prevent another carnage like that in Northumberland, where seven died after a carpet caught fire in the smoking carriage and the windows, locked from the outside, too thick and gluey to break, ensured that the only escape route was no escape at all but a blind chance tumble headfirst into an oil fire. Tragedy. Picture it—

You picture it. You have the elements and you have the time. You build the train and you people it. And then you climb aboard.

The trains, you say, they're out of sequence. Keep your eye on the trains and don't waste time connecting them. Don't worry if they don't line up.

You are facing the wrong way—backwards.

Still you can follow this, especially if you know about trains and care enough to link what you see to what you know and what you know to what you might predict, beginning with the train, this train, with its pick-and-mix carriages, its steam engine, humpbacked, huge and spouting, a great whale thrusting into onrushing countryside (or so will shout the hyperbole the yellowest tabloid of them all come the morning when news of this catastrophe, in all of its wild inaccuracy, explodes). Thirty miles distant, a switchman wipes his slurry nose, yawns.

It is autumn, September. It is evening. The girl waits at the train station, out of sight, squatting, rocking heel to toe. Dory. Her hair is three shades of red. She is slightly nearsighted. Traps have sprung in her chest. Bits of feather in her hands. Her ribs squeeze. Breath shortens. Too late—that thought in her head for good.

I have done a terrible, terrible thing.

This passage is the secret beginning of the letter Dory writes, a letter she is still writing. Secret because sometimes it is part of the letter and sometimes it is not. How does she do this? With a flap over the lines like a pop-up book. With the flap open the letter has this hidden lever: the crime that begins and ends the story and suspends it in place, the whole under linear pressure, all the elements groomed one way. How odd that Dory of all people would work in this manner. What did Ruth used to call her? A swerver. Like that short-finned fish that swims only at angles even if it would rather go straight, even if its food is directly before it. The time-wasting fish, *Pisces eratus*, one of Nature's wan jokes.

She has been writing this letter a long time, though her interest in it has grown and waned and like all tedious work it has spent its share of time shelved beneath more immediate pleasures. In the years she spent with Ruth, before and after their daughter, she managed to set aside this letter and the part of her life it indexed. Ruth, in her tall and world-embracing abstractedness, made a condition of her lack of interest in Dory's past. They would be new to one another, she declared. Forward-looking, clean-skinned. Ruth renounced her surgeries and history of failure with pets. Dory forgot her experiments with yarn-based hobbies and the worst part of the worst year of her life. Well, Ruth managed her end.

Among her correspondence this letter is unique. For one thing, it is unfinished. Rough. For another it is what Dory would call expository. It sets out to tell a story, to align a lot of cross-ways facts. Themes? Forgiveness, maybe. This is one of three or four themes she returns to that offer complexity, scope. Wanting. Self-deception. Wisdom, hard-won. In this version of the letter, with the lever up and the secret gaping, Dory considers what she has come to call her tragedy. Tragedy—a not unproblematic term, spoilt by a single flaw that irks the gods. But Dory's tragedy is not bookended by her greatness and her flaw. Tragedy, in that sense, scarcely applies to her at all. Error, then. Or lapse. The exact circumstances of her lapse and the reasons for it have pre-occupied Dory in later years. With each addition to this letter they have become more clear but they are never quite clear. She has always intended, once she has drafted her letter fully, exactly, to copy it out nicely and follow through, post it to someone, it doesn't matter who, enter it into the public record. But who besides Dory would bother, would make the effort to rescue and reassemble her letter from this slumber of invitations and bills she has pasted into this old book she has kept from her girl-hood? *Girlhood*—a word from her girlhood that has been replaced with harder, meaner, more knowing words. The lexicon itself has been got at, Dory thinks. Coarsened. Scraped away. Not one or two words but all of them. Perhaps this is part of the intractability of the letter she is writing: that the words she began it with are exhausted, no longer able to cut the world at its joints.

She pauses to note where she is: long brown settee with a parsley-coloured cushion, corner desk with fly-addled water in a glass shaped like stacked gumdrops, portable fan, tissues. These details she adds in a neat descending string down the page's left margin. Setting the scene. In her bathtub a collapsible rack with a blanket on it she has just hand-washed and laid dripping. What had got into it? The water ran brown for three full rinses and finally she gave up. And here nearly a day has passed and it drips still. Too heavy by far for her to wring. It is the very devil, achieving a fit between her present thoughts and feelings, her state, as she writes, and those of whoever might one day read this. When she started this letter as a girl of twelve Dory had a habit of annotation. When a thing proved difficult or tedious to describe she left it out to be filled in later with a little indicating curlicue in the margin and the date of revision. Sometimes, rarely, she went back.

Going back. Revision. Isn't that what she is guilty of here? She has decided to focus and to exclude. One year. One summer. Every time she sits down now she tops and tails the letter, trims a little more off each end. And here she is with fewer than eighty pages and the rest in a red leather box hinged by magnets misoriented so they oppose one another and the box won't shut, slackjacked yokel with her life's work spilling from its gawp—

Noise on the street. Tractor? Cloud like a fish. Her swollen arthritic hands seem stuffed with wet cotton; heavy, bulging. At one o'clock, lunch.

It is autumn, September. It is evening—

She opens the folder, looks for the tabs in yellow. Red, yellow, blue, black. She brought little with her on this trip—her mortivacation, her daughter called it, in her cool elsewhere voice. Speaking to her face to face was like phoning long-distance, just as expensive and remote. Tilly, who has always done everything with the enormous diffidence that Ruth obtained for her with a wide and indulgent education, is pregnant by one of the artist-roughnecks she finds herself dating—inadvertently, virally, man-thrax, she calls it—and has begun to phone Dory in panics not about her actual situation but about its analogues in the larger world. She sends newspaper articles about famines and carcinogens, the slow infiltration of fruit. She exaggerates sideswipes into full-bore accidents and says "me and the . . ." pausing so Dory will understand that now there is a child involved and it is serious. Dory endured this for two months and then let it be known that she would be away through the beginning of the month and only in emergencies reachable by a third party who had access to her phone. Then she left.

Station, leaving. Leaving is one of the great themes.

It is autumn, September. It is evening. The girl
waits at the train station

There is something unsettling about this passage. For one, it is not her usual style. Processional. She would call it processional, grave. It is less a description than a posture, she thinks. Ruth, who died last year, maintained that posture was the human constant: anatomical, cognitive, moral, sensual. Ruth, who shrunk like a leech when touched in the last few months. Who could no longer tolerate light. Whose scalp came away with the hand towel.

And if I need you? asked Tilly.

To obey her, Dory thinks, is to never again be unobliged.

One month, Dory said, hung up.

The girl waits

Dory tapes the flap open, notes where she was, reads over the last sentence, begins:

Dory is six and leaving the town she was born in. The day before the day they leave Dory says goodbye to her three friends in West Roger: Dougie, Judith and Seth's mother. Dory and Seth do not get along but this doesn't faze his mother, for whom Dory is a valued companion: similarly afflicted, used to listening, reassuringly plain.

Well, I'll take brains over beauty, Seth's mother says. Lasts longer and costs less.

When Dory drops by for the last time, Seth's mother goes to a lot of trouble, fixing her a milky English tea and a stack of carob brownies in the shape of noughts and crosses that Dory has to eat with a fork wrong-handed because Seth's mother has trapped her left to stroke and pet while sniffling and murmuring about eating up and how delicious and hasn't someone got a hollow leg while Dory stuffs herself with two whole games of noughts and crosses and Seth picks his nose onto the Saturday comics. Beetle Bailey. Dagwood. Ol' Rum Skunk.

When Dory has to go Seth pulls his finger out long enough for his mother to take a Polaroid of the two of them upright and unhappy, blinded by the five-bar flash.

Say "caw" like a crow, she instructs them. Don't move, don't *breathe*; you're blurring.

Seth slopes off, and Seth's mother hands Dory a parcel and a sheaf of stamped SAEs.

Poor Seth, she says, clicks her tongue. He'll miss you. He is a human oyster and you are the sand in his shell. Write to me, but not if you're happy. If you're happy I can wait.

Dougie's dad is a doctor who hands out penny lollipops like they're going out of style. He gives them to kids with chicken pox, kids with new back teeth, kids who fall off bridges and ladders and log piles and bikes, kids hit by BBs, bed-wetters and scab-pickers, the virally ill. He is a candy machine with a stethoscope, a coin-op MD.

Dougie wears his hair slicked up and has chronic boils along his forehead and neck that swell or shrink with his mood. Today he comes by with an angel food cake he can't quit staring at. Dory wants to leave him something. She finds him a pail of plastic soldiers, hand-painted, sporting identical chalky faces except for one, a German Kommandant. His is a red tattoo.

Izzee the leader?

I guess, says Dory. You can have him. All of them.

Uminuminum, Dougie says.

Thank you for playing with me—

But Dougie is rumbling the bucket. Some of 'em is doubles, he says. This 'n' this I got.

Judith is a fierce girl with a pook-out tum and a mouth that has always unsettled Dory, darker than the rest of her face, a bumblebee's black mask. Now she grates arrowroot biscuits across her teeth, spiderlegging drool.

D'you wanna hear something really really funny?

I guess.

Didja hear the one about the broken pencil?

No.

It's pointless.

Dancing round, squeaking her white rubber soles.

Hey Dory!

Huh yeah?

Well willya *watch* me?

They play Judith's own game: Favourite Ladies. These Favourite Ladies are beautiful and house-proud, they ride horses with mop manes stinking of pine cleanser. Dory is Kind Lady and Judith is Brave Lady. Kind Lady loses her mount to things in the woods and wails from a tree to be rescued by Brave Lady and spelled into life. After which they lounge in the shade moss and plot elegant suppers until Judith gets hungry enough to head home.

Peas and tinned sockeye, she says. I spread it on toast.

Judith has a goodbye card, a fat valentine on red cardboard sparkling with sequins puffed onto white wood glue.

It's a beating heart, she says.

Inside the beating heart are two regular hearts mounted on pink, folded-paper springs. *Will You Be My Valentine?* is crossed out and in its place Judith has written: *Judith Judith Judith.* Three times for luck, Judith squeaks, then blowkisses, runs off, fishing in her pockets then grating grating grating at her cookie flocked with lint.

Dory stays up late, cross-legged among the boxes and packing tape, staring at her bare washed walls. There she had a magazine picture of a northern winter. Atop an ice crest a wolf, looking like the kind of creature she would like to be: structured, agile, weighty; not with baby fat but with meaning.

They move five times in four years for the sake of three jobs and a one-time opportunity. Each of the three jobs turns out to be unsuitable and the one-time opportunity disappears into the pockets of a veterinary-supplies associate who takes fifty dollars for a "starter set" containing salt tablets, gloves with insect parts embedded in them and a book on equine welfare from the Court of King James.

No matter. They leave again. Barnett, her father, plans it beautifully. He is an old hand. He comes home from work outraged. Once again he has been passed over. Two of them do the main sales and the other, a nephew of the firm's owner, is promoted to a position fit for a man twice his age. Then Barnett waits while June comes slowly to the boil. Barnett. June. Dory. Dory and Barnett and June. How often has she seen it? Barnett has only to say he's feeling changey and June, like him a leaver by disposition, begins in her mind the unwinding of things from their places that will evolve into packing and unpacking somewhere new. For June and Barnett, leaving is an act of imagination, the axle of the wheeling self-revisions that came as a gift of war. In this great project Dory is a hindrance. She is small, slow. She wishes for impractical things. Home, companionship, a working knowledge of some town. So she is given tasks suited to her. Hold the packing tape. Find the caps for the permanent markers. Roll paper towel into strips to cushion dishes.

Where are we going?

Your father's horizons, says June affectionately, expand to fit the space.

Barnett lets his beard grow up to his glasses and down to his chest. June buys a series of fruit-coloured dresses without waists which agitate the neighbours. In a photograph Dory finds years later there they are: Barnett grinning, mad-bearded, head tilted to one side as though he is presenting something; June serious but with eyes focused very precisely; Dory with thick glasses slipping off her lopsided ear, some of her hair in motion as though she had been twisting her head with incredible force, no no no no no. But she does not remember this, picture or locution. She can't remember saying no as a child, not once.

Finally, at the age of eleven, Dory sets down roots. She and her mother and father now live in the town of Absinthe at the old orchards at Lount's Point. The new house is really an old house with eight rooms not including the cellar and back and front stairs connected by a corridor with a wall-mount laundry chute that still has laundry in it, someone's striped pyjamas, hemmed by mice and moths. Striped blue flannel waist 38 and a tiny filmy thing for a baby so short the arms meet the legs practically. There is a plate and a mug in the dish rack, a packet of biscuits dissolved to crumbs, and in the icebox a carton of orange juice and some hard cheese and a clutch of quilted towelling. Casement windows crammed with flies.

Are you sure? June asks. Is this the house we came cross-country for?

June was a nurse in the London Blitz. Klaxons, rubble, hot tea, hymns in the underground. These lodestone memories have protected her. Now she wears a raincoat in spite of the heat, a blue raincoat with a fitted belt and seamless slant pockets for her hands. With her unerring radar for proving a point she slits open the box marked Miscellany and produces the real estate sheet and reads passages Barnett has underlined: character, charm and Greek proportions; all-day light.

This carpet is like chewing gum, she says. These windows—what do they remind me of? Lead in a wound.

She curls a finger along the baseboard spiky with finishing nails.

You had it appraised, she says, tugging at the carpet with her heel.

A conservatory! shouts Barnett from the darkness at the rear of the house. Barnett. June. Barnett and June and Dory.

Manor house, you said. Beautifully preserved . . .

Rose bushes! calls Barnett. This you must—

Remodelled, says June, testing the first of the stairs. Bathroom *en suite*.

Come *on*, come *on*, warbles Barnett. A hornet has stung me for luck.

Old and new things; the house is full of them just as though the old owner packed and left in a hurry, and never checked under the beds to find the undoing of the owner before him and the owner before that. Dory finds an egg timer and a radio valve in the kitchen and in the pantry sixteen damp bricks of Cow Brand baking soda and an enormous roll of silver foil with patterns etched onto it by a pick. There is a half glass of greenish water on the shelf by her bed and a clothespin mounted in plaster and a Bible turned backwards, spine to the wall. Unable to sleep in this thrill, in the heat, she lies on the bedcovers watching the back-slanting light, its shapely abstractions, a man made of wire—

I saw something, she tells June, at breakfast. Last night, on the wall.

You will excuse the charring. The stove is old. Primitive even, says June, smearing porridge into shallow bowls. It has neither dials nor thermometer. It does not cook the food but rather succours it. Like the St. John's Ambulance this stove first does no harm. Present it with a slab of raw meat and three hours later its condition is unchanged. But for all that, it is capricious. Offer it porridge or a fresh egg and it incinerates them in a flash.

I was up I don't know the middle of the night; when the moon hit the wall I saw a man there a wire man—

You do not surprise me, June says. I fully believe this to have been a slaughterhouse. Move in, go mad, do murder. Do not mind the lights, June continues. Avert your eyes if they should seem to flicker. And consume your gruel. All of it, she says. You must gather strength for pitonning the staircase. Be sure to leave the kitchen by the left-most door, she says. Beneath the right door lies a fault line. I forecast the very grimmest consequences, she says, of looking at anything too hard.

—a man made of wire, a book inside a book—

Please, says June, fingers at her temples. Please please please please please!

What had she seen? The man composed of wire and meshing, metal easing into flesh. The book inside a book. She asks Barnett to fit a curtain for the window, and later she explores the attic and cold cellar, the shed in the yard. Piles and piles of old books with hangnail spines and blurred covers, matched badminton racquets in screw-down frames and a blue bucket full of mysterious rocks with numbers on them in discs of green felt. The rudder from a yacht. She establishes bases across the house, in the shed, in the rock isles of the property line, rushes between them, swapping markers and treasures. The mixed trees arch their backs and shimmy, making runes of the choppy lawn.

Here Barnett will raise fruit trees on the few places not ruined by a winter which couldn't make its mind up if it was coming or going. These are good, specialized acres, perfect for fruit: apples, pears, cherry and berry canes. This is one reason he chose the place.

The good Lord gave us facets, Barnett says.

Barnett isn't bookish. He has ideas and he has bearing. He is well groomed and upright, he speaks with a clear, low tone he has memorized from gramophone records teaching elocution in which shopworn thespians recite Shakespeare and Shaw and implore God to save their Queen. His bearing is the scaffold for his chief ambitions: to have his picture in the newspaper, to enter public service, to bequeath a piece of land.

When Barnett becomes uneasy he makes a mental picture. In his new picture he stands smiling by a tree with an apple in his hand. Beside him, bushel baskets and his wife and child. Sun like a tick. Appaloosa orchards.

Have faith, he tells Dory. Look *forwards*.

Barnett knows nothing about growing. He does not understand about watering, culling, pesticides. He does not know how many plants make a row, how many rows make a section, how many sections an orchard. Other people know these things; he can always ask them. The former owner of these orchards has promised Barnett a swift and plentiful harvest. All he has to do is wait for this bounty to weigh the trees down. In the brochure he has borrowed this dream from, cherries make a carpet to the sea.

Absinthe is a sickle round the bay. There is a main street, a park-to-be and rows of shops whose functions are clear in their windows: brunette dummies in skirts and trousers with scarves grooved into their necks. Hammers and saws, blue denim overalls, gleaming wheelbarrows. An enormous pill in red and white enamel set in a stoppered jar. There are places to buy boots and shoes and to have surveys done and wills made, to have photographs printed and framed, to have boats repaired, a library on two floors with plush brown beanbags and thin, straight scrivener's chairs and eleven loosely related books in French in which the boys carry satchels and the girls wear sunflower hats. There are two banks on corners and a liquor store with a parking lot and the town's lone illuminated sign.

There is the world of the town, and the world of the forest that refuses to absolve it; between the two everything is off-kilter. The insects and the animals, the terrain and weather too. Bedrock becomes swamp in hot zones where mock wasps breed in their millions in the crowns of blue spruce, jigging in high columns, laying their eggs as a thin foam in the needles and then diving into the lake to become long beetles shunting along underwater tracks. Spiders check their airborne traplines. Budworms with angelic faces. Bounding martens. Specular bears.

Because it is summer and because she is new here and must make friends as she finds them and because she hasn't yet found them Dory is often at home. She goes to bed in tomorrow's clothing and gets up as early as she can to plummet through breakfast and then to the shed and the rocks and the creek with its frogspawn and rope of current and only then is her day really begun. But should she not beat the dawn and should her parents be awake she is called for and kept in and included in their day. So today Dory and Barnett and June drive to the new development southwards of the lake, a twenty-acre hoop the council hadn't bothered to clean up after the stubble left by clearcut. Small, smartly tailored in red brick, green roofs, slim chimneys, pocket lawns, straight paved drives.

Where are the pixies? asks June.

Since building started Barnett has come here one or two afternoons. Perhaps he is not a grower at all; perhaps he is an architect. He has watched them scoop and level the land and lay foundations in cement-and-iron blocks and unpack pine skeletons and assemble and clad them with drywall and a rind of brick and seal the roofs with great tarpaper sheets over bendy bright copper flashing and finish with patented green asphalt shingles to build this small-scale city, stacked at the top of the rise with painted lampposts and pretty street signs: *Pelican Way, Proudfoot Crescent, Reindeer Ridge.*

What are we? Rural road six, Barnett says. Pelican Way it is not.

On the highway they are selling billboard space. Everywhere signs rise above the fields advertising grain silo facilities, spare acreage, fresh grade-A eggs. *Dad's Snacking Wheats. Heartland Cattle Feed. Rest Easy at the White Mill Lodge (Hot Water and All Conveniences).*

Down on the construction site men on silver ladders snap eavestroughing into place, long pre-painted pipes running to ground. There is a choice of white or beige or brown trims, island or wall-mount kitchen, French or sliding patio doors. People visit the model homes and test the water pressure and the thickness of the paint, the depth of tiling. Last Tuesday two kids were found in a show home rutting on the Posturepedic bed. Filth and soiled linen, cigarette scars on the cream broadloom—they're calling it Randy Ridge.

Sometimes, says June, I don't know who is the greater child. She is bored, irritated, flicks at her metal hair slides. She spins the lid of her stainless-steel thermos, another cup of bitter, kelpy tea.

We're sightseeing, Barnett tells her.

It is a marvellous spectacle, she says. What was it you particularly wanted us to see?

Look around you, says Barnett. This is the new.

There is this about the construction: though she watches and watches there is a difference between what she sees the men do and what they are actually doing. It's magic, an abscess in the everyday that delights and disturbs all at once.

Barnett waits until the whistle sounds for sandwich break, reverses out of the lane.

Here, Dory thinks, is the first of the springs for the lever that opens and closes the secret in her letter. The suburb in its infancy, her father's fascination with it, anticipatory, voracious.

June with her tea like a caustic, straight back an inch from the seat. Within three days of arriving in Absinthe June set up her own private study. She tacked autumn fabric to the walls and a picture of a Scottish crofter and his flock of piebald sheep. She went about making the house a home as she imagined it, and as always with her the activity grew unstable, corrupted. To fit in she bought a food mill, an apron, pattern of perennials with ladies' heads, marigolds and tulips and violas like thunderheads under impossible hairdos. She joined the Women's Institute, chased prizes for pastry and jam.

And all this time, Dory thinks, June was unhappy, distressed in the bone. She spent her adult life travelling, from England to the New World, from one end of the country to another, from one town to the next, in the teeth of her own stern and easily contented parents, for whom overreaching was the most comprehensive sin. Disappointment collected in her like iron filings, weighed her down until she became antic in her compensations and Barnett grew more anxious in his efforts to balance her out. Her parents operated a feedback loop in the wrong direction. They made each other worse.

Barnett reverses out of the lane at the construction site and June turns on him—hot tea, scarf of vapour—and says harshly, distinctly:

The strain, you said; the strain—

Dory is carrying books, armloads and armloads, from the little house to the main one. Leatherbound, clothbound and coverless, some shed pages and some contain pages belonging to other books entirely. One or two she sets aside to browse later—*The Queen in Her Amber, Adventures in the Hinterlands*. June is fraught in the kitchen, shouting about the goddamn sieves the goddamn sieves—

Everything in this place is broken or breaking. June cannot cope.

There, there; leave them there, June says, jags with a spatula at empty floor.

Thirty, forty trips. Picture and wildlife and storybooks. One celebrating the life of an orca named Imu, a great black-and-white teardop of a beast who each day eats a tonne of fish. Imu and huge bales of mackerel. Imu leaping for his supper. Imu and a stack of 3,000 hotdogs. Imu returning to nature, diving in arcs on his way to his pod. Tearful farewells, whaley joy also, memories of beach balls and hamburger steak.

There is a set of books following the adventures of Jane, a doughty young pioneer who lives first in a wagon, then in a cabin, under a falls, on a homestead, finally in town. Nothing worries Jane, not wolves or bears or locusts or panting old men. She merely tucks into her pouch of needles and sews them all out of harm's way. God, graft and a clean sure stitch—this is the key to roughing it in the bush. Dory hates Jane. Still, when finally Jane marries a young farmer, non-drinking, non-smoking, horsey Gilbert Macon, and her mother, not yet forty but blind, embroiders the lid of the hope chest, Dory cries.

There is a series set in America and published in the Saturday magazines. The prairie scout Andrews and René Red Fox the Kiowa tracking phenomenon and old Gus their wise prospector mentor. Here they are in a silver creek breaking up a gun-running ring. Here again, camped among the purple sage, on the trail of disease-carrying horse thieves. Here pistol-whipped and left to die in an old streak mine full of bats and phosphorescence while the Haray brothers make off with the swag from nine stagecoach raids.

Pistol-whipped, Dory tells Eff. For hours!

Eff is small and bright and warlike. So bright that she shimmers and is lost. She circles, moving to the left.

That way, she explains, I can see to punch.

She steps fearless into one of Dory's schoolyard tormentors and lays him low.

Don't mention it, she says. Really. It's something I enjoy.

Eff always wears the same sort of sweater, the same style of overalls over waxed boots. Blue. Her hair troubles her, it is an occupying force, forever making demands and issuing orders. Her hair is strong, cracks like whips. She ties it round her books and locks her desk with it. Her lashes thud when they fall. Dory wonders how she can carry all of this weight, the boots and the jeans and the hair, how tiring it must be to haul around. And yet Eff flashes, like so much purposeful light.

Hi pilgrim, Eff says when they first meet. I'm practically next door.

Dory loves the spacious, lawless West, the few trees, the lingering scents to track by. The villains who hate to shave, the tough, slangy singers and showgirls, quiet René and feisty Gus, tall, rangy Andrews and his unfussy goodness like a belt through his cowboy's blue jeans.

He nearly makes nice respectable, says Eff.

They read these together, act out the parts, alter scenes to suit. They trade around roles—Eff, hand on heart, loves the saloon girls, she is creative with swears and can make the word drink last a minute. They limit themselves to a daily chapter so as not to use them up too fast.

There are cookbooks: Beeton and Marriot and Mme. Angeneau, full of graphs and charts and notations and rules. Apple In-And-Out, Marrow Patties, Jugged Hare, Six-Squab Pudding, Muggett Pie, Firmity or Frumity (A Mothering Sunday Favourite). One must never serve vegetables cold or with something cold or mix sauces or play hostess in the clothes one has cooked in. Smiling aids the flavour of a meal. And love—love is a seasoning.

With love, she tells Eff, handing over an oatmeal square.

Why thank you, my dear, says Eff.

After Church Pudding, Glamour Sweet Dish, Good Daughter's Pudding. Spatchcooked Fowl & Rabbit (it is an improvement to a Rabbit especially to bread-crumb it, and serve with cold tartare sauce).

There are boarding-school novels, set in England, during the reign of the Queen. Everyone is in a "form" and much talk is given to games and pyjamas, japes and midnight feasts. There is a dark horse, a scholarship girl. An orphan.

An orphan, Dory says wistfully.

Another of the springs of her secret lever. The man made of wire—a very old, very dim, very browned photograph on the front of the book inside a book. Really, a zipped leather pouch, book-sized, containing a book to match it. She opens it alone, quickly and with eyes half shut, very thin paper with the lines of the pencil raised on one side. Then she puts it in a box beneath her bed and drapes the box with a blanket. Some treasures are charms to be contained.

Dory has a birthday. They have liver and onions and mash and fool and a cake made by June with a coin in the middle and icing combed into braids.

Pioneer Jane! Dory says.

I gambled on the proportions, June says. Did frontierswomen French-glaze?

Barnett has produced and hung a blotted watercolour rendition of *The Startled Fawn* in her room and gives her as well a folding easel and boxes of charcoals and brushes and paints. From June's sister a set of Ogilvie's Classics, mechanically separated versions of great books. June has bought a scarf decorated with figures of women themselves wearing scarves and—provokingly, Dory thinks—a magnetic town with a magnetic church.

It holds six times its own weight, reads Barnett, from the back of the box.

The magnetic town features black lines and mountain ranges and trees and cars and people who are red and black and yellow and blue button magnets.

Everything now is magnetic, June says. It is the ferrous age.

I think what you do is you build your own town, Barnett says. "Kids! Explore!" it reads. Would you call that an imperative? he asks June.

A double imperative, I should think.

"Kids, explore"; a double imperative, Barnett says. That's it for instructions, he says.

Let me see it, says Dory.

Well, I expect that the black lines are streets, he says. Or regions. Regions, he says. There's all kinds of flexibility, he says, peering at the side of the box. That's a heckuva thing, he says to June.

It stood out from the dust in the shop.

I'd like to see, says Dory.

Somethingsomethingsomething Christopher Columbus, reads Barnett without his glasses. They're really pitching this, he says.

The church's front doors open and inside is room for a preacher and his parishioners (included) and one stained-glass window, all affixed through the miracle of modern magnets.

Scots Presbyterian, says June. In the Pentecostal version everyone falls down.

I'm going upstairs, says Dory. I'm taking my town and my cake.

Later June comes into Dory's room. She wears her lemon house-coat and a terry diaper for a headscarf and smokes out the window so Dory won't have to feign coughing.

We took the most tremendous care of you, she says. When you were very very small. You got hotter and hotter, you convulsed—Well. You ought to bathe after playing in swamps. The soles of your feet are absolutely Dantean, June says. We ought to hire an angel to sit vigil at the door.

That was some cake, says Dory.

Yes. Well, we are all approximations, June says. The most tremendous care, she says; from the window, from smoke.

Eff gives her a spyglass and a pair of adapted gloves that she knitted herself out of discards, part brown and part blue, reinforced about the knuckles.

Actually I stole them, says Eff. If it bugs you I'll have them back.

Eff is at Dory's, she is always at Dory's, though she refuses to come inside.

Big houses dilute me, she says. They give me the shits.

So Eff comes over to Dory's and stays outside and never lets Dory follow her home.

Nothing to see there, she tells her. God's own mess.

She lives somewhere over the hill and off the mill road, near the lagoon. The bayou.

The where?

It doesn't matter, does it? Eff says. So long as I appear.

Dory introduces Eff to the shed and the rocks and the creek and the laundry chute. They roam the fields and scrubland sweeping at drowsy insects. They cut beetles into cross-section to see their looped insides. They groom each other, combing hair and tickling backs.

Why do people wonder where they came from? Eff asks. Muck unto muck.

It's a question, Dory says.

Will you go eff yourself is a question, says Eff.

Mmm.

My mom and dad, italics, were fools to have me, Eff says. What have we wrought, etc., she says.

I was made in a bomb shelter, says Dory. They did it standing up.

I knew a Stevie who smoked gasoline, Eff says. He went ever so blue and he died.

Oh, Dory says.

He was a nice enough boy, Eff says. What happened was awful. He did it on a dare. That was the deal: if he did it, I kissed him.

Did you—

My word is my bond. Sure, I kissed him, Eff says. It was messy, to say the least.

They sit in the leaky evening light. Dory thinks of the gasoline eating up Stevie's good looks, the manic flames browsing, Eff with human charcoal on her lips.

Sometimes Dory plays with a boy from school named Frazer who lives on the third floor above the hardware and garden shop. The shop smells of earth and grease and so does Frazer in his playday uniform of gym shorts with a stripe down the thigh. They don't talk much. Frazer hardly speaks. They sit on a bench and pare leaves down to fish spines. Frazer is soft as an oat, he eats bread dipped in whipping cream and skinned apples he wraps in a handkerchief sectioned with the flags of the world. BrazilChinaDenmarkGreece.

All his books have pages missing. In their place he has pasted his own speculations, pictures and words. Dinosaurs sporting, a kite with the face of a man. Frazer's apartment smells of fried liver and tarragon. His mother speaks French, smokes in French, careless and dramatic, using the cigarette like a long fountain pen to write with. There are burns on every wall and grease spots where she has melted butter through a strain. Frazer with butter on his breath, frightened of umbrellas (spiny, ship-like, liable to whisk one away). He's weird but impressive, Dory thinks, one of those who draws poison to himself without thinking, and so improves the lot of the rest.

She waits to introduce Eff to Frazer. Properly, that is.

I despise that boy, Eff says. I loathe him for the faces he makes.

He can't help it, Dory says. It's his nerves.

It never, Eff says.

Well it is. His face just goes that way.

It's not normal.

It isn't on purpose!

Frazer is terrified. Zzzt, he tells Dory in an agitated whisper. Mmf. Tzlot.

Calmly, Eff undoes a wasp.

We're going to the river and you're coming, Dory says. You promised. You swore.

He gives in, marches over to Eff, hand out stiff as a pike, face tacked into place. Plsdtmt, he says.

Enchanté, says Eff.

Frazer's face performs an upward ripple; his features soften and collapse and then reform in an altogether different pattern.

That boy is a positive gargoyle, says Eff.

Dory explores. She and Eff and Frazer take one of the dim and twisting paths treacherous with rock knots and the root spew of old, incontinent trees. Pine weep makes their hands hot and sticky and the river can be heard but not seen.

It's that way, Eff says.

They pass the beams of a burnt-out cottage, log stumps and smoked stone and an iron grating from the fireplace that spelled the word *Love*.

Which was their name, the family's name, Eff explains. It

burned down with the nurse and the dogs. You'll be pleased to know you've moved to a fire alley, she says. Everything round here goes up.

The river is in pitched argument. It roars and answers, queries and deafens, it cares for nothing but itself. It is near, and then veers off again.

That way, says Eff.

They stop to gnaw at apples and a block of white cheese Frazer has brought in his pocket. The sharp cheese tames and sweetens the apples, tickles their mouths.

Christ almighty, says Eff. Save us from this boy and his cheese.

The river moves somewhere near them but never near enough to see. Once Frazer spots it, but by the time they reach it only a wet thread remains.

Eff scuffs the ground with her boots. It could be anything, she says.

They have been all afternoon in the woods. Dory shivers in her jacket and wishes she had longer, steeper legs and then she would kick trees out of the way and carry the river on one banked toe and stride home triumphant.

An hour passes, and another, and they are no closer to water and they are resolutely lost. Frazer runs at a bright slash visible down the hill, seam of quartz in the bedrock, dips his hands, tries to refresh himself, splashes wildly at hard crystal. His face is blown by crosscut breezes, his eyes and nose and mouth alike disappear and it makes Dory feel seasick to watch him scrabble at the rock, gulp from his empty, dusty hands.

Get that wind-faced boy away from me, Eff hisses. Now— or I'll corpse him!

Then she is beating him, almost gently, swiping her knuckles across his face and neck and head and caved back, spiking his rear with her boot, plucking his ketchup hair.

Shut up, she chants. Shut up, fucker, shut up—

Eff is a little murderer. She is covered in Frazer juice and she is elated and withdrawn and she circles them, muttering, taking measurements. She needs to find the river, Dory thinks, because she said she would and this promise kept backs up all those others, the broken others, that freeze the air like ghouls. Dory has to peel Eff off Frazer and then they leave him to recover while they supine—*supine*—on the flat dry rocks, Dory on her side arranging heated crayfish claws in speckle blue red purple, Eff on her stomach pincered between two rocks; she is thin, Dory sees, so thin that Dory can see the rudders of her spine. Great tenderness. She leans in for a kiss but Eff grabs her fingers, bends them back hard.

You must never, never presume, she says.

It is evening when they find the water and find their way home.

You, says Eff. You—Cheese Boy. Throw this rock. Throw it, she says. Just shut your eyes, and pitch.

He throws the rock, it travels forever, lands with a splash.

T'river, says Frazer, shiny with joy.

That, says Eff, is what we call practical magic.

Frazer. Frazer is the third of the springs in the lever, Dory thinks now. His high U-shaped shoes imported from Europe, the clumped tousled hair like a classical statue, Hercules or Pan, and wasn't he needy without knowing it? The truest way of being needy and the most damning. His mouth always a little open, spit strings like the cords of a drawbridge at either corner and his thirty-two plus four extra teeth all leaning into each other as if for protection. Face like the sky, like a weather system. June called him mimsy.

It is the middle of the week and Dory has switched her phone off. She has begun to sell their house, covertly, although it is her right to sell it and she is perfectly justified in doing so. Nine rooms on two floors with blind corners, six neat themed rooms and a seventh, the largest, where Ruth spread herself out gloriously in an archipelago of books and papers and fruit rinds and seedling plants designed to grow in low light. One bathroom where Dory hung her sketch of a man whose walking stick had fused with his hat. And Dory's room, tiny and round and wooden like a brandy cask, with a bookshelf and a rolltop desk and her box for mementoes that Barnett had given her for the collections he presumed a child must have, bottle-caps or doll clothes, photos of oneself. Strips of pine of different colours and a sliding lid that stuck. Two rooms between them even though they might have used them all. What modesty.

Throw it away. What will she do with the bits she can't use? She used to think she must remember everything and then discard the unimportant, proceeding by logic instead of raw feel. Previous versions of the letter have included maps and legends, attempts to fix the space in line with her belief that it matters where one person, one thing is in relation to another. That when she writes that the town of Absinthe was above the town of Zane she is implying a certain relation and this relation might not, in fact, hold. Ruth. Where was Dory and where was Ruth? The big and the small room. Messiness and thrift. But hadn't there been in Ruth's messiness a decided generosity and a little—what? call it menace—in Dory's thrift? And in the letter too this problem of relations, of events and actors sitting side by side. Frazer is a spring in the lever—why? What part had Frazer, really, to play? And yet Dory has never been able to think this story through in the absence of Frazer, his imported shoes, his face, his cack-handed attempts at drawing, his need. Had she thought she was rescuing Frazer? Was that it, in the end?

In the morning Dory is old and bruised. Her feet are like split melons, oozy and huge, and her eyes are brimmed with dust and crushed needles and her hands are cracked and filthy.

Only a cat who has taken vows would drag you in, says June.

She is supervising Barnett who is supervising the tarring of the trees, to prevent the creep-rot and parachute worms and tunnel bugs and demolition beetles with their charged eggs. Stumps will be scraped and painted with the thick and reeking tar. Afterwards, the orchards will seem like so many men dressing for dinner. Tuxedo trousers. Web belts.

These fellows are good workers, Barnett says. That one, Rudi, keeps owls.

She finds Frazer in the schoolyard grazing a peppermint stick. He starts when he sees her, looks round.

The Terror is still in bed, Dory says.

Skrk, says Frazer.

We'll hear her coming.

Frazer's face has great powers of recovery. He looks fresh and swabbed. He has been to church and apologized for his past week's sins. Looking. Wanting. Lying about the number of pages he has read in the Book Race. He has made his mother a tureen of milky coffee and a rack of toasted brown bread. He has hilled dry food into the dog and cat bowls, checked the water and the wood. The horse next door has died in his sleep.

It is a sunny day and the boys are about, and Frazer is preparing to be beaten. Already, there are a few warning shouts. Then the boys, the Element, will arrive in a mass of scarves and teeth and hollers and they will seize Frazer and beat him to the ground until he has squeezed himself up so tight that he no longer presents a surface.

Last year Frazer was taken ill. He lay in a fever and the Element went about fighting aimlessly, smashing windows, setting fire to livestock, cutting the guy-lines of boats. The police were called in and had their car tires bled.

Finally Frazer got well. There was silence when he returned to the schoolyard. He was surrounded almost instantly. When he began to tremble they left off and he felt his hair smoothed and his jeans dusted off and he felt their tears everywhere on him, fifteen boys sobbing in their gladness at having him back.

Well, says Dory. I'm going to the depot and collecting deer fur.

Xzyt, says Frazer, and prepares to deliver himself to the Element, united in their violence and their love.

⊕

Dory is careful. Today, for a prolonged, horrifying minute, she stepped out of time. She was in the garden shed reading about the Great Plains tribes and she was reading about the adventures of Professor Dauntless and his atomic spacehoppers and suddenly the shed was full of people slight as radiograms moving and speaking in the cool outlandish way of people from the future whose technology and society she cannot possibly understand. It is a terrible time-shifting shape-shifting afternoon and she runs from the shed where Barnett courts an infant white pine.

Come with me, he says. I'm off to buy beets.

They drive to the market and its great chilly apple cellars with stacked bushel baskets, wire racks of pies and soda biscuits, white pan loaves and shelves of preserves in tubby jars done up in gingham.

When they return June offers them biscuits baked in the image of the Lady of Shallot.

To Barnett she says: Thirteen.

Biscuits. The strain. Thirteen. In the perpetual skirmish between Barnett and June this must be seen—though Dory isn't sure how—as an act of reprisal, one in a series of new and unsettling routines. June uses the facilities before seven in the morning or not at all, preferring to strain and grimace and periodically arch like a cat to redistribute her bladder or bowels. She sets aside her books and articles for a basket full of clothes needing mending. She has unpacked a sewing machine with a hair-trigger treadle and spare needle cups.

Let me, Barnett says, increasingly desperately, when there is something to be done.

Now in the kitchen June plaits pastry ropes in and out of a wooden trivet. Her sleeves are bunched at her elbows and her back is bent.

I'm going out, Dory says.

Shh, you are *grating*, says June.

Their teacher, Mr. Mason, teaches them a little wildly about the heart and soul. The heart is the seat of sensation, the soul of high thinking. By way of example Mr. Mason offers several passages of music he rates as very fine. As the music plays Dory imagines Eff as an open vein, thin and blue and pouring. She is pouring but her face, cycling, is visible along her every inch. When Eff reaches Dory's heart there is a tremor and a snag. Dory is expanding; Eff is pumping her out. When Dory is called upon for a recitation she sings the melody from one of the pieces Mr. Mason has just played. Her classmates despise her but she thinks she has learned something. It is possible to be what someone wants, and to show them the way in wanting it.

When she sleeps that night Dory dreams of a perfect silence. She does not see or hear or smell or taste or feel anything. Her nerves have been gathered and snipped. But this is not the silence of death. Her awareness is so sharp it is like travelling. All the things in the world are still as she moves among them. She has cut time free from space. It is not space and its contents that generate noise but time, its spinning and creaking, creeping and grinding. At a slice Dory has managed what all the scientists and priests could not. She wakes but the dream has left a residue. The dream has shown her that she must make a cut but not where she should make it.

Downstairs June contends with the radio.

What was ever influential about chastity? she wonders.

When I was—Dory begins.

Oh no, June says.

Did I—

You were a perfectly normal, contented child, June says. No one ever commented on you. Whatever you get up to now is not our exclusive fault.

MERRICK

I arrive at the Home of Lemuel Merrick—I Become
Acquainted With His Ways—An Unusual House—The
Town of Moar and its Distinct Advantages—Who Am I?—
Biographical Sketch—A Mysterious Woman—
Terminal Machines—Civil Unrest—An Amputation

Who am I indeed? I met Merrick by accident. He gave me
his card. He represented the end of a certain trajectory
during which I stepped from one life to another—easily, as I
thought.

I write these lines in the frontispiece of the one book I have
with me on the night I sail. Waiting for the purser to take this
blasted commemorative photograph, a perk of travelling first
class. I am carried from my chair to the deck and from there to
my cabin and from there and from there—for that I must thank
Merrick. I spent less than a year with Merrick. I served him, I
nursed him, I stole from him and I left him. And yet there is
about that time a tremendous force, a pendulum at full stretch.

And these? asks a porter, a vector in pressed whites. He carries twin long map tins, wrapped and waterproofed against the
corroding salt air.

Yes, I say. Be careful with them—

Still, barks the purser from beneath his black hood. Stay very still, he says.

I am not yet with him a week. I am to cook some and scribe some and manage his affairs. I am hardly literary, but I turn a neat phrase, have a fairly quick hand, a docile temperament and a fungal imagination, qualities admirably suited to the private secretary or This Year's Novelist—a creature I know well. The house, once dear, is worthless now, having slumped like an old Duke to a pocked and reeking approximation of its former grandeur: a Blue and a Malt and a Rose room with handmade wallpaper and a broken-up triptych of rugs, several portraits probably unpaid for, marble basins, blown-glass sconces, two full sets of decorated stairs—the battle for Carthage, entwined lovers haunted by Zeus—bespoke billiard ivories used as doorstops. One wing seemingly abandoned at the superstructure phase now provides a spiky habitat to an ancient race of King George pigeons, wan and doomed, that emerge from their eggs with a biblical regularity, cycle through fledge and adolescence in what seems a matter of hours and die soon afterwards in a cretonne of slime and feathers with an air of having grasped Life, pronounced upon it, and expired with the truth on their lips. There are very few conveniences: no central fire, no shower (not even a proper iron bath-basin) and chipped and pitted chamber-pots of a quality not seen outside of a workhouse since twenty years ago Our Lord.

Identical doors lead to the four wings of the house, with scullery and pantry downstairs. There is little decoration besides the unnatural profusion of mildew and rot, which in places has arranged itself ornamentally, as though assisted by some vegetable aesthetic, a painterly yearning on the part of the spores. In truth the house is less a building than an incremental disintegration.

Daily the foundations heave and subside and the flanks shake until some doors are seized shut and some open; pipes and superstructure burst their sheathing and invade the open spaces of the hall and main rooms. Indeed, the house seems something alive, bemused and rheumatic, forever stretching and repositioning in search of muscular peace.

For all its overgrowth the house is oddly streamlined. Routes, clear and unobstructed, run between Merrick's rooms and his laboratory and the nick in the wall where he takes his food. These parts of the house have been stripped of anything that might divert him from his purpose. Walking once without a candle I reach to steady myself and feel a friction along the walls where strips of felt have been tacked as runners. The laboratory door has pricks of phosphorescence; one can travel in the dark. There are bookcases mounted on turnstiles. Watercans with spigots and holstered drinking cups. It is lit not by candles but by a selection of waxen fruit and flora which burn with a pleasing sweet odour and a highly coloured light (I have thus far identified apple, apricot, avocado, banana, boysenberry, cassava, hops, pineapple, jackfruit, kumquat, lemon, plum, potato, quince, radish, shaddock, tangelo tomato, turnip, walnut and yam).

The history of this place is disrupted and vague. It was built in the previous century by a wealthy tobaccaneer who, a connoisseur of surprises, specified a mansion in which no guest could know what lay more than a few feet ahead. He had his builders install oblique corners and false ceilings and rigged follies and illusions: revolving staircases, a waterfall made of glass. When he died and too little was left of his estate to undo his eccentricities, room after room was abandoned and the household confined themselves to the first floor and garden with its novel greenhouse in the shape of a lyre. The family contracted further and three sisters lived here. Devout, isolated, they embarked upon a permanent fast and were found finally by a priest come for funds to refurbish a stained-glass Simon of Cyrene. The sisters, all dead, lay serenely in the kitchen by the hearth. They left behind their journal, a collaborative effort that treated seriously the metaphor of a garden of souls. Planting, tending, vigilant feeding and watering would return the earth to Eden.

We continue to hope for ascension, wrote Evvy, the last to die. *This starving is tiresome. But we persist.*

September to September—I will spend nearly a year with Merrick. His health will fail, the house will be ransacked, we will move, and I will leave him. But for now, I settle in.

I come to Merrick with, I admit, few options. I am orphaned, with few friends beyond some remote though fecund cousins breeding genteelly, and had before my accident lived alone. Solitude has its perils for an imaginative person; it encourages a delight in oddness, in excess, and may contribute to unwhole-some self-regard—though it should be noted that true revelation (scientific, spiritual) generally is experienced alone.

For instance: I had a room in a house of thirteen rooms. One Wednesday I awoke and opened my window onto the busy thoroughfare beneath and found that I could see right through the mass of the crowd, through its divisions and permutations, through its hats and cloaks and constituent bodies, through fat and muscle and bone to something like the human will manifest, all of our wanting and striving revealed in a cipher-like pattern of dashes and dots. I watched from my window and at night walked to a coffee house to remain until closing. I came gradu-ally to the certain knowledge that I occupied a position in the providential reckoning, that I had been singled out as an agent of salvation. I asked myself, whom would I save?

Months later, following a prolonged recuperation from an injury that was both sudden and severe, I applied by calling card to the home of Lemuel Merrick, Esquire.

My interview runs three sentences.

You are free now?

I am free now. There was some question—

You have writing? Write me a line, anything. Good. Good. You will do.

I write for him the opening sentence of this year's novel, the incomparable *West Byrne*, that salt-drenched tale of a naval cad and the heiress who endures him. That marine testament to suffering in petticoats. That elongated handkerchief of a book, full of poisoned clergymen and ravens shrieking among the limes—

Good, good. You are excessive. But you'll do.

And so I fit myself into the stencil of this other life.

Merrick does not inquire further; indeed, he takes no interest in me. I am the agent of his suppers, his wall-calendar, his correspondence-machine. I make copies of the blueprints by which his ingenuities are constructed. Merrick has a positive phobia of competitors and makes frequent hints as to the likelihood of spies among his circle; and since I *am* his circle, I take care. The strongbox he stores his papers in is ringed with tiny charges of soot so that he will know if they have been troubled, and the doors to his laboratory are thick with locks in the shapes of oxen and osprey and other monitory creatures. I am left in no doubt—curled-up pages, tiny corrections—that he supervises my work closely. His annotation consists of one or two lines of facts concerning the genesis of each creation, the specific problem of mechanics, electricity or motion each addresses, and a log of its construction. I take notes, arrange appointments, draft letters of business, copy learned articles to his colleagues in America, Switzerland and France, etch a sign for the trade entrance forbidding posting of notes and issue sundry stern or evasive replies to his creditors in the sharp, quarrying style he prefers—a style, I fear, singularly without rhetorical merit. A gentleman in debt ought to be *loquacious*, full of inventive and graceful explanations. Not so Lemuel Merrick. He scans what I write, affixes his queer lightning bolt signature, then recedes until the light fades and it is supper time.

I am transcribing this, my account, on the plain backs of Merrick's discarded blueprints. The paper is of the highest quality and takes the ink with little drift or blotting. I am able to work very small and very crowded and still keep things neat.

I have little enough with me, when Merrick takes me in. Razor, clothing, a book or two. Tomkins's *Algebra*, Brewster's *Physics*, Ramsay's *Leading Men*, an unread Chapman's *Homer*. My schoolmasters proselytized the usefulness of these classic texts and I find they were right. The *Algebra* I use to line the drawers, and Ramsay's eight volumes help steady my bedposts. Homer lights my room at night for two weeks when the wax runs out. Eventually I am left with Inkster's cheerless admonitions for the young. That compendium of half-truths, hearsay and fine, Anglican bigotry. *We will notice today the feet of animals. The Cow is intended to inhabit soft localities, meadows and river banks; hence, its cloven feet. Then, in the Mole we find all the legs short. Its forefeet are shovel-shaped and fixed obliquely, and are worked by powerful muscles. (Object: the Mole does not impede its own progress by casting the dirt in front of it—here draw a lesson for Humanity.)*

The frontispiece includes a portrait of Inkster, sitting, quill poised, hard at his sermon, stern and well situated, plain in the sight of God. These books, and a railway watch I keep on a wire in my coat.

I write a letter home. I say that I am settled into the most extraordinary place and with the most extraordinary man. I say the town is pleasant and the countryside near. I make everything decent and harmless and engagingly odd. I wonder, is my aunt well? I wonder, is it temperate? My aunt, who will read this letter, was proposed to as a girl. A lieutenant stopped by a baby carriage she was minding in the park. She remembers that he stood at an angle, less like an officer than a stake in croquet. He had brown eyes and precise, umlaut scarring. When I first leave her home to go to work my aunt takes everything she has felt for thirty-seven years and has it stamped into the back of a railway watch sold to mark a bicentenary. *Grapple!* implores the watch.

As an employer Merrick is gracious enough. He desires that I am comfortable and inquires about my rooms in a determined and naïve manner and hopes I will be happy here and not be overwhelmed.

You must not exceed yourself, he says.

His hair and his skin are uncommonly bright, as bright as his language, as bright as his gilt library and the polished copper tubes of the laboratory where he spends his time. He is tall. There is about his legs and torso a stretched quality, as though elastic flesh had been pulled to its limit and left there to harden. His small grey eyes are set wide on his head. He is not quite master of his expressions and means to show one face and ends up with another. Sometimes I see powerful emotions pass in sequence over his features, cycling as precisely as soldiers marching for review. He feels by rotation, I think, not because he is reacting to a direct stimulus. I could not make him angry, if anger were not his next scheduled mood.

I am not alone in his service. There is Izzie, a vestigial maid, who manifests extreme variations of attitude and dress like some chart of human evolution—crouching, loping, walking—and who carries within her the atavistic memory of all servants, all duties, a compact history of labour at four foot ten. There is someone I never meet who comes in the night to tend the great ovens and chimneys and whose creosote presence persists between visits like a spoor. There is old Rostern, who has charge of the stables, a long, wet bristle of a man combed into a green suit.

I am aware from the start of the limited resources. Everything is reused. Merrick writes on all sides of his pages, vegetable peelings are reconstituted as a weak fuel, I blend the few spices with an edible solvent to make a kind of potable eau de cologne to season our suppers, Merrick and I and then Izzie take turns in the tin bath, dented and rusting, smashed tallow soap.

With my injuries I require more time than most to fulfill my duties. Passing from floor to floor and room to room necessitates careful planning. Bedroom, kitchen, dining room, library. Kindling, coal, plates, cutlery, glassware, one at a time. Still, there is merit in suffering, we are told. Honour. We recoup through our burdens our better, more authentic selves. Excessive, Merrick called me. I am excessive. I set myself against the Inksters of the world. Humanity—who would not add a little burnish in order to emphasize a tale's humanity? Think of Eyland's heroine in his *Grace Confirmed*, our lady of the emeralds, exhausted and strip-mined by childbirth, drawn on a wire between drawing room and nursery, all the while desperate for a quaff of claret and a clatter on a horse. In this year's novel, *wanting* alone constitutes an outrage against the way of things, punishable by disfigurement—eyeful of vitriol, at a minimum. I admit I am excessive. Certainly I want. I have come in the spirit of this year's novel—I began with its very first lines.

As I learn my job it grows lighter. Preparing the fires takes longest, the coal slipping from the tongs, the dry fuel shedding, the matches igniting and as swiftly eclipsed; one in three is bad. A household is a type of machinery, prone to rust and overheating, constitutionally inclined towards chaos, to be rested and lubricated when the running is hard. Today I ask for eggs and flour and corn and a bird. I will pluck and clean and slake the bird with port and ginger and pack its cavities with onion, corn and sage. It will roast until the first clear perspiration and then I shall serve it with potatoes poached in milk. This is one of forty dishes I can manage. Twenty, really, plus variations. Thus far I have made a mutton, a bird pie, sundry bakes and puddings and a soup of snape, a dense flatfish that flourishes in cold oceans. All passed muster, though Merrick scarcely eats. Food for him is a cerebral lubricant. He starts, chirrups, drums upon the table. Once, he drew with a fingertip in gravy upon his nap: ley lines and a concatenation of blottings in the centre I did not understand. A map? A route? A collision? He rose and disappeared and it was Tuesday, perhaps, before I next saw him.

By nights I listen to the commotion on the street, and sometimes I throw open the windows and treat the multitudes to Inkster. *Weeding commences. In Flanders, this is performed by the women and the children, who are provided with coarse cloths, and who are enjoined to creep along on hands and knees. This is not so injurious to the young plants as is walking on them. The weeders are also particular with recourse to their position to the wind. They turn toward the wind, so that the flax, which has just been bent down by them, will be raised again. Any delay in weeding proves fatal to the young plants, as they will bruise and die when grown too high. It is for these reasons that the flax is known as the Lord's fleece.*

Observant Inkster, thick-breeched and zealous, among the flax workers of little Belgium, sketching their backs as they break.

A high odour is constant round this place: metal, oil, sulphur, solvent, beeswax, paraffin. It nearly suffocates me when once a week I go to pay the trade at the rear door, an iron-gated trap in the wall. Enormous twin brothers, the Pargetters, are responsible for the transportation of goods from the loading door to the laboratory. The elder of this pair is the more articulate; the younger relies on a vocabulary of gruesome winks and tilts of his cap, a grey, knitted atrocity streaked dark with a variety of venerable greases (in Rood's *Dark Manacles*, the weird and silent footman is found on inspection to be minus his tongue, excised at birth by his abject mother so that she may never have the pleasure of hearing his voice, the daughter of an Earl). The Pargetters form a human road down which the laden carts travel and I supervise and check the contents against the bill and generally move things along. Increasingly I am seconded to new tasks: finances, research. What is a Griffin? How many dorsal bones in the common Grey Porpoise? Who sat in such-and-such a seat on the Birkenhead express on the seventh of September, 1855? Naturally I read the papers I copy, and piece together what I can.

I ask for new coal and a clock for the kitchen and today they deliver great knuckles of yellowish dry coal, scraps of timber and dipper matches, lamp and cooking oil and one or two aromatic boughs. Merrick, evasive, tells me clocks are at a premium here and I do not ask again. Time here loses its purchase, and soon I cannot say what week it is, how old I am, whether it is day or night.

The town of Moar is midway between two settlements. It is the world centre of wax food and flower manufacture. Fruit, buns, fish, roses. Wax busts of the nobility. Wax approximations of the greatest battles of the sea. Wax apostles and wax saints, injection-dyed features perspiring in alcoves, in the sun. Wax, with its curious mixture of density and vulnerability to the elements; anything may be made of it, but nothing made of it lasts. In Moar one may stroll into any one of twenty waxworks and procure fine wax articles and receive a disquisition on the patent method. The fruits are hollow. Cunningly, a plaster mould is poured around the live fruit. When dry, it is cut in two and the fruit removed. Molten wax is then poured into the two-part mould and the mould shaken. When opened, a hollow fruit likeness is obtained which subsequently is painted. The skill, I am informed, lies in the colouring and texturing. The paraffin dust and the oil make a paint for the buildings and slipcovers for the people and articles of the town, and the sky itself seems cast from some discarded mould. The dense factory pall exerts a traction on perception; one notices less, and less surely.

The tradesmen and their families live unseen in curling tracts with short wooden hems. They burn a paste of oil and coal dust that leaves huge handprints on the fronts of their houses, and the gap between settlements makes a collar round the hill. Years ago there was money in the mediaeval ironworks and very little thereafter, and the castle was tenanted until subsidence caused it to chuckle, gulp and steadily inhale itself. It has never been raised but sits broken in its socket, muddles in its new-made moat.

Merrick's house sits on Windmill Rise, a dim, damp prospect. Its proximity to the waxworks puts it in the path of the coloured vapours that sift gradually down throughout the day until the world is a cool tea-brown. It has become my habit to sit up by the light of a breadfruit and set down the day's events. My window provides a view of the town in its botched cascade from the cathedral to the chain-makers' cottages, smoking links at the base of the hill choked by the railyards. I watch the locomotives. These are not legendary trains that join distant coasts and reunite peoples; that strive. These have little eloquence or charm. They are squat and functional, serving short, closed routes, driven hard and seldom rested, tended like carthorses.

I watch the trains, and I watch as sector by sector the town is burnt. Before dawn agents torch the street below, house by house, handing out corn sacks for belongings, shouting all-clears as they lay straw and pitch at the base of the walls. Tenants scurry from their lodgings, terrified, coughing; syringed-out, silent, half-dressed children, veering-off women and men used to eviction, they do not struggle much. This is the philanthropic element in its all-knowing benevolent pomp, theologically obliged to do good works so long as they do not promote pleasure. They have maps identifying the location and attributes of the social residuum: pestilence flourishes in this parish, idleness in that; a third germinates pickpockets with an overdeveloped lower lip. Between Moar and the world is exact correspondence, they argue; change in one will mean change in the other. The marshals provide warning. They come to the door, where there is a door, and knock.

Though my own sash is lowered and locked I can hear them. The shouting, the terror—that clear, serrated tone. Kindling igniting at the pulse of a building. Varied wordless screaming. Hard, spaced knocks.

Ideal servants, it is said, resemble flypaper: they are discreet, they are efficient, and everything sticks. I have no confidants to gossip with, am passing efficient, and I determine to be wonderfully sticky. On those rare occasions when I venture from the house I am invariably asked about Merrick's provenance, as if he were part of the family silver. Where had he come from? That question, again and again. Places, after all, are harbingers of their people, marking them by accent and essential character as their own. I claim no authority as an interpreter of men, but here is the history of Merrick as I found him in his mansion on the hills of Moar:

Lemuel Merrick is born into a family of weavers but shows little interest in this craft. For the new machines that threaten this ancient livelihood, however, he displays a remarkable gift. He serves his apprenticeship at Peebles, the greatest of the mechanical shops. Days of winding wire onto wooden spools. Baths for beaten gold, for copper cooling, for leaching the tarnish from silver, for buffing precious stones. Bins and bins: spoke gimbals, spread gimbals; starfish and fork and frame gears; long and short and cotter pins; crown-wheel escapements; levers; spun amber catgut; tiny bellows; tubes and rods of different diameters bought by the length; derailleurs and chains shrouded and unshrouded; pulleys *grand* and *demi-grand* and *petit*; grommets for thirty-six gauges of wire and the wire itself, copper or dull alloy, coiled or wound into balls like infants' fists; collars and crowns; picks, springs; an alphabet of screws; custom winding keys—each catalogued in a huge cloth-covered ledger.

For months he is allowed only piecework, polishing broad casings for men's watches, checking the grooves in the crowns, keeping the wire clippers and the etching knives sharp. Foot-pumping a stream of fresh air to clear the dust from a thousand lettered clock faces and sanding invisible imperfections from their domed glass doors.

Clockwork. Upright grandfathers, ornamental one-offs, mahogany compacts to be hung from a wall. The chimes are the most trouble, copper discs minuetted upon by tiny felt hammers, the armature must be correct for the hammers to strike properly. On more luxurious models rotating cams drive a set of pins to pluck harp strings; the tones echo, one atop the other; sometimes he stops in the midst of testing, utterly overcome.

There is a great demand for gimcracks of the kind that illuminate the weddings and summer parties of the upper thousands, and (by now) the middle ten thousands able to bid on ancient country houses and silver plate. The weddings require the aerial bouquet of rockets fired from stands, fire fountains driven by steam and timed to the second. Fashionable parties demand water serpents, floating pylons of coloured fire. He diagrams and assembles shafting and piping, the butterfly valves, the conduits to control the heat, fine mesh guides affixed to the spouts that produce magical patterns and distributed shapes: Roman candles and St. Mary's steeples, an eternal flame.

At last released from his apprenticeship, Merrick produces, by his own pocket, one or two trifles which catch on: a bird chorus; a blessing priest; a stooped, fugued Cedar of Lebanon with a name carved into a bough. A mustard-powder merchant owns an expensive machine in need of a rebuilding, an automaton that cheats at cards; when Merrick is able to get it running, other invitations follow. A great man, friend of the mustard king, asks Merrick to his factory, a modern and humane place where young men and women have the opportunity to aid the forward progress of the race, twelve hours a day, save Sundays. Merrick can see merely by watching just what within a movement is required for that movement. If the ladies working the seams would only sit at a new angle and draw their thread from the right and not the left, they might raise their speed and decrease their effort. If barley, instead of being heaped in huge shoes in separate sheds, were kept in silos next to the fires, and if the men were trained on tubular barrows—just patented, in Rutherford—and if the peat were sliced in the round . . .

The workers, with their awkward, fallible bodies and want of technique, frustrate Merrick. How much better to have only hands and forearms here and there a canopy of subtle fingers. Imagine it—a specialized labour purpose-built for the task at hand! He offers to factory owners a scalable formula, each action broken down and readjusted, perfect working bodies unhampered by mind or soul.

The first of his improving machines is a gift to the manufacturers of preserves and jellies, resembling a forest of hands, palms down, each with a rubber grip with four or so inches of play. At intervals timed to coincide with the filling and levelling of a jar of jam each hand compresses, screws down and springs back, and a lid is affixed securely. Compress, screw down, spring back—a commerce and a social politics in one.

Although there is no record of their courting, Merrick exerts himself to marry the woman who has for years kept his books. Rose Ames is a widow and mother of a girl of six. How do they live? Rose is very tall. Gentle. Just after New Year, Rose and her daughter travel to the Continent. Why? They take the waters and the mountain air. Then, sometime between Easter and September, somewhere between Switzerland and Moar, Rose and her daughter disappear.

This is the story as I learn it—incomplete. There is in Merrick's life as in his movements a quality of ellipsis, of passages indicated but left out. In a second-floor room, cold, disused, there is a formal painting and a wooden ark, pairs of animals rudely suggestive of their species, bodies pinched and everywhere adjusted the better to fit in their gloomy conveyance. On the bed, beneath the dun-coloured blanket, a coloured blanket with neatly turned tassels, and inside the ark a mosaic floor—there are, I see now, a thousand tiny touches that must have enlivened the space and the life. And not Rose's hand, as I believed, but Merrick's. Why did this surprise me? Why should not a man who loves details learn to prize the details of a person above a thing? What is a child, after all, but soft matter, tending perhaps in one or another direction but hard and fast in none? Is it so surprising then that Merrick, that arch-tinkerer, that blueprint-follower, should have wished to improve Rose Ames's girl?

Infrequently, Merrick tells me something of himself. He grew up in a living corduroy of uncles and aunts. An uncle who, believing himself to have suffered a brain injury, wore a bandage round his head at all times except for the nightly reading of the Bible from 7:45 to 8:00, during which he would gravely unwind the gauze, comb a part into his hair, listen to the selection until the clock rang in the hour.

He would exclaim, and reapply the dressing.

There was a park belonging to another relative where Merrick as a child watched swans and ducks strike complicated attitudes and imagined beneath their plumage illuminated bones. On his seventh birthday, a much younger girl held squatting over a drain in the street by a man, ragged and bearded, she with tattered red gloves, midstream she looks up, straight at Merrick.

I have gloves. They are red, she says.

He closes his eyes, kneads at the corners, and for a moment I seem to see into his skull, through the surrounding whir and tumble, a mechanized life-drawing, the very image of a man.

Fifteen years ago my mother, the luckless Calvinist, fainted upon witnessing an eclipse, her hands in her basin, unwashed. It was the shame of it that did for her, meeting the Rapture in her soaking nightgown, bloated by cabbage soup. My father, a shipping clerk, left a note for me, then stowed away and died—that was the year of shipwrecks. My aunt took in sewing and china in enormous quantities and eventually there was so much taken in that something must go out by way of equalizing the household volume, and so it was determined that I should be apprenticed to a sharp gentleman, Catnatch, who had a fine, tested means of breaking a boy, and when he had broken me he thought it best to get a little work for his trouble. I became a general clerk, then a chandler's clerk, and thereby found my way out of Catnatch's rathouse and into a warehouse by the sea.

I was clever (and what's better, not easily bored) and I studied to become a schoolmaster in the mornings and evenings and worked hard for very little the rest of the day. In the chandlery I rose to a position of responsibility in my firm. I had two men under me and one man above. One of the men under was whittled and small, freckled skull and high shoulders. Symons. I watched Symons as he made mistakes, entering the right sum in the wrong column, miscarrying in long addition, making sevens into ones. I watched him flail about and it occurred to me that he was stealing, brilliantly; that each broad, clumsy error concealed a modest theft. Pennies, at first. Then larger and larger sums. I admired his craft. Under my supervision he flowered. Forged bank draughts. Altered cheques. Such audacity! Such nerve! I am a creature of broad affections and I loved him. It was wonderful,

I thought, that I could love a man so debased! Pity is a strong relish; its danger lies in our forgetting that it is fashioned, not felt. When the thefts were reported Symons was let go. He took his coat and was escorted to the door. I was called for, and asked to explain my insufficiencies. I said that I was fond of chocolates and that Symons had brought me chocolates and that he had thought enough of me—of my cupidity, my lovesickness—to bring me chocolates and to watch me as I ate.

I left without a reference. I had nowhere to go.

I think of the office now as I draw a bath and watch the draughts play over the water: high desks, tapered stools, the scrape of elbow on foolscap. An ink-stained window we nicknamed the Nile. The firm worked by dealing its tasks out between the men so that no man knew the exact business of his fellows—

Three knocks on the door.

Sir?

Barely into the crossing and already I am sampling these luxuries, room service suppers, a blond boy to polish my watch.

I said that I came here by accident; well, accident or fate. I would be Merrick's Nemesis. I would jolt him from his path.

Merrick seldom sleeps. I hear him, or worse, wake in his wake, certain he has been by. Soon a curious suspension overtakes us, wherein we inhabit a half-life slower and duller than ordinary wakefulness but more determined and active than sleep. We exist between times, between states; leached of all urgency and care— I notice once that the fire has leapt the grate and watch, distantly, as it nibbles the border and rug. We creep about breakfasting at midnight and I am aware of a sidereal tug, the pressure of organic time upon our sparse routines. I do not shift my bowels for weeks and weeks, and a graze with a knife on a Thursday takes until Sunday to bleed. Conversations begun in one after-noon are hung neatly to cure and picked up again days later with no advance or decay.

I sit up with Izzie once or twice—ever evolving, she is in a sanguine, Paleolithic temper—and ask her questions to which she responds in glottals and shrugs. I ask:

Is he mad?

And Izzie allows that indeed he might be, but are any of us better?

I ask:

What happened to make him so?

And there comes upon Izzie a general disassociation of her limbs from her nerves and for several minutes she jitters expressively before settling into her customary incipient rictus.

What directly? I ask again.

And am given by Izzie to understand that some things is best left as is.

I say goodnight to Izzie, climb to my bed. I have come to hate the nightly cacophony from the laboratory, squealing, hissing, crashing, scraping, burning, a soft vegetable rub like grass at right angles. These sounds refuse elaboration; of different pitches and separate families, they seem to belong to different moments. I collect wax from the candles to pack in warm clots in my ears so that I hear my own digestion, the circulation of my blood. This makes me present to myself in the most incisive, uncomfortable manner, a thoroughgoing tinnitus, and I think it will never be silent and I very nearly scream.

I woke where I was, in the night. Why had I woken? I found a match, lit a pear, made my way to the top of the stairs, looked down.

Merrick. He sat. He sat and drummed one finger. He half

rose, sat again. Drummed. There was the creak of the house letting out its belly, and he started from the brow, one long line of him unscrolling: face, throat, breast, loins, legs, toes. He half rose, sat without settling, drummed long, short. Dashes and dots. Then he rose, decided, stood, paced once to the wall and turned, pressed his back to it, stood up flush. He rested and counted. Counted, quietly. Drummed. Walked across the room, paced, counted. Turned back to the wall. Thrust one arm out like a bayonet. Mechanical sounds, charnel sounds, terrible. Stopped, drummed. The entire sequence was repeated: pacing, turning, lunging, charging. A collision and a pause. Then he sat down as before and drummed one finger. Subsided.

I watched. And, eventually, slept. Woke with that long reverberation in the mind that accompanies any serious discovery, though I was baffled as to its meaning. In the map I drew of the events of that night there are two figures, myself and Merrick, a twist of flesh in a nightcap, directing events with his breath.

I make the pudding called Conundrum. I do this as an edible diversion, a palatable screen. I salt brazils, plump currants and fat Australian sultanas. Shave cinnamon and soak cloves in a smattering of sugar and brandy. I fashion tiers of sponge. Whip my batter to a shine and fold it over, leave it to half rise. Then into the oven to brown.

I slave over this pudding. Merrick barely tastes it.

Good?

Mmm.

I serve it twice and then retire it. It sits in its cheesecloth hood upon the butcher's block and I pass it a hundred times before it subsides, sweetly, into air.

Meantime I am patient. I keep my duties. I leave his meals under cover by his laboratory. I transcribe and copy and tidy the remaining rooms. Izzie comes and goes, and when she is gone the house is warmer by two or three degrees and a teaspoon is missing from the silverware. Though she does little work, I enjoy her company. If there is such a thing as wit in Nature then Izzie is its near edge.

In the news: it rains frogs on the coast. A travelling fair is charged with the abduction of seven drovers. Lord Welland is heckled by weavers who lost their jobs to the automatic looms.

As the clearances continue we are besieged by the vermin escaping the tenement fires, seeking haven from the burning wreckage of the streets. Insects seethe on the baseboards and door frames, drop softly from the walls. I lay traps with jam and paper and in the mornings these are brown and spheroid, mountain ranges with a million upquivering legs. Mice with scarlet tails, enormous beetles with profound and searching antennae who feed on dust, collect it, rolling it before them in vast, grey-edged wheels or dragging it on legs specially adapted for the purpose. These creatures, whose policy it is to stand fast, then perambulate swiftly over terrain while pedalling their strange and bulky cargo, fascinate me. The same specimen will work a stretch of floor persistently, to and fro. They shine like bits of mirror I can see myself in, a bit of man.

Before I came here I met with an accident. I was injured and lost my legs at the knee. Merrick does not mind this. He is that rare fellow for whom deformity is neither a cruel trial nor an opportunity. He sees in my caesurae what others see in canvas and marble and bronze—aesthetic potential. Not an amputation—a lack—but a pristine space to build in.

The surgeon who does the initial work is an efficient Frenchman, tall, built on an incline, rising to a steep forehead and raked hair the colour of salt. He wears glasses and tiny protruding cones from his ears and leather bands round his wrists and ankles—he is reinforced at every one of his joints. He carries his tools and instruments with a cunning strap that holds papers bound in oilskin comprising the fashions and patterns he cuts from. As he works he makes gnomic pronouncements, as if he has come only recently to the language by way of a manual of genteel correspondence or opera politesse.

Fortunately you have no atrophy, he says. Your thighs retain their heft.

Or: Your pleasure is my assurance.

Or: Do not unman yourself with screams.

The Frenchman asks what I work at. He has a system for reintroducing part-men back into the world by matching their limb to their labour—I might have a hook or a plier or a knife or a mitt for a hand, a stake or a post or a right angle for a foot. There is a woman he shows me whose left foot is a leather needle and whose right foot is a scissors so that she complements herself and soon becomes the quickest seamstress of her shift.

I was to be a teacher, I tell him. Have you a bit for that?

Before I am attended to I am given a regimen of exercises that will prepare my legs for their new termination. I am taught to shiver my muscles one by one in series. I am taught to seize, and release. I am shown pictures of men the Frenchman has seen cured. Throughout he is impatient with my fear.

I should have died; why did I not die?

Huh, what a palaver over nothing at all, he says. What a lot of herky-jerky. Look, he says, examine what is possible!

What is possible? The men in the pictures stroll the city in custom calfskin boots, looking as though nothing more than a club luncheon weighs upon their minds. I can too. I can farm, ice-skate, pick at a mine, dance stoically, properly, run for a train. I can kick a ball and anchor a tug-of-war. I can ride to hounds and rescue a child from a river. Balance—I can walk a tightrope, pivot on a tether, a hundred times. Stability—I can stand comfortably in the line of fire to set an example for my men. Durability—I can leap up and down stairs day in and day out for a lifetime, then screw down and become statuary.

The Frenchman doesn't linger. He fits me, cuts me, moves on.

These are the legs I walk on, stiff turnip greens. Veterans' crutches; sturdy, heavy, bolted, that leave hard boluses in my arm crooks and calluses on my hands. I swing as I stride, like a well-bucket. At night I loose the straps, ease the reeking stumps from their rough sockets, pick splinters from the flesh.

You will still feel them, the Frenchman said. Simply cast it from your mind.

Yes, I feel them. I lie on my back and picture my legs whole and whittle away at them, slice by slice, and it makes no difference; that is the Frenchman's curse.

At night I enjoy the entertainment provided by the philanthropic element. The town burns for its own good and the idle population is reallocated in a round of clumsy shuffles. As soon as the ash dries they are at it, putting up terraces in place of tenements. The hammers and saws and barrows sum to produce a vibration that rattles loose objects and undoes the locks of the house. We stutter about. Our teeth grind to powder. I bite my tongue in my sleep. One by one the rooms are closed off. I toast bread over what's left of a wax coronation, Denmark's Crown Prince, dressed in his naval blues and taking stock of his soft armadas as they are aspirated by the sea. Our cutlery rests in an inkwell.

Merrick works constantly. Though he has obligations to his commissioning customers, few as they are now, he directs his efforts to several figures incorporating a new principle of his exclusive design: an argument, realized mechanically. Each of these machines has a dual core with opposing orientations, like two brushes with their bristles slanted north and south, and these dither with each other and through that physical disagreement produce a friction and a sum that allows complicated behaviour with relative mechanical simplicity. Merrick braves the gusts and ash outdoors to test his mechanical aeronaut, an androgynous figure boasting balsa limbs and a bell skirting to catch the wind and ladder down the atmosphere. This fanciful creation secretes in a tube rocket and is propelled by gunpowder. Exclaims, striking terra firma, "Land ho!"

Next is a vase. He has it turned locally on a pottery wheel and glazed thickly to produce that consistent sheen so much more desirable in the woodsy darkness of a well-draped parlour. Heavy. Into the base of the vase a miniature version of his hen and her cockerel, the careful, picking dance, the mannered bowing, the split-second twining of necks. Painted, on the inside. The sun and the wheat and the dunes of grain. The whitewash fencing. With an ear to the vase the whirring and choking of the gears is apparent.

I have invoiced and booked payment for dozens of these figures. The child painter (7), the nightingale (13), a parlourmaid pursued by a footman upstairs and down through a clock (4). While ingenious, they are but piecework to him—he assembles them by numbered parts and can manage five in a day.

He shows me a dragonfly with working wings and organs. In a small vitrine his creature captures and methodically chews a blowfly, then a duodenal muscle contracts the matter into a dimpled metal barrel containing a mixture of digestive acids and passes it into a copper gut lined with hardening compounds which are then excreted as pellets of regular size. A body for Merrick is a set of separate functions, each highly developed, which work in the main harmoniously. From basic behaviours are derived tremendously difficult ones; so that complexity is aggregate, simplicity stacked up.

Here, he says. A walking machine.

A rolling cylinder supports two woman-sized limbs hinged at the ankle and the knee and the hip, flexing along the base of the feet so that the knee leads and the hip and foot follow. Balanced as it is on the narrowest possible pivot point, the entire mechanism is forever falling; walking for us is merely falling curtailed.

By now he works only on new pieces. Existing orders go unfilled, past-due bills unpaid. As each tradesman and supplier refuses him or starts proceedings against him, Merrick auctions off another of our dwindling stock of rooms. The house becomes a rolling line of credit; bondsmen and auctioneers come for the furniture and hangings and finally the walls. They take the rugs and the panelling. They take all but one set of stairs. My task is to inventory what is left in the place, and arrange the best price for it.

Immovables excepted, we are down to a fresco and assorted pots and pans. I expect a month's worth of coal for the painting and have managed to secure a capon in exchange for one of the lamps.

This grows serious, I tell him. Can you find no work?

What about the library?

Your books?

Sell them. Sell everything—everything, mind. I must have three months.

It pains me to open the library to that wolf pack. They chase the gilt and the morocco and ignore the words between. In less than a day they have stripped the room to its brickwork, to the floors, and beneath them—they harvest the mushrooms at three pence a head. One entrepreneur solemnly unwraps oilcloth from a long sharp corkscrew, drills speculatively into the cellar floor.

It is stone.

To *you*, he says, taps his nose.

We have bought ourselves three months and Merrick labours with remarkable intensity. First, the irises. Copper stems, silk blossoms each made up of a dozen or so individual petals linked by thread. As the shaft turns these are separated to simulate blooming, simulate withering. But after seventy such repetitions, the thread will wear through and the petals will drop onto the brown acidic bed that will leach them of their colour, dissolve them unto dust.

These irises make a tempting nectar for the doves, a sweet lacquer that coats their beaks and will be worked into their feathers. From their cotes the doves descend on painted rods to muse among the flowers, pecking six times, preening for one minute, rising back to their branch to bill and coo.

Watch, says Merrick. Now—

As I watch the machines begin to fail. The iris nectar has changed its formulation, become acidic. It strips metal from its copper stamen, its nectar darkens, it chokes the doves, introduces harsh skips into their song, makes treacle of their feathers, weakens the branches of the trees they roost in.

There, Merrick says.

These trees provide shade for an artist at her easel on the banks, all blush and porcelain. With an air of exquisite concentration she makes one of eight separate sketches: sky, dove, tree, stream, fish, house, fire and a cunning portrait of herself, brush in hand, painting herself, brush in hand, painting. From her paintbox she selects a regal blue, creates a bare wash of sky, chilled white space, leans back to assess the effect. The first few times she is wound she cycles through her repertoire without complaint. But eventually, and by design, she will fixate on one or another of these objects. Now it seems she is interested only in the sky. She paints it obsessively, sky over sky over sky, until the sharpened bristles finally pierce the canvas and she can jab at it no more. Each convulsive thrust of her arm moves her closer to the bank and the water and soon enough she is in it and drowning, her painting arm swirling at the silt. Her corpse in the river is the start of a dam.

The house beneath the sky the artist captures so sparely belongs to a village, rustic jewel. A smith wields his bellows. A horse pulls a carriage, a street-sweeper doffs his cap. Beside them the dammed and rising river, the float of blond air. The smithy fills with water and the water catches fire.

The last one, says Merrick. Look closely.

I see a doll's house, its roof able to open and close, operating on hydraulic principles. With a seizure it lifts and skates sideways to reveal a series of rooms briefly illuminated by torches and chandeliers set into walls—panelled walls, papered walls, plaster walls. The library and parlour and conservatory and baths and scullery that comprise the lower floors of the house. Not a doll's house, not a real house. In the dining room, a maid lights and snuffs a candle. In the scullery, a misshapen cook at his pot.

Me, I say.

In the upstairs bath a pewter tub spouts and foams and from this roiling a dark head emerges to muddle the water, dive down again. The base that holds the mechanisms has several ports that permit the insertion of new parts and tools for the myriad adjustments required for smooth operation. At the fancy of the owner, the house can thrive, or burn.

It works in any order. Hundreds of combinations, all terminal.

Left unflooded, the town catches fire, pours oil onto the stream, ignites the artist, scorches the irises, chokes the dove. It is nearness that contaminates, proximity that kills.

The logic is a defiled logic. To sit beside another object, another system, is to cause it. The artist drops her easel and a village is washed away. Malign fate is designed into life. At last, a God who bears out his critics. And a world as cruel as it seems.

Should anyone call, I am away, Merrick tells me.

Until when?

Indefinitely.

I work as he works, ceaselessly. I am his agent, his advocate, his minion and, not least, his courage. I find buyers for the trees in the garden, for the kitchen stove. I embroider promises so outlandish, so beautifully formed, that one plaintiff collapses her lawsuit and another gives us four dozen fresh eggs. Always before me the hope of Merrick's artistry turned to practical ends: two slender, responsive filament legs to replace the crude spikes the Frenchman stuck me with, that rattle and pinch so that I am in a constant state of nervous agitation, aware only of what is immediately beneath me. Little mouths, ulcerated, at the bends of my knees.

I wait, as Rose might not have, the patient wife at Merrick's side. I tell myself that I choose to do it.

The materials for his most recent and ambitious device take up a third of the laboratory. The musculature, cartilage, voice box, brain and breathing apparatus. The hand alone has twenty separate bones.

He scrapes calves' hide until it is transparent, inscribes upon it the faint tracery of veins, conductive wire stranded into floss. Gears and cams and levers are reduced in size until they can perform ten times the work in a tenth of the space. All long bones and struts are hollowed out.

The designs have changed for good. It ought to be enough, when a man has such a skill, simply to display it, again and again. But Merrick could no longer build the toys that had once amused him. His art followed his temperament. And his temperament had turned.

It is part of his ongoing project, I see now, of simplifying each element of his designs while increasing their complexity overall. For the first time since I have known him he is not working towards an object but a pattern, an arrangement of ideas, and since these ideas are still nascent and resources are few, he aims for economy and cuts out as much as he builds, removing excess parts, extraneous movements. The secondary alimentary, which once used several valves, now makes do with one. The nerves that fed the thumb and shoulder are plucked, one by one, until the bare minimum remain. The elastics above the eyes are pared and shortened. The skull gains four inches of swelling room.

Merrick now does not move so much as elongate in various dimensions. He can stretch to a door or up a flight of stairs without shifting his core. More than once I fancy that Merrick is not present at all, that I am alone in this house, inventing him as he invents me. The laboratory fires burn constantly, fed by cheap coke. He forgoes shaving, bathing, clean clothes. His open shirt shows cresting sores along his ribcage. His eyes stream yellow and cake. He eats strained soup and soft bread. Once, he coughs a tooth.

We are losing custom. To fulfill an order Merrick sends a bird that is one twisted wire and a paper triangle for a beak. It does not play, it does not sing. He has sent out a child painter made of a copper tube and a horsehair. A flautist, three fingers welded to a length of pipe.

When I convey a client's indignation he is unsympathetic.

Essence is simple. When will they learn?

A clock that is a splinter of glass on a cog. Water lilies that make do with a single flake of leaf. The rearing horse in its glade—

It is a coal, says the bewildered buyer, a barrister in the City.

It is described as a horse, I am forced to tell him. In a glade, I believe.

This is a coal in a cabbage leaf. Look; it is absurd!

I am with him throughout. The philanthropic element works its miracles with enthusiasm and on every side of us the town burns, the carts roll and the hammers descend. Merrick leaves his laboratory to sift the rubble for things he can burn or melt or transmogrify. The dust obscures the weather. Finally when there is nothing left to burn or melt or transmogrify, Merrick, like one of his infernal machines, comes to a stop. He weighs eight stone. Pale blotched skin—he might have been exsanguinated, tapped and bled. Close as I am, I notice his strong, metallic odour. He will not let me see him undressed.

We are sitting quietly in the kitchen when I hear it.

Listen, I say. The door.

A soft insistent knocking.

They have come for us, I say.

Shh, says Merrick, alert now, attentive.

They have come, I say. Shall we—

No, Merrick says. He rises to answer it, is gone a few moments, returns.

It is nothing; I knew him, he says.

That night marks the worst of Merrick's mental absences. He speaks but will not answer my questions and makes no sense. He talks of a visitor, a man terribly burned and disfigured, who came in the night and left behind a pencil drawing, the plan for an astonishing machine. The drawing was novel, incomplete, giving the dimensions and materials very exactly while leaving the workings out.

He has an idea for a mechanical parable, a clockwork moral tale. A girl trapped in a room, she is meticulous, he says. Meticulous, and brave.

He raves, burns, babbles. He is like a skillet in my hands.

He says: I saw it. I was there. I saw the clock, the lamp had failed. It was terrible, terrible. We have met before, he says. Have we met before?

Yes, I tell him.

Serpent! Asp!

Izzie and I move the bed to the kitchens where it is cool. She more agitated than I have ever seen her, in the midst of a kinetic filibuster, forestalling Merrick's end.

I am with him. I alone am beside him through it all. Smudged once more onto Merrick; our need like a latch, like a lock.

Before the fever breaks Merrick breaks, cycling through his programs indiscriminately.

Yes yes come in, he says. Well by that I mean, he says. His face is blank but mobile, changing expressions faster than I can register them. His limbs shoot and withdraw and a stain emerges where he has wet himself An electrical storm takes place within him; when I lay a cloth to his forehead it sparks.

This is my past, he says. My past—

The fever eases and he is exhausted and cold, a dense, clear vapour puffing from him, cognitive content, a thinking steam. It is as though he has found a way to partition his faculties— thoughts, wants, memories—within himself but is unable to control them; they compound and dissolve mid-air in the room I have lined with quilting and scented with cloves—how home-spun I have become, how useless.

I am alone in the upstairs rooms. Outside, crashing hammers and low flames, the clatter! The doors are shaken open. I leave my chamber and without thinking walk into its opposite. Merrick's room. I see my watch and a hundred clocks, wooden skirts flung open, empty bellies displayed. Gutted. To what end?

I am downstairs. The laboratory too is open—I tug once, and am in.

And I see it—a foot, its broad sweep, its least articulation. Its finish of tinted rubber gives it the colour of life. Lifelike, and truer than life. The divine extremity, the appendage that gave us the gift of walking upright, in the silhouette of God. It is beau-

tiful, the most lovely of the things he has made. I think: this is
gratitude. He has built it for me!

In infancy, the bones are composed entirely of gelatine. At the centre of
each bone, is a tube or hollow; this secures strength and lightness.

The slender fluted ankle. The arched and sculpted metatarsal.
Tendons running on tracks. Polished jigsaw toes so perfect they
seem to be moving, to have always been moving.

Amazing, I say.

In clasping our wrist, what is the hard substance we feel? Bones.

Inkster in the bleak crofts of Scotland, performing his ruthless Christian archaeology, saying grace by each brae before
piercing the earth with his shovels, sifting bodies from the dust.

Of long bones we have examples in the bones of the arm and leg. Of
round bones we have instances in the ankle, the extremities of the bones in
the upper part of the leg, and those of the arm. Of broad and flat bones
such as those of the knee and of the shoulder blades. Bones are porous. This
might be experimentally demonstrated by forcing air through them, if only
suitable machinery might be found.

When I wake, Merrick has taken my legs.

THE TRAIN

Thirty miles distant, a switchman wipes his slurry nose, yawns.

You have made it this far. One or two have made their excuses and left—appointments, fatigue—but the room is still half full. What have you covered? The girl, the bereft young man, the inventor and his drudge. And the accident, the train.

An impediment, you said.

This is a story of trains and it is a story of impediments. Twin tracks precisely spaced, close enough to touch but never touching. Tracks that join one space to another, one town to the next. Tracks that divide one space from another, that divide towns from themselves, that block views, that without warning end with a quick dip of track into concrete into earth a few feet from the ocean, near a tree holed by lightning in the woods. Trains that do not run. That meet, tragically, on summer evenings.

They called the crash an inferno, you say. The smoke went all the way to London, skimming down the Thames.

You are telling this story and you are watching their eyes. Their eyes and their arms as they cross and stretch them, shake their fingers out. Any mistake you catch in time can be corrected and they are your guides for this. Already they have some questions.

What connects the inventor to the girl?

Which house is the injured man in?

Who should we focus on? Who'll pay off?

Slow down, you tell them. We're halfway through.

You have laid things out. You have begun each of the four stories. You have cut across and between them. Now you return to the train, to the accident. The train and the train it strikes. What don't you know about this? Research. You have done your research. Accumulated and numbered facts and laid them out across your sallow non-slip floors, set them on push-pins into the story you are telling now: the train and its accident, the accident and its consequences.

The train you begin with is scheduled. The train it collides with is an overflow made up of Sunday school children and chaperones on excursion. Children line the narrow carriages. They jostle. Lean uphill. They complain of hunger and feign incontinence and swoon in the heat, the closeness. Their chaperones wear stout coats and scrupulous footwear and make quick, devastating connections between landscape and scripture and the duties of small boys and girls. The day is the hottest of the summer. One of the vicars, Shortleigh, seizes on this—the scenery, the heat, all proof of the sympathetic artistry of Providence, sculpting and colouring and tending the land. The group hews to a schedule. When they reach the end of the train they will dismount and walk from the station to the cemetery where a bishop is interred. There one of the children, daughter of an advocate, will place a posy of flowers she has, immensely carefully and fearfully, transported upright in a vase.

Nowhere is the special attitude to disaster that you expect to see, knowing what you know—the orientation towards east or west, the attention paid on that day, at that time, to the detail of the weather, to the conversation underway, to the premonition concerning this or that child or relative, to that minute tear in the weave of events that will afterwards assert itself—why did we? Why did we not?

This long train, this second train, heavy, perhaps under-powered, crests a hill and pauses, shuddering, just below the peak. This specially priced excursion has attracted attention, and of the several thousand passengers number hundreds neither children, chaperones, nor attendees of any chartered Sunday school known in the land. These men crowd the carriages, spill over into the engine room or van. To ride in the van is forbidden but these men care nothing for that. They have bottles with them. They drink with the guards and brakemen and play cards. It is one of these men who first sounds the alarm barely two miles from their departure point. Leaning out for a puff he hears the whip of snapped chain between carriages.

John, you have a wandering brake-chain, he says. See there—it has burst its hinge.

Inside, the vicar and his chaperones address their flock on the idea of the modicum.

Perfection is at once no less and no more than what the soul requires, explains the vicar. Beware corruption occasioned by over-sufficiency. Beware corruption occasioned by want. Conscience is the soul's barometer, says the vicar, forgets himself briefly, smiles.

Bugger bugger bugger, says the engineman, drops what remains of the broken chain on the tracks. Hot as cinders in the van, on the train. The railway watch. The forty carriages. Already they have lost two minutes and on this bloody day of all.

Mark this two minutes—it will come back. Months and even years after, women and men will argue about that first two minutes and one last minute more to be added on within the hour. Three minutes, telescoped across the centuries all the way to now. It is in these three minutes that everything happens. The girl, the bereft young man, the inventor and his drudge. One to kill, one to languish, one to decide.

You pay attention. You have in sight the first train and in mind the second. But there is a third train, and a fourth. The third, decommissioned, stands in a short valley between two towns. At midnight its driver obeys a signal from the main dispatch, turns off the engine and the lights, checks his instruments, stretches and opens the door, steps down the grille steps and onto the brief gully between the tracks. The fourth—we will come to that, you say.

How do you generate the stories you tell? The broad strokes? Details? How do you adjudicate them? Decide which is worth pursuing and what goes where? Partly you think it's a question of wiring. Your brain has reconnected itself in surprising ways. Some things were preserved just fine; others had their ends dissolved, their beginnings spliced into other beginnings. You sat in your living room with your memory cards before you, unlabelled pictures: old man, another man, a young girl, a train. You had these cards, you were told to look closely.

An old man.

A thin man.

A girl.

A young man weeping.

A steam train.

The pictures—look at the pictures, you were told. What are they wearing? Doing?

You were told: Give them names, but not just any names. Nothing then was "just any." You were told: Names, and characteristics. These might be in the form of an adjective, or noun. Sue is nice. Edward is a fireman. Use your imagination, you were told. Play with order, play with sense, but whatever you do maintain connections. And here's where the shuffle happened.

The old man in a labcoat.

The man in the sea to his knees.

The girl on a cushion.
The young man weeping.
The steam train receding.
The steam train—well, you knew about the train.

MERRICK

*A Shocking Incident Explained—More Misfortune—We
Move Houses—Looking for Work—Merrick, Redux—
I Make Connections—In Merrick's Railyard—
Departures and Farewells*

What did I say, after all? What have I left out?

I said: "Merrick has taken my legs." I might have said:
"I gave them to him."

I have been with Merrick some months now and it is clear
that we will not continue here. We live in one room. We go out
now only to forage with the others in the ashes remaining from
the philanthropic gesture. Bits of wool, leather, whole bricks, any
form of fuel or raw material. I've sold Homer's spine and
Ramsay's plate engravings. Merrick shows me a ledger in which
he has kept track of my wages and other monies owed.

You will not always suffer through my acquaintance, he says.

He is preoccupied. His laboratory is thick with figures and
topographical biopsies: samples of the continents, flora and
fauna, the core of a deer, cross-section of the atmosphere, triangular ocean, sedimentary rock.

What is it?

He smiles and chatters, he is tremendously excited. Partly

recovered now from his illness, he does not pause to sleep. When I roll from my bed at dawn he is working and when I shut my eyes at night he works still. The number of pieces in his workroom dwindles steadily despite a corresponding feeling of increased density in the room, though I cannot see the object that absorbs all of his materials and energies. I have become his below-stairs secretary, fetching, positioning, diverting.

I do not listen but I hear you, he says. Your nattering squares the mind.

I recite what I know best. Braithwaite's *Anxious Hours*, Mrs. Duggan's *An Undone Bride*. Torrence's *Elegies* and Henderson's masterly translation of Glacous's *Fragments*, which tell the story of a red world intermediate between ours and the gods', a red world full of red things and red people thinking and doing redly. For Glacous, all wisdom is found in analogy. Inkster.

Beavers, when vexed, will cry like young children.

O Inkster, happy Inkster; doughty Orkneyman, armchair sailor, scourge of sloth and ignorance and getting above oneself. You will learn something, Merrick, if not about loss. You will learn something. About the home life of the beaver, about processing flax.

Beavers, when vexed, will cry like young children. So much so, that a gentleman, about to shoot some of them, refrained from so doing, as the cries of these creatures reminded him of his own small son.

Meanwhile the Frenchman's masterpiece is coming undone. The scars split like curtains until the bone is nearly through. I find myself locked into one position, and only by minute and ordered agitations of my muscles am I able to release the limb. Merrick finds me frozen in place on an errand, carrying a bin of ashes. He walks slowly round me, then ducks to trace the joint, the scar.

Good God. I am no surgeon, he says. But I can do better for you than that.

—

Alone upstairs, Merrick's harvest of clockwork, the laboratory open, the beautiful foot. Inkster and bone shards—Merrick with my legs.

He sits at the foot of my bed and taps the legs gently. Then he tumbles me into a chair and we move through the house in the darkness.

And I am in the laboratory, in nighttime, under the sun.

Not the sun, I realize, once I have my bearings, but a gigantic globe suspended from the ceiling above a compact station of drawers, a central bank of flasks and scales and valve burners, racks of phials and jars and beakers, a giant iron press, a deep kiln oven, a watchmaker's table and suite of tools, clamps and pre-cut strings and wires in hanging baskets, several bolts of cloth. As my eyes adjust I see to my right a thin, deep river, a miniature landscape of hills and downs and a sickle of beach. Just past this bucolic scene there is a hanging woman and a smaller girl, harnessed forms, walking in place to test some theory of locomotion, their heads an afterthought, plugs of old straw.

Merrick cleans my limbs. He wears a cloth over his mouth and nose and applies one to me, soaked in spirit, that burns and then freezes. He has set out his various instruments in the order in which they are to be exercised, hefting and tabling them in rehearsal. He immerses his hands in a steaming basin and dries them, steadily regards me.

Now, he says.

The disinfectant has dispersed, evaporated. He taps a path downside my knees to locate the point of sensation, runs his fingers along the withered convex of my knees, flexes the joints, measures circumference.

I had better trim these leg-ends, he says. I'll need a straight edge.

With a pencil he draws on the limb above the cut. The broad

shape and the exact pattern of overlap, the wound's awkward overgrowth to be meshed with metal in a new configuration.

I am drenched in spirit, in draught after draught of laudanum, a dream of instruments and the hedge of a saw. I feel a pin in one leg-socket and its slow withdrawal, slitting of the ventral side and a slow, aching loosening of the fluids that wash the centre bone; the careful trimming of the bone, the twining of some new fibrous material into the topknots of exposed nerves.

The agony is tremendous. The saw discards as much flesh as it cuts and the seam of its cut is replaced by air, which upon touching the severed nerve endings appropriates their function until the room is all air, all nerve. I am sure I must faint as the morbid tissue is cut away yet I feel it done and I have not fainted. It is as though I have stepped aside from my body into an adjacent room from which I am able to watch all that happens and register the sensations whilst feeling nothing at all. A meticulous stitching hand has he, I think, there he is through the joint; then the last draught takes effect and I am farther and farther away—

Even now the memory of the procedure far more intensely than the actual injury lingers. I have been sawn a thousand times since with no diminution of intensity, no dimming of the edges that usually accompanies our imaginative reliving of a scene. The specificity of these memories: the raw, pungent stink of the room, its rough mottled walls; the sharp, linear shock of incision; the insistent dragging of the saw; the spray of blood and gore; the frothing tissue upon the floor; the obscene outline of its path in the sawdust. When I shunted about on the stumps afterwards—the pain! It was like treading on my eyes. Every grain of gravel, each cobble, rug or bit of turf was transmitted the length of my spine so that I made a kind of travelling microscope, with a lens wired straight to my brain.

For days after I lay in my cot, waking for long enough to pick at the vile mash and milk delivered by Merrick in his distracted manner. Things have shifted again during my long sleep. The room is empty. Walls, doors, ceiling, stray moulding and corner heaps. I have been moved. Still prone I follow Merrick's instructions. I assert the straps and test the weight of the leg raised. I sit up in bed and hold one leg across my lap and learn its functions and its tics. The knee flexes. The leg shaft narrows to a perfect ball, designed no doubt for the socket of its companion foot, though for now Merrick has fitted me with what might be a pair of modified wooden shoe trees. Still, I can walk on these legs, these lightweight miracles in steel. I plant and step—why not?—pirouette!

They have taken the south wall for the bricking. We have set up in the basement scullery, the last full room. Men have come for the leaded windows. The foundation stones are to be cut and carted away. The wallpaper is stripped from the Blue and the Malt and the Rose rooms, the three rugs sold as a lot. The turnstiles and drinking fountains are sold. The stairs are sold piecemeal with the battle scenes heading to Lancashire and the doomed Greek lovers to a doctor in Rouen. King George pigeons are captured and sold, six as breeding pairs.

The mould is scraped and sold to brewers. The eaves and drains are chopped and sold by the foot and the shingles lifted; those intact are sold in bundles and the broken ones are ground into a kind of builder's meal. The greenhouse is bought by a barrister and moved pane by pane to his estate, and the bobbled mice follow it. The phosphorescence is scraped from the walls and sold to a surveying firm. The old umbrellas are skinned and sold.

We have been visited by the philanthropic brotherhood. They have recommended that we leave the house.

Gentlemen, my apologies. We are light on chairs, says Merrick.

They are surprised by the state of the house and, I think, by the understanding that Merrick and I share. A tall and bearded specimen outlines the attractions of the new properties to be built on the hill.

These feature a very modern ambience, he says. Classical proportions, all-day light.

Another man carries a register.

Full name, date of birth, he says.

The next morning Izzie appears with her motley bag, curtsies uncertainly.

Ah, says Merrick. You make your way to Tor?

And Izzie shudders in a northerly direction.

You have connections there?

And Izzie releases an upward sigh.

There is a smith, Daniels, who will remember me, says Merrick. Look him up and inquire after fourteen shillings, and if you get it, keep it, he says.

Izzie contorts gently and disappears; in her wake a haze of dust, Precambrian.

Well, says Merrick. That she stayed on as long as she did.

By February we have no fuel or food beyond that which we can borrow or scavenge. There is nothing to do but prepare ourselves. In the mornings Merrick tinkers with his designs, makes adjustments to the legs he has constructed for me, a set screw, a hinge. They bend and torque and are beautifully balanced. My stumps sit in cups like lenses, convex and smooth. Straps run to my shoulders and are controlled by muscular movements there. The mechanism is concealed beneath twin hatches and wrapped in a rough fabric. I teach myself to manage stairs and to stand on one leg and to turn rapidly and not to crush what I tread on. At night they rest in tripods upside down.

I am at that point in Inkster where the credo of unthinking obedience subtly shifts from the Lord to the group. Here the great man apostrophizes the qualities of the collegial insects: ants, bees. Good old Inkster—at last a species that perfectly answers his needs.

Bees are divided into three parts: the head, the chest, and the abdomen, or stomach; including a very peculiar stinger, used for defence; a besom-shaped trunk in order to extract the honey from flowers; tongue which may be flattened like a trowel or sharpened like a pencil (shew the wisdom and goodness of God in thus providing even insects with so wonderful a system of contrivances). The bee's body is covered with short hairs; hence, to collect the dust with which it makes that substance called "bee bread." Its abdomen collects the intestines and also the honey bag, the venom bag, and the sting (the honey bag, which contains the honey, will be familiar to those country children who have killed bees for the honey—here denounce cruel habits, and shew that the mischievous one is, in reality, only destroying the works of God). The sting of bees is purely defensive; they never use it to attack an enemy.

Downstairs a knock at the door.

Bees teach us to be industrious (refer to the hymn, "How doth the little busy bee," etc.); they teach us to be loyal (fond of the sovereign); they teach us to be fond of our homes; they are models of cleanliness; they are fond of fresh air; they are early risers; they are peaceful; they are very sympathetic (they feel for each other, and have been seen to carry a wounded one out of the hive into the sunshine, lick him with their tongue, roll him over and over, and, at sunset, carry him back again into the hive).

They knock again at the door. Very fast and loud.

This time it is certain. They have come for us, I say.

Perhaps, says Merrick. He trembles where he sits.

Will you answer it? Will I?

Again. Then, three hard, spaced knocks.

Merrick sits up very straight; again I have the impression that he has decided something, even that he is eager. Again the knock at the door. Again. Again. Then—nothing.

I write: *This waiting is tiresome. But we persist.*

In the morning there is the mark on the door, the smudge in a circle like the iris of an eye that marks the house for demolition and affords us three days to pack and be gone. Merrick acts with a speed and authority I had not credited him with. Within the day we have vast crates delivered to the door. Men hired by the hour number parts, roll them in cloth, settle them inside the crates. I make maps in order to keep track of what goes where. By the second morning the work is done and arrangements are made for conveyance.

Merrick has taken a storage depot in the nearby town of Welton to keep his inventory in. Great sprung drays come for the crates to be loaded using hoists of Merrick's devising that are broken down and packed into long, flat, sturdy boxes that become the sides of the rented carts. The workers take their dinners and Merrick and I tour the house in case we have missed anything. I see bites out of doors, pitted floors and shadows where furniture once stood, and it occurs to me that even these shapes are designed; there is South America, the long slump of Chile and the finger of Ecuador. The walls, the fittings, the corridors, bare floor and carpets. Together, in order, they are the shapes of the continents and oceans, land masses and rivers, forests and mountains; an elemental, unencumbered map of the world.

I recall this night as a series of branching ellipses. We wait. We are underway. Wait. Cross. Wait. Wait at the door for the moon to rise. A horse stirs the water at the rear of a scoop barge. A man in a filthy collar picks spinrushes into a sack at his belt. We are in the close, then we are at the ponds, then in a dark and vicious avenue with rolling cobbles, high windows. Sudden indentations, crude paths slash vertically between streets gargoyled with sleeping men. The night is warm and damp, swatches of fog and pools of still water. There is a film on my lips. Our column moves awkwardly, yawing side to side like a pig ship.

Merrick wears his clothing in layers. Three shirts, three waistcoats, overcoat and oilskin and tall hat. He is excited by the trip. He steps in place and agitates his fingers and pierces the earth with his stick. He walks ahead and circles back and weaves between us and walks ahead. I have never before walked with him. His stride is long and uneven, syncopated, his eyes shift, elongate. Suffused with a weird, lilting energy, he all but leaps about us.

The carts buckle beneath their weight and the Pargetters, conscripted for the occasion, stagger before them, driving four wiry old nags forward hoof by hoof. I see a beak protruding from one untucked canvas corner. Navigating one wattled back lane we trail bright gimbals from a hole in a sack. At the short neck of the lane we find a commotion—one Dr. Roland preaching on the fusion of Socialism and Temperance from a wagon he lives in. All work shared among all men, the river of liquor set alight—keen is the affliction of gin upon us now, the brimstone of alcohol and berries.

Listen, brothers, says Dr. Roland. There is time, there is a little time. All of us once lived among them in the desires of our flesh, following the wishes of the flesh and the impulses, and we were by nature children of wrath, like the rest. But God, who is rich in mercy, because of the great love He had for us, even when we were dead in our transgressions, brought us to life—

The fog descends with us and tampers with the light until faces are flattened to so many calling-card portraits. An old man in waistcoats. Another cut off at the knees by a band of fog so thick and green it might be sea-water. A girl selling pin-cushions. A hollow-eyed youth with his tonics set out on their bright red case:

What will it what won't it cheap and long-lasting, he says. The gout the luff the palsy of the liver the red bumps the swelling we don't mention the rheumatic you've never you've never, missus, not once in your life! Clings to a tumour and wrestles it off would you settle for something drawn straight from the well? Lumbago smallsey what do you mean you've tried everything, sir? Babies grow fat on it ladies grow thin complaints of the complexion intractable rashes superannuated fevers a runty tool—

Our route through Moar is a long, lateral perambulation—I am never aware of the grade. The town by night is a series of friezes, ruined and appalling: parish church, workhouse, hospital, a beggar cradling a bird. We exit the high street, begin our descent into the chain-maker's coils, the lowest quarter of the town. Already the air is thick and hot and the path is treacherous with the oil-and-earth mixture the chain-makers use as mortar and to slick the way for wheeled forges. Ragged narrow unfinished houses like blackened teeth, some without roofs. The heat and noise are infernal, made more so by the uncertain sideways illumination cast by hundreds of open fires. Figures appear in loops and ovals, slowly, link by link. Children's faces are wicked and lined. Chain, the raw stuff of it, is everywhere: chain buckles up the chimneys; there are chain knockers for the doors and a chain bower in front of the largest dwelling on the street.

The depot stands at the wrist of a wide crescent like a set of spread arms. It is deserted. The tracks of a large dog. We wait and finally a man in a bright-green coat emerges with a notebook. He is tall, stropped like a razor, smooth and sharp. He speaks to Merrick briefly and waves us on.

The horses will not proceed underground. Merrick has disappeared. It takes the Pargetters and two scruffy boys to shift the things onto long carts on tracks. Box after box, laddered by beams and nails. When the work is done the Pargetters unclip from the carts tools—picks, mallets, iron locks. They hammer the latches into the stone walls and clamp the locks. Then they pour wax into the lock barrels and set a red string over the wax.

Merrick and I continue our journey alone. The thoroughfare is a steep road lit haphazardly by the brittle fires of the chain-makers. My legs, designed for flatter surfaces, catch and bend in the road and I must lever myself from step to step like a stilt-walker. There is acid in my joints. I cannot keep up with Merrick as he strides ahead, head down, but I cannot rest without risking a tumble.

I mange a step. Merrick waits. Step. Wait. And so we proceed.

The edge of the city in winter. Separate rooms at the end of the hall. The edge of the city, wallpaper glued imperfectly onto the panels of the world. What colours there are survive in the faces of citizens plying their trades in the warehouses and railyards and cafés and fishing vessels and stockyards and laundries, in winter, though the body craves dormancy, though the streets are iced an inch thick.

The cold makes for good logic. It adulterates revenge. The passions thrive in hot places; here they are a luxury consuming resources better spent on foraging, on banking energy and heat. It is dark by four, a persistent wind, birds drift by like pencil shavings. Propped on the soft bank of the river, the houses are forever in danger of losing their foundations. People are splay-footed, bottom-heavy; they pitch themselves against the steep streets and struggle through their days. Here, one's twists are anticipated in the landscape.

We live thinly. Merrick rises early to go to his draughty work-shop with its banked crates and groaning stove, walks back with the clerks in rough suits and one-ply coats, no proof against this weather. These city men are made of fog, they subsist on sand-wiches and scrambled eggs, hoard cheap, strong builder's tea in tin caddies displaying the royal warrant. Sometimes I walk the lanes. I keep to the walls and frequently look behind me. There is a graciousness in angles this acute, the elegant distortion that accompanies any really telling rise and fall. I watch the gait of the women and pay attention to their ankles and booted feet. Something this delicate, perhaps, for me.

In the news: the Norwegian princess disappears. A woman in the north gives birth to thirteen rabbits. I continue my labours on Merrick's collected papers, the painstaking transfer of his ideas onto naval stock that can be folded up small as a stamp.

Isolated and bored, Merrick grows introspective. What is his achievement? His legacy? The automata—clever, but irrelevant in this new age. I read the blueprints as I copy and I wonder whether Merrick has genius or only facility. What distinguishes the landmark from the toy? What in Merrick's race of machines recommends him to posterity?

He concentrates now on causation, the production of coincidence by mechanical means. A simple proposition: if/then. If x then y. The world in all its irregularity managed and foreseen. If the temperature rises a switch is tripped. If the switch is tripped a magnet moves. If a magnet is moved current is generated. If a current is generated a circuit is closed. If the circuit is closed a pulley is stretched, a mouth opens. Merrick's intuition is that ifs and thens are physical destinies, allowing his creations to be mechanically aware of themselves.

Alone among his fellows, Merrick eschews the brain for the body. A thing is not how it thinks but how it acts. So Merrick makes empty brains and clever bodies, the heads of his figures are air and paint. When designing a body for walking, the proper motions are more important than having somewhere in mind to walk to.

I did not know it then but Merrick had ceased to make things. Instead he is telling stories, working out a combinatory system, a mechanical narration, comprising self-sufficient blocks. Each block will have a function and each function will permit a limited range of variation within the boundaries Merrick sets.

This system will generate, eventually, a life sufficiently complete and structured that Merrick will be able to live it.

In his project Merrick has specific fears. He fears that he will awake and forget how one thing properly connects to another. What does this fear issue from? His long-held theory of love: make an object whole for a moment, then take bits away until it lacks.

⊕

It is spring, then summer, and I have grown impatient. I cannot forget the pain and shock of Merrick's surgery, it was the worst thing I have endured. And yet, I confess, I adored it. I lay twitching in the swill of tissue and fluids and was happier than I have ever been. I knew I had found that supervening desire that informs and displaces all others. I longed to be cut and fitted; to be undone and rearranged. I would remember that first time always—it was extraordinary.

I spend days stumping round Welton finding models for my new parts; miners' feet, fencers' shoulders, the teaspout neck of Lady Gadd. I will confront Merrick. I will lay out my plans.

Feet and toes; be delicate, I will say. Filigree, not bolts.

But why stop at the extremities when the rest is so imperfectly designed? Hips seize; kidneys calcify; livers overflow; hearts stop.

I draw arms and ears and limbs and organs in the margins of Inkster. Human at first and later my own improvements, chimeras of flesh and metal. How like deeds are bones.

⊕

Here, he says. This, and this. One copy, seal it, he says.

The plan he hands me calls for several inches or several plates of homogeneous thickness; he has used layers and layers in its construction. Unfolded, and again, and again, a million times, it will replace the ground we walk upon. I see it. Banks of pins and switches permit adjustments infinitesimal and profound: pull a rod on a spring and a fire erupts. The smoke fills the horizon. The lake boils. The river rises.

The imprint of a city and a field and fodder animals, versions of the cows and sheep we are familiar with. Most of the buildings remain unfinished. There is a sun and moon and one or two notable constellations. Fold. Fold. The eastern mirror of this city, all bulbs and cupolas and humpbacked beasts and the scent of breeze and spices. The noise of markets.

Fold, Fold. Fold—a broken sheet of ocean. Fold—a lighthouse's distant revolutions. Fold—a pod of deep-jawed whales. Fold—a wedding underway. Fold—a floating grand piano.

I am amazed. I am. Here is order shaped by breakdown, splinter, eruption and chance. Independence of function. Modularity. Accident; accident or fate. The difference between the merely mechanical and the authentically sublime.

A dream: I hear an ambling grinding and threshing, a scraping on the floor. I see Merrick in the alcove. He turns, in his hand a clutch of wires—tipped, I ascertain, with varying colours. As he moves there is a faltering on the floor behind him and I see the jerky unnatural digits of a quadrangular machine with a horrible discus for its face. Not one, but ten such monstrosities. Merrick turns left and they follow him. Not a herd but a race, I realize, and he is their avatar.

September to August—I have spent nearly one year with Merrick. The house has gone, his health is failing. As soon as I can I will leave him. But first there is the debt I am owed.

August passes and I reach my limit. What have I come here for? What have I achieved? He is ruined; I see he is ruined.

Recurrent fever, thickness in his lungs, spew on the handker-chiefs bloodier by the day. I doubt he can live out the year. And even so, would I trust his palsied hands to perform their old miracles? His memory is atrocious, his eyes are failing, he works entirely from my copies of the blueprints and calls on me constantly to read these aloud. New feet? Ridiculous. I have long since missed my chance.

But I am not without resources. I have been shameless in my bookkeeping and illness has made him incautious. I have a sum put by and, just as in Last Year's Novel, a plan that will see justice done. What tools does one depend on, for undoing another's life? What knives and picks? What ballpeens? I am not vengeful by nature, I might not have gone through with it, even then, had he given me my feet. Had he asked my name.

The interview ran three sentences.

You are free now?

I am free now. There was some question—

You have writing? Write me a line, anything. Good. Good. You will do.

I take a cab to the East Gate, tip the warehouse master half a crown.

Second from the end, he says.

When I find it I knock on the door.

As I wait I think: if I wished, I could tell Merrick a story. About a woman, Rose Ames, and her six-year-old girl. At Brontyn Station, waiting for a train. Capped, quite respectable. Early, as usual for her. What else? A busy day. The trains are full. Summer has disrobed gracefully and handed off to autumn and the station is full of exhausted country-house guests, students returning to their colleges, tradesmen on their circuits heading west-northwest.

The train—where is it? A beauty; new engine, new carriage, a sleeper, an observation car, down from Inverness, a very great distance, it has still the glisten of mountains about it, of burns, of glens and lochs and savagery, of being coolly lost. Or so she fancies—she is full of fancies! The child, we'll say, alternates between sitting quietly and singing verse upon verse about the denizens of a farm. A rabbit, a rooster, some pigs. There is a man sharing the bench with them. He materialized here suddenly and found himself at home. He offers her peaches—he bought too many at market—delicious, just-ripe globes of pink and red, thin-hided and full of golden juice; will she share them, she and the girl? Silently, messily, they eat.

This man—what should we call him? Call him Dysart, after myself. Dysart. That will do. So the gentleman is Dysart, the lady is Rose.

Rawlins Dysart. Few advantages but a rising man. He has worked hard at his studies, clerked in the City, qualified as a schoolmaster in the Physical Sciences (Classics at a pinch). This week he won his first posting at a good small school with a progressive Master who believes in the mixing of rank with file and whose radical ideas, borne out by results, are sure to be widely adopted. Dysart has a suit of grey flannel that brings the colour to his eyes and an unwaxed moustache. He speaks cautiously, moves slowly, is quick to bow.

These are familiar habits. He has been trained, Dysart. He has been trained as a dog or bear is trained and to much the same end: to forget it has been trained at all. He loves his work; why not? It is a noble thing to be entrusted with the minds of the young and curious, to have the chance to make of them someone better than ourselves. And who better than him as an example? He is rising, after all. He aspires. He will rise and leave behind crassness, falseness, poorness, cant. Thus does a dog pursue its ball or stick and a bear perform its ambling waltz, and a nice bit of joint at the end of it. And thus does this rising man contemplate his future, just secure enough to be intriguing. And this is where it ought to remain and would remain, by the immutable laws of bears and dogs, if the train were only on time.

But the train is not on time. The train is late. Dysart, were he forthright in his manners, might here confess to a subterfuge. He might say to Rose: I was walking my usual route round the square, past the tobacconist and the park with gold-tipped gates. But today, I turned left. Today I saw you and turned left. And here I am—forgive me.

Of course he says none of these things.

What are his reasons? What might he offer in mitigation, say, in a sitting court of law? That to be trained as a dog and bear are is to learn the habit of being elusive. That even now, despite his recent good fortune, he feels in constant danger of being found out, that all this rising, this relentless rising, is not rising at all but embedding, a casual bronzing of a life in full motion—and he discovers this over peaches on a country platform of a train he is not himself waiting for since his ticket is for Tuesday, two weeks hence.

And what of Rose? And her girl? And the train?

The train was three minutes late.

Three minutes lost between there and here, then and now. Everything depends upon it. Three minutes that Merrick has searched for. That he desperately wants back.

The train, late by now. Like all things expected to come to pass that do not come to pass, its very lateness begins to seem the surprising new dispensation of a life. It is not the train that does not arrive but rather the new prospect of a life that does not include the arrival of this train, that does not depend on it, that relinquishes altogether the possibility of the life in which this train played a part.

What might they have said, Rose and Dysart? It must have been querying and timid. They are strangers, separated by class and sex, bound by conventions of speech and behaviour that might have been wired into them, so reliable are they, so fixed. If x then y.

Good afternoon—

Good afternoon.

If x then y. If Rose takes the peach Dysart offers her, then he will stay.

She takes the peach and they talk about the weather, the unseasonal heat. The number of people at the station today. Newspaper headlines, an execution at Withers at six o'clock.

Taylor, she informs him. Taylor, the Master, who slew his friend.

A famous case. Taylor, the brilliant linguist and botanist, first to apprehend Gaelic roots and the blue lichen (a medicinal), a man of highest principles, who had described a single square foot of Highland turf in a monograph of a hundred pages; who had won the daughter of a local squire through sonorous disquisitions on the amblings of the moon. Taylor, whose friend the merchant was found dead in a cave, his head a hairy pulp.

I would not say "bludgeoning," remarks Taylor in court, having opted to defend himself. "Cranial interruption" more precisely states the case.

He is considered to be brilliant, she says. They are forever being likened to an eagle's. Taylor, I mean. His *eyes*.

Dysart then is able-bodied. Bad lungs, yes. Not the clearest of complexions. Winch nose. Oblong jaw. But he walks, he lifts, he carries. His feet are almost simian, adapted to the low rung of the stool they curl over for eleven long hours in the import house down Scrivener's Lanes, where fine wines and ports are tallied and distributed. His room in a house of thirteen rooms, young men with high collars, older men with higher collars; some ancient specimen with a collar so high and stiff he is actually imperilled by it. Dysart takes his morning meal at five o'clock and his evening at half-seven. Sundays, he sleeps late and takes a newspaper, commits an article to heart. His is a life dedicated to rising; a life shorn of delight and frippery, a solid working life. It is Wednesday, he opens his window to the street below, sees a void at the heart of the crowd—

Oh! says Rose when he asks her destination. What should I say? Home.

The train. A warm day, 28 degrees. Waiting, languor. The peaches, a warm gold curve through the afternoon.

She is lovely, Dysart observes, of the sleeping girl. Her father—

—is dead, says Rose. The man I work for is an archipelago, she says. Isn't that a funny thing to say about a man? We have returned from Switzerland, she says. Zingen—you know it? There is a spa there, she says. The water is green. It is said to effect all manner of improvements, she says. The physical being and the mind.

It is—Dysart begins, after a pause.

We have returned, feeling much better, Rose says. We felt much better, and we came back. But perhaps, she says, feeling her way, perhaps we are too early. The water is potable, she says. Ten full glasses per day.

Dysart senses that she is asking something of him. What? Who is he to Rose? No one, a stranger. And yet, he feels, she is looking to him to decide.

It is sometimes better to observe caution in these matters—

The illuminated waters, the peaches, the soft afternoon. The commotion of the platform and the quiet of the bench.

It is too early, she says. Too soon.

In an instant, it happens—the train arrives. She rises, signals a man for the luggage, presses an envelope into Dysart's hand—it is the work of a moment to complete the handover, and then Rose walks away with the barrels and the sleeping child enveloped, he fancies, in a soft green glow, and he is on the train in sole posses-sion of the Ames compartment—what luxury!—without clothes or shoes or pen or notepaper, without the least idea where he is going or when he will arrive, on the first real adventure of his life.

—

I knock again at the door.

What is Dysart to make of this? Of this strange afternoon, of the conversation he has enjoyed—or has he?—with this woman, and her child. He sits in the carriage, watches the scenery flash from gorge to grain fields to river moraine to the smoking outskirts of the town of Moar. He wonders at the chance that has brought him this far, refuses to allow himself to think of what will come next. Nothing will come next, perhaps; it is no calamity. He recalls her final sentences, the description of the spa, the cave, the waters. An invitation? Has this woman offered something—herself, perhaps—to him? The more he considers, the odder it seems, everything, the meeting, their conversation, her last words, the departure of the train, the crowds banned from the hanging but gathered outside the prison walls, waiting for news of Taylor's passing and his dying words—was he remorseful? Blasphemous? Taylor, the peaches, Rose and her child, his own behaviour. How did he come to be here? Even now he can find no trace of the decisions he must have taken, the choices he surely made.

The train, the train. A few miles short of the marshes, speeding up in accordance with the new instructions, adjusting course and speed to match a master clock standardized to Greenwich from which the time signal issues like an emanation of the stars. He feels the train gather speed, stands up—

No answer. The window is open and I look in. The floor is tiled with blueprints, oilcloth, various devices for weights and measures. Trains. I see trains and train stations and a G-shaped length of track. A figurine in a tan bonnet made of butcher's yarn and another in a waistcoat, seated on a bench. There—a third, smaller figure, deep in her mother's skirts. Other characters are supplied economically by bits of coloured wood. I am surprised to see this scene repeated in several places across the floor.

The burners are gone, and the other apparatus. The tools also. This is not a place for making things. Rather it is a place of disassembly, recombination, dissolve. Everywhere artifice undoes itself. Wingless retching dragonfly, melting flowers, the bald child painter hacking pointlessly at her canvas, overflowing sewers, poisoned dying birds.

The walls are dark and the floor drains steam, difficult to see to the far end of the room where I hear Merrick moving; he seems to be everywhere, throwing switches, presumably, organizing trains. I look closely at the miniature rail ties, the interleaved bridges, and recognize the cheap pine used by the Frenchman, salvaged from my poor old pegs.

Indeed every object here has been cannibalized and repurposed in an uneasy blending of old and new: a nightingale's beak, stem of an iris, the hair of the child painter remade as thatch. There—a navicular. Talus. The parts of the human foot. My beautiful feet amid all this carnage, and I am reminded of the fabric blowing off a corner of the carts the Pargetters drove to reveal the mixture beneath. He has taken it all apart, all apart, for this. A beak, a paintbrush, a larynx. A life's work disassembled to make this ghastly toy train.

Merrick does not break stride, and I see at last where this must be leading, in the dense, sparky air of the warehouse, everything a bit electrified, as Merrick's trains approach each other, exactly as they did on the night.

—and walks. And it is night, by then. The train, with its parts sourced from Scotland, Ireland, France and Germany, its Italian walnut and Swiss plumbing, speaks in fifteen languages at once. Crashing, cacophony, the noise is incredible; for a minute at least Dysart stands in the rubber gullet between carriages and listens, listens to the transfer of effort to bearings and axles, pistons and gearshafts. Marvellous. Everything is marvellous to him. The most insignificant crosscut screw, the rippled carpeting, the middle-note thrumming of wind beneath the train. It is all astonishing, all transformative. The train, the peaches, the afternoon, grains of moonlight at the butt of a glass—he laughs, in the plenitude of this moment, laughs and opens his watch: *Grapple!*

Twenty-twelve.

Twenty-twelve. Dysart remembers the new carriage, the one with the whisked-off slip. Observatory, they called it. At the rear of the train. He walks, to the remaining first-class carriage; the second, the third, the dining car, empty, chairs folded away; finally the club car, where the men play whist and chemin de fer.

Tom, says the dealer, by way of introduction. Draw, gents, he says.

Twenty-eighteen. The train gathers speed. Still late, by two minutes twenty. Still late! There must be a discrepancy between the time on the engineer's watch and the time in the station. Perhaps this is a matter of mechanics. Perhaps it is not—this is the fear that grips the engineer. What if time does not mesh so easily after all? If London time fails to match that of the estuaries, the border provinces? Lost seconds, minutes, hours, days. Ought he to speed up? Slow down? Hold his course? In the galleries, in the card-room, people feel the fluctuations in their stomachs.

Between the last two cars a young man strangely dressed, muttering. And on the tracks, superstructural in the fog, a girl in a raincoat waving her hands slowly up, slowly down.

Dysart is walking, sees ahead the last of the throats between cars, sees the observatory, just as advertised, an enormous bell of glass and steel. He plies the corridor, until twenty-nineteen becomes twenty-twenty and twenty-twenty-one, exactly at the same time, and the switchman sneezes, and his boots slip, and the onrushing train, perfectly calibrated, arrives along the same piece of track, and there, in the twitchy rubber of the space between cars, between times. It is like falling into a lantern, smashing and squeezing and burning and . . . calm. Dysart watches himself and the world slide into lanterns, and when he awakes—

I knock three times on Merrick's warehouse door. Hard, spaced. His concentrated panic. The two approaching trains.

I don't tell this story to Merrick now; I never tell him. Dysart. Rose. She was halfway up the stairs. To leave one train for another is the simplest thing in the world. To leave one life for another is the simplest thing in the world. Rose handed me the ticket and I gave my life for hers. I returned to the platform in the days following the crash. Bandaged and bleeding still I came to the station and followed the search. I watched the men depart in the mornings and return hoarse and grey for tea. I saw the officials of the railway and their court-appointed aides, tagging those belongings and body parts that had been identified and those that would never be claimed.

I watched. I saw Merrick walking after the others, making notes in a book. I had Rose's ticket and now I had Merrick, too. Archipelago, a funny name for a man.

I called on him after a decent interval. The interview ran three lines.

It was formerly supposed that the rattlesnake could fascinate its prey and thus overcome it. This notion however is now exploded, and the fact is that the self-possession of the victim is lost.

I will leave Merrick. I have packed my trunk and map rolls with the collected papers of Lemuel Merrick, Esquire. The originals and the copies, too. It was the work of a moment to remove them and to substitute the blue cloth-bound volume with another I had bought. The work of a moment and a life. We might say: this is destiny, the bone that subtends will. Yes, why not? Destiny. That will do.

The sea is uneasy; the great ship saws and rolls. I draw from my bag an old, plain volume, the pages grey and mottled, stiff with ink and wax.

Some whales would be choked by a penny roll. It must be the case that some other fish, notably a shark, swallowed Jonah, since the whale gullet is so notoriously slender.

Inskter! Prophet! Pedant! Tale-spinner! Imposter! Fortune-hunter! Wax-maker! Improvident moulder of truths! If I were not so superstitious I would cast him into the sea as whale-food, shark-food; his faith would snap their jaws.

I think about other journeys. From my home to my aunt's house and to Catnatch's lair. From Catnatch's to my apartment. From there to Moar. One by one I balance these memories on a very sharp, very true point: on the one side is eternity, on the other is here and now. One by one, I throw them over, cancel them out. Merrick in the centre of his infernal landscape. I knock three times at the door. Hard, spaced. Panic. Sparks. The fire round the track. I watch at the window as he depresses the lever that sends the first train fast round the unswitched track, short one brake, striking the fourth and fifth carriages of the chartered train crossing, torquing from the tracks to explode and burn and maim and kill for the tenth, the hundredth, the thousandth time; perfectly, and to scale.

DORY

In Absinthe the passenger and the freight train are owned by different companies and traverse the town along different tracks. The freight four times daily and the passenger twice, 06:00 and 19:00, ducking under the neck of Minnard's Hill, where in 1919 Robert McAvy, a local man rich from the whitefish, bought twenty acres for an observatory he planned to build but only ever managed to scaffold, forty feet of iron bars and phantom planking dedicated to the study of the Northern Lights.

Minnard's Hill. Dennison. Clouston, Larsson. Wishart. A town of names and namesakes, where children are called Walter and Larry and Doris and June and streets are called Dennison and Clouston and Larsson and sometimes, where family names fall short or councillors bicker, Church or Second or Main.

Minnard's Hill, Dennison, Clouston, Larsson—this is the view from the Bow Hotel. During the summers the men come down from the city on weekends, briefcases and lightweight suits and folded newspapers. They step off—they seem only ever to step off, only ever to arrive—and cross the superheated concrete laid each May to rebuff the delicate insinuations of the ice, pass the lounge with its bench seating and brass fixtures and kiss hello to their wives, sons, daughters, housekeepers, walk the quarter mile to the public docks and hand everyone into the Chris-Craft or Duke or Peterborough, key the ignitions for the short ride home. This is the view from the train, cramped now with journalists and photographers connecting from everywhere, descending into this out-and-out wilderness, this paroxysm of lakes.

There isn't an outcry when the body is discovered. A notice goes up in the Sure2Save and the flower shop and the *Intelligencer* carries the first of its two standard obituaries deployed when the departed is over fifty and has long resided in the town, invoking the wanderer and the polestar and the pioneer dream. His only relations, two cousins, come to oversee the funeral and the sequestering of the body in a White Oaks plot in the shadow of the German cranes clawing out new foundations for row houses abutting the lake. They are irritable, exhausted, walking the town incuriously, checking their watches and dutifully scouting the gift shops and searching in vain for up-to-date national newspapers and making sure that their cars are where they have left them and have not been defaced.

The victim's bed is stripped and cleaned and one loose nut is repaired at the head where his fingers had worked at it. Then the room is sprayed and vacuumed and the pictures swapped, all part of the careful forging of luck. His death will, in less than a week, become a famous death. It will be written about, fretted over, taken as a harbinger for a violent and unsettling new age. But this is all to come. In the room where he died the brand-new ceiling fans have yet to be switched on. The pollen count is up. Tent caterpillars weave their grey haggard bottle-ship sails, feasting on ash and birch and maple, their million mouths churning, the cotton-ball sound as their dead bodies drop.

⊕

Dory has difficulty with this section of her letter. The transition. It's the secret again, aligning all the tiny iron filings, as though everything she did she did to this end: murder. Nothing that happened in these months is innocent with the secret in its place. Everything counts as part of the explanation. What good is it to argue, to say: something came over me, a feeling, and I followed it through? How can there be rehabilitation without remorse? Yet here she is.

The events themselves are straightforward. School ends for the year. The liberated summer-camp hum. Jump-ups and curling irons. Bronze and silver fitness medals. Jubilee coins. A renowned mezzo visits the town and gives a recital in the arena. A dance with balloons with gold and silver shake inside them, planets that have swallowed their atmospheres. A filtered kiss from Teddy Sakic. The renaming of Allan's Drugstore to Town Drug Mart. A general increase in the use of the suffix "mart." Swimming in a heated indoor pool cultured with chlorine gas. Episcopalian minister, blind. These are some of the things Dory remembers. There will be others. Some telling, some inconsequential. Out of sequence, like bingo calls. Rise in the price of a licorice stick. Tina Douglas falling asleep with her hair in a sink of peroxide. Finding the town Eff calls Zane.

Ephemera. Barnett bleeding from his hand, a small cut, and wiping and wiping and wiping and wiping it and Dory going to him and closing his fist in hers and June saying later: I'm glad you were there. He panics. If blood can get out, then what can get in? Breaching, spilling—he frets.

Dory sets her pen on the thickly lacquered old desk she writes on here. School desk? Perhaps—it is overbuilt, with a half-inch pencil gutter and dungeon hinges, a desk to sit up straight at. Outside dark clouds riding low as cow bellies. She has only a few days left. On Sunday she went to a heritage house in town that was celebrating its hundredth birthday. There were beeswax candles and slices of pioneer cake. A woman made bread in the coal stove and a man in costume who took his costume seriously gave tours of the house and explained how its first owners had lived there: what they cooked, how they slept and entertained themselves. It turned out that they cooked what they could grow, herd or scavenge, slept briefly between crises, diverted themselves with musical evenings of hymns and airs on a two-octave patent piano and those passages of Scripture concerning sacrifice and the piquant desolation of life on earth.

By our standards these were hard lives, says their guide.

Five rooms downstairs, five rooms up, and a broad low attic, as though each room held another on its shoulders, temporarily, as it thought. Simple construction, a house born as shelter and later gussied up.

On her list Dory has banking and shopping—chicken breasts, dried prunes, skim milk—and postcards to Tilly, who is struggling, and to a dear friend of Ruth's who, unhappy, a drinker, hopes to look her up when she is back in town and unite and focus their sorrows, Dory's and his, on Ruth. And so the world intrudes on Dory as it did on these people in their house of 1855 when the snow blew up to the roofline and they had to dig the mortar from the chimney in order to mole their way out.

A long winter, wrote Paive, the lady of the house. We have lost all directions but North.

Dory has cut five more pages from the eighty she has left. She has the ghost town to go, and Freddy, of course. Freddy Fychan, murdered by Dory, of Barnett and June.

—a terrible, terrible thing.

Were these, as the guide said, hard and barren lives? How did he know that? How could he arrive at the truth of those lives by recovering their recipe for rye bread? She feels the shock of overlap, the man and the woman, their raised edges, their different tempos, jutting against hers in this small room.

Ruth had chosen the name, Tilly. Tilly from Mathilda, the middle of a name scooped out. It was a hard labour. They were forced to make incisions and Ruth thrashed across the bed and seemed at times to think she had produced a child and at other times to believe she had lost it. The nurse brought Dory a paper to sign and she felt all of the gestures executed at that moment in the world funnelling in upon her, saw clearly the line drawn from the newborn to Ruth to her, saw and felt it tighten like a bit of cord. Tilly. A tourniquet name. It was not that Ruth had wanted a child more or that she had done the main work, though she had. It was not that the child would come to replace her in Ruth's affections, democratic as they were. Ruth was unconscious, hours yet from holding the newborn, and all that time Dory made herself watch it and waited to feel something for it and instead thought about supper and thoroughly washing her hands. Her hands. The wounds in Ruth's body. The pale fur on the babe. Tilly. The name of Ruth's Welsh Valleys grandmother who acted the part of Rosalind on the West End stage in 1904. A bit of taffy under a red bob.

Where has she put them? Those awful soft salted cookies that form round her teeth like a dentist's mould. The staunch aromatic tea. Pen . . . pen . . .

There—she has snapped it. Pen tip through paper to the pages beneath, the ink spills from its plastic intubation, the page is ruined. Another one. It occurs to her that this is the pattern: pages worn through, stained with vinegar, curling with damp. Over forty years she has made in this manuscript tears that cannot be repaired. Three, five, eighteen pages lost. All along she has been destroying it.

There are other pens.

Eff and Dory make a discovery. Twenty minutes of ducking and winding and battling through the dense bush on the town's west side, over scrub and stumpland, there is another town, a mixed-up mirror of their own.

There is a special railway with long, low carriages. The mine was worked and families lived in rows of upright houses with clerical features; tall, narrow, nodding off. A model town. Each street looks the same distance from the main town square. Houses abut a grassy common. The bank says Bank. The shops say Shop. Running alongside the street are narrow gutters here and there covered by long stones. Everything is encroached upon, overgrown. Saplings flourish in the eaves and gutters, the roofs. They have to scuff away the mash of leaves and grubs to find the sidewalks.

They enter the bank through the collapsed siding. The supporting frilled columns inside are intact, and the wide shallow stairs. At the base of the stairs a pair of teller's cages fed through velvet ropes. Ledgers and deposit slips are mouldy and the chairs have been hollowed by mice. Pens sit fused to inkwells. They race chairs on castors and decide what they will burn.

I hate to light the blotters, says Eff. They're historical and they'll smoke.

This is YOUR town, reads Dory. It's the coming attractions, she says. Christmas Concert. Bingo with the Elks. Refreshment and Fine Wines.

Veddy genteel, says Eff.

Dory is still reading. They had a library and a choir, she says. In the summer there was a festival of plays.

There is a doctor's office with an eye-chart and a height-chart and a triangular mallet and a colourful diagram of the healthy body, man, woman, child. Posters of children from when the main distinction was brunette and blond: lifting shirts for the stethoscope, swishing their teeth. From the bank to the shops to the school the town can be read like the bands of a tree.

Mercury in the river, says Eff. One sip, you've got a planet in your veins.

All of them?

Maybe things . . . deteriorated, says Eff.

They start to spend more time here. Eff breaks into the shops with a chisel and squares of Scotch tape. They crack almonds in the barrels and paint with molasses and pee into drainpipes; there is excitement in all this activity, in the chances they feel they take. They sit and the spiders weave them in. They explore the town: the school, the service station with its windows smashed, cash register plucked of its numbers all but one.

Four, lucky four, says Dory.

The shelves tilt and the tiles erupt. There is a thin grease on all surfaces. The school is up a long slope. In the yard logs are bolted to more logs to form a splintery cat's cradle. Tibia of an ancient swing set.

Under the schoolhouse Eff keeps a game brought from Germany with an enormous octagonal board and all the trimmings: dice, pickup sticks, checkers, snakes and ladders, cards for Bavarian Old Maid. The drawings are elaborate and weird, children in high trousers with their thumbs snipped off, gold-toothed balladeering cats.

They can see three separate classrooms, identically fitted, with swing desks and high slate-boards and narrow aisles. On the teacher's desk a stack of student reports, not yet filled in.

Harmony is one of the categories. And *Deference*.

Dory volunteers. She is at the end of her school year and no ticks yet under Public Service except a pan of bake sale flapjacks and the orange drink she pours at the Concert for Bethlehem. She may choose between the litter patrol or pushing the book-mobile at the Elland Hospice.

You can steal from a bookmobile, Eff points out.

Charity in Absinthe is safe in the hands of the Cream of the town, a sniffing minty mass, wavy hairdos and dresses freshly ironed each morning by patient mothers bearing uterine scars.

If you shot one the lot would die, says Eff. Like Medusa, she says. Without the guts.

The Cream love Public Service. Some of it joins Girl Guides and prepares for domesticity by the light of a plastic fire. Some devotes itself to mysteries of nail varnish and never-run hose.

The women *I* like, Eff says, kick men downstairs for fun.

The Cream perpetuates itself through sleepovers and pot-latch: heirloom clown erasers and bits of cheap jewellery. It is best viewed on Saturdays, and after school, when the boys gather, the Element, swearing and hurling stones as if by hered-ity, an itch upon the anterior brain.

Don't, says the Cream. Don't!

So this is evolution, says Eff. Patty-cake and Highland danc-ing and going by Annie, not Anne.

The volunteer organizer wants to show Dory just everything.

And over here, she says. And over here. And oh, over here of course.

Her name is Maeve. She is not a nurse proper, though she trained as one.

The whole course. Three times, says Maeve.

Oh, says Dory.

I could practically teach it, says Maeve.

Could you, Dory says.

Some places are different, Maeve says. They're after the exam, the degree. They don't mind that here, she says. Whereas I consider flexibility a virtue.

Maeve's face is the colour of mince. She wears a vest over her shoulder and a lily corsage to brighten herself up and is strict about tea breaks. Dory isn't just a volunteer but part of a team, Maeve emphasizes, with responsibilities and opportunities for the deployment of grace.

Over there is the dispensary. Dory is not meant to be here. This once. Rack after rack. Metal syringes in their jackets. Brown jars. Pills in boxes, and tubes, and loose in tacky piles. Over there are the long wards, the regular and the locked. There are the showers, eight heads on a wall, and the deep stand-up baths. Dory looks and listens and smells. There are the wheelies and the lounge full of books about wars and magazines of gardens and tribes of Africa and Asia. *Cities in a spin. Land of the midnight sun.* Crayons in plastic crates that lock with an oversized key, the sort of thing Farmer John might whip from a back pocket.

There is no end of cottage homes and poached-egg sunsets. One lady sees a lighthouse sidling up to a storm. One sees a chestnut colt. One sees herself in a mirror, old in the left side of her face and young in the right.

That one I like, says Dory.

That is a depiction of the human spirit, Maeve says. She is authoritative on the human spirit. It pops up in the strangest places, true as a hymn.

Those who leave this world are never far away, Maeve says. They know. They know.

When the human spirit fails, there is a sound of collapsing, a bird sound.

It is a terrible thing to witness, sighs Maeve.

The floor here is slick with the human spirit. It coats the windowsills and blows into the corners of the rooms. Sour faces, sulky words, getting above oneself all weaken the human spirit.

Smiles and prayer strengthen it. Dory is to be pleasant always. To brighten is a mercy.

For two weeks Dory walks the wards in Maeve's pocket. She looks after the paints and picks up the cards after canasta. Smiles and chats. Brightens. She tends a Scottish lady with a recurring illness she will not discuss. She tapes pictures to the sides of a clear tent occupied by a madwoman who sleeps in a crouch and spits on her fingers and draws on the sides of the tent. Not words but frugal quirks of code. Dory shows her the pictures in the books and when she sees one she likes, she croons.

Dory does well and the hospice is short-staffed and so in only her third week Dory is given charge of Mr. Freddy Fychan, a fat and irascible man barely contained by his clothes and wearing tiny glasses with lenses that are nearly opaque. He stutters horribly. There is a story on the ward that Freddy has lived in the hospice all his life, that he was born here, that he is prone to apathy and sits like a gem in the claw of his chair and glistens. Dory's job is to draw him out. Today she promotes wellness through fingerpainting.

I have all the primaries and some pastels in the popular blues.

Bring me darkness, says Freddy, waves at the blinds.

The nice thing about this paint, it washes right off.

"Dear New Girl," composes Freddy. Bugger painting. Have a mint.

They chew quietly on spearmint glaciers and Freddy falls asleep.

Freddy keeps a journal. He makes constant repairs to his clothes, embroidering, unsuitably, the collars of his shirts. He attributes inner lives to the cats that hunt the grounds.

He runs on a track, says Dory.

Eff says nothing.

Like a kid, says Dory. He's more of a kid than we are, she says.

Let him have it. Youth is death.

Dory keeps house. June spends the month of January on the west coast with her sister Dinah who runs a glamour school for dogs. They have a woman in to do the main cleaning and cook a week's meals in a night. Dory does everything else.

Barnett on his own is stark and tuneless. He reads the ads from the *National Geographic*. This is the world of things and states that lie just outside their grasp. The selected leather of that year's Dodge, the freedom of long-distance telephoning. Dory picks up after him and ping-pongs between the hospice and home and school in the sudden awkward knowledge that in the war between June and Barnett she has always been the cause.

And then, with a few words, she and Barnett swing crazily off course.

How does it happen? What comes first? In the letter she is writing it is one of the most often revisited passages, the fourth of the springs in the secret lever. Andreas. Dory. Barnett. June. It is Barnett who brings it up.

On their way to school he asks whether she would like to have a brother.

Would I?

Yes.

She looks at him. Would I?

Yes, he says, and it's settled. She would like a new brother; she can't have a new brother, so Barnett provides Andreas.

Soon Andreas appears, a mocked-up snapshot, drab bug-eyed puff in a christening dress. Older than Dory, thirteen this year. He has ash hair, a mischievous squint, strong arms and legs. His grin is white icicles. He is camera-shy.

It is a game they play. They imagine Andreas's room and things: a longbow; a toy boat with sails made from scrap lumber;

dumpy clay candle-holders he fired and painted blue and red. Andreas swims and rows and runs and plays an instrument—

Piano, Dory says.

—the violin. Every night, he is in bed by nine. No arguments.

The game is oddball interesting, but it doesn't stop where it ought.

He's not quite right, my dad, she tells Eff.

She has a card from Andreas, upright handwriting, in pen. She learns about his friends: Otto, Suzanne, his Scotch Terrier (Dory is forbidden pets), his exploits in the Rovers, chess club, school band.

When she is finished reading it Barnett takes the card away.

They grow him up. Andreas and his accessories. The wallpaper changes to reflect his age and new interests. Posters, an electric train. A wood-and-foam glider with detachable decals. Balls. Bedroom door fitted with a bulletin board of events in the town—floor hockey, Cub Scouts, artificial respiration.

He's coming apart, Dory says.

So does everything, says Eff. We had a squirrel round our place. It had mange so bad it shed its heart.

It seems to Dory that Barnett is going mad, but not in his own way. He is going mad in June's way, as though she has left him instructions and he is carrying them out. The game ends. Andreas has died in the bath, drowned in a fit brought on by a flicker in the bulb. Barnett is precise about the boy's position (arms in, feet in, the diamond of his knees akimbo) and the sounds he makes (gurgle soft, gurgle chokey, tapping tapping tapping scraping). He takes her to the tub and partly unscrews the light bulb and has her pay attention to the flicker and the *shtu-phut shtu-phut* noise. He points out where Andreas's hands and feet and head were. Calm—Barnett is calm, anecdotal. He is telling her a fish story.

We didn't hear anything, he says. That was what alerted us. Your mother—

The day the time the weather, the bitter smelting fog.

This is the watch I was wearing, he is telling Dory when she leaves.

In March, June returns with salmon jerky and various jams and a perfect knitted shawl with a mountain pattern. She carries journals about school teaching. She wears a wax of joy. This, she proclaims, is a fresh start. She strolls about the yard in an elaborate hat and picks lilies into a basket. Then she washes and hems each flower petal with a complicated self-hiding stitch.

Dory thinks that what Barnett and June do is start fresh with one another, over and over; to recognize this in progress is to cripple it, or worse.

The flower's soft parts tear, the stem splits and oozes milky water. When June is finished the flower is stiff at the edges, squashed and bent.

This is what I missed, back there in civilization, she says, smiles. Natural beauty.

A man and a woman come to Dory's school and stay for two periods. They have carousel slides and film strips on the subject of the world of the future. The world of the future will be silver and streamlined. The people in cities will stand on moving sidewalks and cars will know not to crash and everywhere peace will reign—this is how the woman puts it. The cities they show have swoopy buildings with shuttles racing up and down the side. There is a hamburger stand with mechanical servers and a museum with exhibits that discuss themselves and pictures that tell you just how they were made.

The man of the future will slice time like a radish, says the film strip. Past, present, future. Everything you say or do will make sense in any direction. So much for grammar! says the strip, winks across twenty-four frames.

The movie camera, says the film strip, the very one that made this film you are watching. Some day a man will carry it in his pocket or wear on his wrist like a watch.

Dory looks at the henpecked white ceilings and thinks of a world of silver fluting with dashing cars and intelligent hamburger stands. A man with a city on his watch—

Here, says the dream man, extends his mechanical hand, amiably whirring.

The man made of wire. The book inside a book.

Pleased to meet you, the hand says.

Where is it? Under her bed? In Zane?

This will not be a world without problems, warns the film strip. New challenges abound. Somewhere are teams of scientists who sit in the hills and think about people. Fifty billion people, the film strip says. How will we feed them? Look, says the film strip, and a man on screen whips a scarf from an aquarium tank in which locusts crawl and tamper with one another.

This is New Jersey, the film strip says, and stalls.

Dory does not know New Jersey or the number fifty billion. She does not remember, later, what else the man or the woman said, the pictures in the carousel, the rough-edged film strips like industrial ladders. *Abound* was the word they had used. A lively jumping word, a word for daisies.

The what?

Abounding, says Dory. Teeming. In their numbers and hordes.

Where?

New Jersey, says Dory.

New Jersey? So what?

Fifty billion people, says Dory. They will eat the paper from the walls.

Billion? That's handy, Eff says. Can they change my sisters' nappies?

Dory is haunted by fifty billion people, in New Jersey or wherever. Sipping the planet dry.

The future. How about a buzzer that went off whenever anyone thought of you, she says. It would light up; it would have the name. You would *know*, Dory says.

What would that change? Eff says. Knowing?

May. Dory and Eff have eggs to take home. These eggs have names and hair colours and infant clothing. It is an exercise. They are to be cared for and kept intact and uneaten until the following Monday, when they will be baptized in a ceremony to be led by Mrs. Dyck.

Eff operates. I'm going to start with a sewing needle, she says. Then I'm going to suck the bastard dry.

The eggs this week, and next week the primitive dolls that plug into the wall and spit up and mess themselves. It is a natal semester. There is a tremendous will to acquaint these girls with the filthy shrieking perils of motherhood, to instill in them a useful mortal fear. So: the eggs and the dolls, the fragile, born-too-soon dolls. Dory is assigned a baby withdrawing and Eff a baby bleeding.

Can it not sit elsewhere? Barnett wants to know.

He is reading up on novice geophysics. There are problems with the new development. The land it is on, which was thought to be limestone, is in fact what they call "false bedrock," a cap of hard rock that has been eroded underneath. Anyone with a twenty-inch auger would have discovered this but the geologist paid by the firm and the town did not have such an auger.

Many of the houses will not sink and some will; it is a lottery. At least two have begun the slow tumble as frame by frame the front corners disappear into the soil and the floors split cleanly along the joists. As the bay window dips underground the townspeople begin to appear in numbers, setting out umbrellas and fold-away tables, nylon mesh lawn chairs and a good book.

By the middle of the summer the audience will number in the hundreds and include boys selling frankfurters and ice-cold drinks. When the slumping first roof touches Pelican Way's signature red gravel, a huge cheer goes up from the crowds.

Barnett takes this seriously. Typically, he has begun to treat the new development as his own endeavour. He is up late worrying about the sinkholes and floats a number of suggestions on how to improve the design of the hydraulic jacks.

He'd take the blame for Jesus if he could, said Dory's Aunt Dinah of Barnett. It's a way of calling attention to himself.

It isn't, Dory thinks. Barnett can be concerned about things as far as his imagination carries, and there is no difference in his reaction to the evaporation of silage on a neighbour's farm and the paralyzing stroke of his Uncle Fuddy. Were he alone in the world he would invent a species to fret about. But he is noble in this, he takes no pleasure in things gone wrong.

At suppertime Dory's egg is the centrepiece and it unabashedly wants. It makes no noise or movement. Instead, it wants awkwardly and silently from its dished coaster next to the mash. What does it want? This is unclear. Feeding, through its grainy hard surfaces. Warmth. Companionship. The Cream has fashioned cunning slings and cradles for its eggs in comfortable fabrics and soothing hues. Flannels and cottons and merino woollens in blue and pink and white. Dory's egg sits in its coaster. Peach-coloured yarn hair is glued to one end, felt feet to the other. Across it a swaddle of pale wadding June has tugged from a medicine bottle. By the intermittent light of the chandelier that nobody likes the egg sparkles with tiny chips of Miltown.

June knits a cervix out of three kinds of wool.

The eggs of the Cream sleep peacefully that night; Dory can hear their rolling oval snores. She gets up and transfers the thing to the laundry hamper. In the layers of stitched-up socks it is suffocated silent and she can sleep.

—

On Monday Mrs. Dyck performs her inspection. Some of their eggs are pronounced happy and healthy and some are sorely dead. Eff's is healthy and Dory's is dead.

Double-crosser, says Dory.

I couldn't kill it, says Eff. I wanted to, goddamn it, but I just froze up.

The chalice of water is brought in and Mrs. Dyck dips each living egg at the feet and gives it a name from her book. Judah, Emmeline, Roger, Maureen. Then they are retired to the café and the baby dolls are handed out. Eff's is topped up with a sickly mixture and bleeds on its side, on its stomach, upside down. It bleeds and nods its head mechanically and she props it up with stick and tape and whips shingles at its head. Dory's baby turns its head from side to side seventy times an hour. It avoids her. It pulls away.

You're smart, strong girls and these are problem kiddies, says Mrs. Dyck as she signs them out. I know you'll do just fine.

Sometimes Dory watches the baby turning and twice she picks it up, rubbery and scarred. The left side of its face is reflective, the other opaque.

Eff has left her a note in the shed pigeonhole. *Zane. Twilight. Bring the brats.*

The apple has not yet fallen and Barnett is in the orchards with his long boots on. These and the slicker and the look in his eye are what make him a farmer and not a dude.

He paces, leaving mud stains and atmospheric colic behind him; the floors themselves grow fitful and discomposed. On the early apples everything hinges, though last week it was something else.

I'm eating elsewhere, Dory tells June.

She is talking to her radio. No one has gout any more.

Here: taste one, take a few with you, says Barnett, hands her a hard pinstriped apple. They're Spartans and they're *crisp*.

Everything around her clots. June's correspondence courses, absorbed into the nation's post. Roasts become stews when the oven mysteriously recalibrates. The icebox's contents are upholstered in a pigeon-coloured down. Glasses and mirrors sweat. The lawn doubles in height and Barnett finds a scythe and swings uneasily, stripped to the waist, waiting for the peasants to fill in along the horizon. June knits a tea cozy in the colours of Flanders fields.

Ten or so days of intense heat by day and storms at night, scissors lightning snipping trees and power stations. Caterpillars hatch in their billions, feeding in a kind of amplified static, turning balconies into live wriggling ropes, hoodworms like thin nuns in their plush habits worrying the ends of the trees. There were one or two visible and then Dory saw them regularly, and then when trying to cajole herself to sleep she wonders at the wind and then realizes it is the hoodworms eating, billions of them, the swarms of New Jersey here humping along the branches and out onto the buds.

June draws all the curtains and plays the radio between stations to make white noise. Barnett buys huge tarpaulins for the orchards and berry patches that the worms form phalanxes around and duck beneath so that the tarps themselves seem mobile and his choice is to peg them down with the worms beneath or simply start over with what they leave uneaten.

The *Intelligencer* runs God-fearing headlines and, ominously, an early map of the town.

Finally the hoodworms descend. They are surprisingly quiet about it. Dory is watching the sandcherry tree from her window when she notices a vertical blur about its edges, and as her eyes become accustomed she sees that this blur is in fact the swift, clean movement of a billion worms sliding on worm-ropes down the sides of the trees, never plummeting, never colliding, until they drop gently onto the ground, point their snoods to orient themselves and bump off along the ground. They do not move randomly. They are always at something green. By that afternoon the trees are bare of worms and people are out with brooms and shovels to clear their steps and railings.

For the rest of that day the worms are on the ground, and then without warning they duck their heads and go beneath it. They burrow and till, and those on wood splinter themselves and those on stone liquefy. They do not seek out soil. They just duck and duck whatever surface is immediately below them until they get through it or die.

In Dory's dream the people of the future lie on their backs with awful thirsts while she walks among them pouring water into their mouths and throats—you can only take that which you can fit in your throats, and this has given them enormous articulated mouths and long and capacious necks. One of the flying men descends to her. He hovers, stands. His jetpack produces a shaky flame. Then he undoes his metal gloves and shows her the rash on his hand. Dory understands that it is his lot to be infected. He touches his skin to hers.

Dory ministers. At the hospice she helps Freddy Fychan make a finger puppet from artificial fur and google eyes with stick-on backs.

My dear, I am exhausted. I am simply *undone*, says Freddy. It is no good asking for my aid in this project. What do you call it?

A googly, Dory says.

Let me direct you in this enterprise. Eight eyes. Eight, I tell you. But spread them about. Ah, he says, as she works on it. I see that the creature is smiling.

They all smile, Dory says. It's in the instructions, she says.

Hang the instructions. Is it within your powers to construct an "O" mouth?

Sure, Dory says.

Do it. Cut it. Tint it. Stick it on. Let our monster be curious. Permit him to greet his world open-mouthed, famished for experience and Life. Let—

Dory raises the puppet, claps its furry star hands.

It lives. It breathes, says Freddy. You are not a candystriper; you are a Rodin.

They suck on semisweet chocolate and Dory tells Freddy about Zane. The school and bank and gymkhana trophies they found in an upstairs room.

It takes longer than it ought, says Dory. The path is so scanty that half the time we have no idea where we are.

One sympathizes, says Freddy Fychan.

All the trees are bent, says Dory. Even the reeds. Have you seen that?

The great Sibelius could bend one's soul.

There are five streets, says Dory. We've counted. She takes Freddy's hand, slots in the thick-nib marker.

This is the bank and this is the shop with the bits of linen and this shop has wood stacked. These are houses and this is the school. The steps of all the houses point to the school, she says. Not the church. But there is a church, she says. Everything in it is rectangles.

I sang alto during Latin mass, Freddy says. I sang in Latin. My cousin trained as a priest, you see, a Catholic priest, and was much given to the old mass. Ernest. He conjured sweets and toys and quality miniatures of the saints. He performed Catholic magic.

I have a new book, Dory says. Erle Stanley Gardner. A corker, according to Maeve.

Freddy sighs. "Think of a psalm, don't tell me which," Ernest said. I chose Ephesians 15. "Ephesians 15," he said, and there it was, the very page, in his hand, and I goggled. "There are no miracles," he said. "None but faith." He tumbled his rosary silently, the beads were black and soft. "Here is a shilling," he said. And there were three shillings, and there they were again, in the toe of my shoe. "There are no miracles," he said, drawing a scarf from his mouth. "None but belief."

I went there alone once, says Dory. Zane. Everything there is stopped up. The creek and the wells and the gutters and the rain-barrels, she says. The mud has something in it that stings. We thought it had bankrupted or flooded or burned. But there's no trace of any of that, she says. It's as though everything swelled and stopped moving. Moving, she says. Freddy sleeps.

June develops systems for keeping things clean—smocked countertops, draped furniture, hooded taps and fixtures. She appears from time to time in the hall archway and stands very still. Again she takes up her needle. She rips the buttons from Barnett's shirts and stitches them back on in fanciful patterns—fish, crescent moon—on the sleeves, breast, back, collar. She sews shut the tops of his socks.

Dory comes upon them suddenly at the room atop the stairs. Barnett is dressed absurdly, in too-short pants and a too-small sweater. June has her hair up in a bow. A bow! She examines her belly with a concentrated love that Dory has never seen.

I can feel it, she whispers. Wait—

Dory narrates. Her year in Speech & Drama is to put on a play written by their teacher, Mrs. Yonge. Mrs. Yonge is a short, snappy, curly-haired woman in wide trousers who came to this town with the husband she describes as flat. She leaps around, belly bare, the hair on her arms long enough to comb. She is uncompromising in her lipstick. Dory has spoken only once in Speech & Drama and then without thinking, remarking in response to a question she had not really listened to that Daisy Buchanan was sweet. Now she is to be cultivated by Mrs. Yonge.

To be cultivated by Mrs. Yonge is to be pursued by her. Asked to stay after class and "open up." Assigned poems which are especially dear to Mrs. Yonge about women of extraordinary talent and passionate feelings mired in dull men. The more Dory tries to elude Mrs. Yonge the more she is beset by her.

She is my Nemesis.

Well I quite like her, Eff says. I think she's zingy.

Mrs. Yonge has Dory read in class. She makes references to their conversations that no one but Dory could possibly understand. She makes her conversion of Dory a fully public thing. Hers becomes the class Dory most dreads.

In Mrs. Yonge's play a rural petting zoo becomes a metaphor for a town. A young doe—small, snappy, curly-headed—is captured by Hunter and brought to the zoo where she is kept. There, Doe, Rabbit, Horse, Cow, Duck and Chorus meditate upon the terrible price paid by the spirit which suppresses itself in the name of Bourgeois Life. The play ends with a rousing speech by Duck, a call to join and raise their voices until the locks rattle free from their cages.

Hark, says Dory-as-Narrator. Hark—is that Freedom you hear?

You're doing terribly well, of course, says Mrs. Yonge. You have what we call "gravitas."

Gravitas, zippy. What is happening to her? To Eff—she is changing!—to Eff?

Dory is with Freddy Fychan presiding over a marriage of popsicle sticks and white glue. From a mimeographed diagram she constructs the chimney of a popsicle log cabin while he paints glue onto his fingernails, picks it off like a skin.

Do you want to paint it?

Under no circumstances, Freddy says. You're upset.

I want to leave. No. I want to be able to leave.

Freddy rolls his enormous hands. I am Fate's creature, he says. Nothing keeps me here.

The popsicle cabin is assembled and curing and Dory lazes in her chair.

I was taken by my parents to see a Polish psychologist to cure my nerves, says Freddy. Anything might set me off. I had grown over-thin. I became so very thin, almost a single layer. "Does this frighten you, boy?" asked the Polish psychologist, showing me a portrait of the devil. "This?" Banging on his desk, baring his stinking teeth. No. Rather, it was the fear that I missed the meanings of the world, that I was never sure. I could never be sure, I could never be sure again. However hard I tried, my nerves were ever in the way.

She lets Freddy finish. What will we do about you? she asks.

Freddy shuffles under his pillow, hands her his monster. Its eyes slide on their dry glue, there is a hole in its side where he has worried it.

One feels no special fondness for the arts and crafts, he says. The enthusiasm of it. The unbridled reliance on glue.

Maeve thinks it brightens things up, says Dory.

Arson brightens things up, says Freddy. But they don't give us matches, he says.

They have begun to people Zane. Some are characters from the books they have stored under the schoolhouse steps. Dory has her people and Eff hers also. Some of Eff's characters Dory has met: a boy with black hair and yellow eyes, a wolf-boy who fixes cars in Pepperville. The population they invent lives on its own, does not pause with their departure. It is a film strip. It runs and runs and they come and watch it and sometimes step in and make corrections.

She writes in her letter the details of the fires they started in the hardware. The windows they climbed through, the picture of a very small serious boy who had a won a piano competition in Pittsburgh, Brahms and Rachmaninoff, at the age of nine. The windows dropped onto nothing at all as though the house were a front, the boy stood in a grey suit and oiled hair and he held his hands palms up before him as if admitting to a crime. Mr. Thomas Pitcher, nine years old.

They contrive to spend all of their time there. They trace each other's outlines with chalk, dig shallow indentations to wallow in and cover these over with boughs. They camp with foam sleeping rolls and a filthy orange tent seven miles into the wind and the horseflies and deerflies; the wind scatters the cooking fire and infuses frankfurters and cherry soda with a milky fine ash.

We are changelings we are salamanders! Eff shouts, grabs Dory, kisses her right through.

Now Dory lies in her room. Eff is changing, and this must be understood and stopped. She thinks she will ask Eff to marry her in a solemn ceremony in the wood, by the altar made by the rock, in the ghost church. The minister will fidget kindly. Eff will spit her nails.

Kiss, don't bite, the bride, the minister will caution. But Eff will bite.

Eff is growing dangerous. She is moody and wants things and then doesn't want them. Nothing happens, she says. She longs for a life in which things happen elegantly and on camera, where lovers come and go, bare-chested and linen-trousered, smoking out of the sides of their mouths. Where vermilion is an everyday colour. She has begun to use words like *organza* and *select*. Dory frets about Eff—she may lose her. If she loses her she will die.

Damn it let's get a little glamour, let's go red, says Eff.

Dory bites hard on a twig while Eff pricks her scalp a thousand times with a pin dipped into a soap bar and then drags a comb through the hair, through the dots of blood.

Not *does* it hurt—*how?* Eff wants to know.

What are we doing? asks Dory.

We're *feeling*, says Eff.

Dory is under house arrest. There has been a meeting at her school. Mr. Keddy, Barnett and June, the Vice-Principal Mr. Geer; short, with perfumed hair and Levantine features, as June puts it. There is some discussion of moving Dory up a grade. Barnett is delighted on behalf of his heredity. June says she assumed schoolkids were graded by height.

Like eggs, she says, smiles beautifully.

This meeting concerns the results of tests Dory has taken that show her to be a prodigy in verbal-written and a numbskull in mathematics.

We look for all-rounders, says Mr. Geer.

Why, then, are they here? There is something else: Dory has written a short story that has caused alarm. Mr. Keddy, rising to the occasion, fairly shivers as he confesses that the piece has troubled him. Sleepless nights.

The assignment, he explains, was A Day in the Life of a Dime.

And from this fertile premise Dory has produced monstrosity.

"Blood Night," reads Mr. Geer.

In the story a priest is attached to a northern people, encroached upon and mistreated by a white mining settlement. The priest hears of a plot to raze the native camp and runs five miles to warn them. He is too late. Corpses litter the encampment. Blood, limbs, filth. A woman eviscerated. An unborn babe. The priest kneels in horror: it is a crisis of his faith in man and God—there.

There. The sound of the men of the camp returning from a successful hunt. They round the corner and see the priest in his terror, wet with gore—

In his hand when he dies, a dime.

There's a coda, says Mr. Geer.

Barnett stands. It's a story, she's ten, he says. She snuck in that dime all right. Your kids are safe with ours.

It's best you knew, says Mr. Geer. He makes it sound promissory.

In the car June turns, looks straight at Dory, holds it for three blocks.

I suppose you're the priest, she says.

⊕

Someone is stealing from the orchards. Barnett, who credits himself with sharp sight, can tell by looking. He counts on his fingers.

Apples, peaches, strawberries, logan, he says.

Three weeks pass and he grows more agitated. He photographs the most productive trees the better to document the looting.

This one you can see, says Barnett, leads them to the borrowed music stand on which he has arranged his photographs. I'd say 20 percent, easy.

By June, with the season nearly on, he is frantic. He bargains for a shotgun and sets up a deer blind in the middle tract in which he will spend the nights watching.

One, you've no clue how to shoot a gun and two, you're sorry clumsy, says June. I will not stand by while you maim yourself.

Dory brings him supper and a pail for slops.

Any sign of them varmints? she asks.

Don't be western, he says. It don't suit.

He stays there in her old cotton baby blanket with torn sateen trim. From her room she can hear him snoring. The gun does not go off.

By the end of the month Barnett is exhausted. Still the fruit thins on the trees. A pale yellow pus on the blueberry scrub is visible from the front gate.

They're not being stolen, they're *dying*, says Eff. What kind of sweaterhead is your dad?

In early July the woman from crop services comes and inspects the trees.

You should never have planted this close, she says. They're killing each other. And what's this? she says, toeing the deer blind. Are you living here?

She takes a sample of the fungus and leaves one for Barnett in a clear plastic bottle with a sealant round the rim. The bottle sits on the dining-room table and makes a pleasant if contagious centrepiece.

If I could spread like that bastard weed I'd be rich, says Barnett. Rich, ubiquitous.

It's a spore, says June. It's carried by wind. Like disappointment.

I'll sell the car and we'll walk everywhere, Barnett says. We'll be healthy and we'll save on gas.

I'll sell the kitchen and we'll live off clover, says June. We'll be sweet and we'll save on digestion.

Ah, says Barnett. I see where this will go.

He trains spotlights on the trees, builds tiny fences round them. He has a pair of glasses he has sent away for that have lenses powerful enough for spores. When Dory tries them on and looks at anything she sees the same dim outline of a skeleton.

That joke has been a long time paying off, he says.

But the—

It helps, he says. It helps.

Freddy Fychan has acquired a dressing gown of stippled purple velvet in which he resembles a corpulent grape. Dory casts his hands in plaster of Paris and listens to Freddy talk about his room full of programs for the concerts he has seen.

One is so very fortunate, he tells her, to have had the opportunity, you know, to have seen so much.

If you know you are crazy, where do you go?

Here, says Freddy. Here is where you go. For six months here I took the shock treatment. I waited in a room full of old magazines. Then I proceeded into another room of massive walls and long-legged trolleys. The nurse had a basket of teeth. When I came out of it they asked me questions to make sure I was all right. Surname and Christian. Name of current prime minister. Weight to the ounce. Then I was made to sit up and drink strong tea and lace up my own shoes. Once a fellow convulsed during his cuppa, and had a fine, sepia obituary. They opened him up and boggled: the tea had dyed him through.

I am telling you that I'm crazy, Dory says.

Welcome, says Freddy. Rattles his plastered hands.

The train will be diverted. The company has found a way to move freight along the border and save itself seven hundred miles. Now the train is running; from the seventh of September it will not. The engineer will receive his signal at midnight and brake gently to the bottom of a rise and check his instruments, get to his feet, stretch and shut off the lights. And that will be the end of the train in Absinthe.

For weeks there is high talk. The town mayor petitions and the train depot employees drift about the station in a blank, dismembered way, and Dory and Eff stare in the windows at the brass fittings and upholstered bar and Eff says:

This is what the Zane station looked like, I imagine, before they closed it down.

Those with cars take trial runs into the country, to the neighbouring towns, just to show that they can do it if they need to, and the army lends a helicopter for use in emergencies alone.

I have no good left in me, Eff says. Now we'll never get out.

Let's leave. Let's do something drastic, and leave, Dory says.

They used to swim in the river in Zane, Eff says. Mercury in the water made 'em bleed. They wanted to drain the river but they were frightened of what they'd find.

Zane points due downhill. It collects things. It collects water and debris and mud and stones and pitch and phosphates. It collects things. It takes the brunt.

What's in the barrels?

Sin, says Eff.

The pox and the polio that visit Absinthe slide downhill along with the drinking and the buried young.

If I were a genius I'd invent a sieve, says Eff. I'd pour this town through it and whatever was left over I'd give the run of the place. The town would be practically empty.

Let's go; why not? Dory says.

You have no rights on earth, says Eff. You were born into suffering and in suffering will you leave.

What about—

Shut it, Eff says. Let's find Frazer, and jiggle his thing till he squirts.

The end of July. Dory wakes to rustling in the bush. She looks out to see Barnett among the trees. He is picking berries, handfuls of bush, clawing ineptly at the trees. His mouth is moving. One or two lights are on. He is picking the trees clean, tipping the pails into bushel baskets, heaving the baskets into barrows lined up like taxicabs at the end of the lane. Blueberries, strawberries, spiders and moths, hatchets of leaf and twig fragments. To his left is the river, clotted with fruit. She stands and watches him, hears a shuffle from down the hall, sees June at her window. Barnett stops, holds a blackberry between finger and thumb, drops it into the pail.

Barnett is a whirlybird. On and off the steady-stool, up and down the ladder. Pots full, tumbling them empty. All night he picks. Twice he sluices his face and neck with cold water. Stretches his eyelids open. By dawn he has picked them clean. In the wind the bruised branches. Everywhere the thin white berry plugs. The ground a muskeg of squashed fruit and leaves.

He carries the bins to the trench, disappears. Soon after she sees at the junction of trench and stream a long raft of berries on the water. Four tin pots on the bank.

June stands by her window. This is very hard, she says.

Before Dory goes to the hospice the next morning she finds June in the kitchen making tea.

Andreas, Dory says. That was his name?

Whose?

I'm so sorry, says Dory. Andreas. My erstwhile brother, she says. The boy preceding me in your affections.

Yes and no, says June.

Yes, no?

It would have been his name. He was born blind, June says. His eyes were bolt white and his mouth was fixed open as though he were drowning, perpetually drowning. He was blind, he was drowning, he hadn't a heart. No heart, no lungs or kidney or liver. He was a perfect baby box but he hadn't anything in him, June says. What did we do? We had a kind doctor then. Cole. He was very helpful but it couldn't be got over. A scooped-out pumpkin. Of course I had worried, but what were we told?

He didn't die, June says. He was never alive. We're talking now and "now" seems like "finally" and it all seems very very important. But then it didn't matter, says June. I mean really. It didn't matter, and we thought it ought to and took steps to make it matter, behaving as though it did, and soon it had begun to and eventually it mattered more than it had any right to; it mattered most of all. We made him and we made *that*, says June. We manufactured mattering out of—what?—guilt, because guilt is shapeless and matter is there. The strain, your father kept saying.

The strain; was it only him it pulled at? Well. We are aware that you will do something but we would rather not, she says carefully, know what it is you plan to do.

I'm not—

My lovely wistful mother, whom you never met, stored her butter in shrouds, June says. Little Turins in the cupboard in stacks of nine. It is a very gentle passing, June says. Butter is one of those things that dished or stored or melted, or infinitely divided, invariably resembles itself. You mustn't think of yourself as *minus* anything, she says. There has been no diminishment on our part. Just . . . mal-focus, she says.

There is a knocking in the vents.

Your father—well. People are jealous of their sorrows, June says. A flavour in the mouth. He thought Andreas belonged to him. Remember him there guarding his strawberries, she says. You think he lives in mourning. What wouldn't that man devote himself to?

It has been weeks since Dory has seen Frazer. She goes to his house and his mother says he is with friends.

What friends?

His new friends, says Frazer's mother. Who now? The fellows with brown hair.

He isn't at the shops or behind the arena or on the *trompe l'oeil* boardwalk or the ponds or the schoolyard or the liquor store or the seven parking lots that rarely call the cops. He isn't on the wetlands path or in Zane—more windows broken there than she recalls, and the church door has been written on: *Bugger Mrs. Innes.*

I can't find him anywhere, she says to Frazer's mother, sleeves rolled and cream cheese on her fingers.

Well he isn't *lost*, you know, she says.

And days since she's seen Eff. Maybe Eff is with Frazer. Eff has found him alone and has taken him somewhere where she will have plenty of time. She will stick him in her or she will go at him with something sharp or tie him up and throw things at him, bottles or biscuits of shale. What can have made Frazer let his guard down? The right lie? A bribe? He is simple and Eff is complicated and what complicated people do is find the weaknesses in simple people and remake them as they choose. She does not, she realizes, even know where Eff lives. Her address. They have always met elsewhere. Dory walks home and leaves a note in the book box telling Eff to meet her and another on the door of the bank.

Three days. Frazer's mother stays behind her door. Eff has come and seen the messages—Dory has checked, they are gone—but has left nothing in reply. Where does she live anyway? She'd hinted in the bush somewhere, one of the communities that pop up in the cutting season and fold up in winter. So, in the bush. What is Eff's last name?

Dory does not see Eff again in August. In September when school starts she is asked to canvass for the autumn concert in which the Sixth Year will give a presentation and funds will be raised for the Porteous Brae Middle School's fold-down parquet floor.

I am a member of the Sixth Year, she tells people. We invite you to support us in our centenary.

Why you don't look past thirty, they say.

She is on Clouston Street at a house with a turret and perfect lawns. She rings the bell—deep, oboe-y—and admires the high arched swingset, the miniature greenhouse.

Hello, I am a member—begins Dory.

Hello, says Eff. She wears a pinafore and her hair is in pigtails.

—of the Sixth Form Centenary, says Dory, in shock.

I'll leave it with my mother, says Eff. Why did you come here? she says. Her face is a combination of very kind and very cold, the cold remaining as something wipes and twists at her features until Dory is looking into a dark-matter pinwheel topped with Eff's hair.

Good day, says the pinwheel, formally.

Then hisses. *Tarnish*, it seems to say. *Tarnish* or *awful* or *get you* or *grapple*, the words matter less than the tone which is horrible, Eff's tone is a horrible thing. It might be *grapple*, Dory thinks—there, Eff has gone—is Eff even her name or is it something altogether more grown-up, distant, like Evangeline?—and what was the word, she can't quite place it, fading now, the vowel circular like the harlequin, the drowning mouth—*grapple*, Eff says, why not?

In Zane someone has gone at the trees. The ash and fern and pin cherry have their crowns cut off. Some of the houses are in distress. The bank smokes a little. The town was never a secret—others have their own plans for it. It is to be played with, and destroyed. She finds in her library under the stairs that her books have been got at, scattered and torn. Mixed in with them she finds a magazine in which a woman pressed over a table is in successive frames stripped of her clothes, her hair is very white, her skin red with blusher. In her mouth is spotted cloth used by farm kids and humanized dogs as baskets for their belongings when running away. *Do me*, says the caption bleeding out of her eye.

Dory collects her books and leaves the magazine. The book inside a book: mass of runny blueprints, a collection of object lessons: *We will notice today the feet of animals. The Cow is intended to inhabit soft localities, meadows and river banks; hence, its cloven feet. Then, in the Mole we find all the legs short. Its forefeet are shovel-shaped and fixed obliquely, and are worked by powerful muscles. (Object: the Mole does not impede its own progress by casting the dirt in front of it—here draw a lesson for Humanity.)*

Humanity! Eff said, spouted her lips: perfect circle, moustache of raspberry jam.

In the school she closes the desks they tore open and erases the swears from the board. On her way home she crosses a horse path, cones of dung and woodchips, and sees beyond a pillar of boys. Muffled screams, tonic cursing, fists and feet and teeth. She looks for Frazer's yellow shoes at the bottom of the squirming pile—she sees him. She has to cross the path before she is by his face, red and compressed like the horn of a funnel. Frazer jabs and scratches from the middle of the pile. He is commanding. He has crossed over for good.

Freddy is failing. Bits of him are coming away. He has a stroke and something happens in his kidneys and from there to various embarrassments and then to a difficulty with his lungs which spurs another stroke; within three days Freddy has slipped into a benign coma from which he now and then emerges to hum.

Strauss, says Dory. Johann II.

To put her ear to his belly is to hear him decomposing. The nurses call him "Sticky" because everything that comes off or out of his body has the power of his hated glue, as though his whole self is concentrated on adhesion, on not falling off the world. When he wakes he is all but transparent.

Get me out, he says to Dory. I crave a harder surface. I find I am sinking in.

She washes and dresses him. He is neatly made, she discovers, all his parts small and fine, nothing like the mottled gross distortions she expected. She pulls on a tunic and his drawers, a suit packed in tissue paper in the long trunk by his bed. Blue, cashmere, monogrammed lapels.

—

Dory breaks the journey into parts. The first part: leaving the hospital and getting clear of the grounds. The second part: managing the path to the river with its waist-high yew and rutted stepways. The third part: remembering what is where in Zane and avoiding the holes and gutters. She has an idea where Freddy would like to go but she'll need to see it. Picturing only ever gets you an idea. But Freddy is heavy and isn't sure he can walk.

I'm going to bed, I'm poorly, she says at supper.

Cold or flu? says Barnett.

"Poorly"? says June.

It is hot, 28 degrees. From the window she can see the slow-motion exit of men from the Old Albion Hotel. Swing door and spilled light, a man stops walking to reach down and wipe exactly the sawdust from one knee.

Stand up and push the chair, she says to Freddy. Push it—it'll hold your weight.

She hips the chair in place while Freddy heaves and snorts, drags one foot after the other until he is beside and then behind the chair, leans over it, sputum dressing his chin like a beard.

That's it, Dory says.

The elevator blinks, blinks, blinks. Opens.

In, she says.

She has no story in mind. They will be leaving and that's it.

In, come on, she says.

The elevator opens and shuts on Dory and Freddy, long rubber lips and hollow doors and then she has pushed the buttons and felt the thing shudder and drop and they are in its shadow and then the lobby where the clerk is one with his magazine. The path is pebbled and the chair catches and shakes.

—

This section she has cut and sutured a hundred times. Freddy, scarf and dressing gown, frightened and exhilarated. And— what? What?

She tears the page she is annotating and beneath it she tucks this fresh lined sheet, yellow. Dory and Freddy leaving the hospice, she walking ahead and checking back, Freddy with his robe round his shoulder manoeuvring his wheelchair with his belly.

Before she died Ruth alternated between a terrible exhilaration and a bleak somnolence in her bed like an urn. In her exhilaration she developed plans for vacations and digressions, abrupt, watershed, that would knit her back into life. Churchill, Zanzibar. Bits of paper, newspaper articles, pamphlets, advertisements, annotated in Ruth's exclamatory hand: *This is us! Why not November? Degree required?* Activities she could do with someone; as if Dory was any kind of insulation. In the end Ruth too was only frightened, just as Freddy was and as Dory will be. Fear, the great leveller. And the optimistic cuttings give way to miracle cures, tabloid quackery, big-pharmaceutical sales pamphlets, white lettering over smiling young mothers who did not after all require a double-mastectomy, low-cholesterol couples hiking by the sea. Attached to one brochure the notes of her calls to the company. *You're in a good place*, says the shaky faint dab that by the end was Ruth's handwriting. Is that all the salesperson told her? Did that qualify as comfort? Advice? *Take things easy. Baby-steps.*

Dory and Freddy leaving the hospice—a long stretch of walking. How to texture this? Trees, ash and poplar, tin cans and tails of kitchen towel, a condom in a circle of campfire ash. The town giving way to the path and all those sharp rocks and gutters made by someone slipping, surfaced roots. The moon full enough to elicit from Freddy a few lines of a poem beaten into him by his Welsh headmaster. Plenty of light to see the path by. Freddy pushing his chair and now and then collapsing, sweat on him like a wax, hauling himself up as though he is beginning to see the importance of the journey. They follow the path even where it is very narrow, even when—this is Dory thinking, trying to do all these things at once, walk forward and in the right direction while managing Freddy, and in among it all trying to plan and to avoid planning (why? culpability?)—the wheels of the chair get stuck.

Was Freddy Fychan not a fat man? Again she is struck by how little he weighs; it is as if his shape and his substance are separate things, connected solely through visual presumption, like a backward-flowing falls.

I'll just catch my breath, says Freddy. His eyes are shut.

Zane is not difficult at all to get to, she finds. For all Eff's secretiveness and emphasis on a hard and twisting journey the route from the hospice is a matter of two paths, both marked and well-worn, a songbird trail and a tagged underground electrical field constructed to supply the developments. Not hidden at all; it had to do with how you came at it, and Eff as always had chosen the most oblique angles. Entering from front-on a twelve-foot sign announces the town—not Zane, but Sabor, a polio-free community. The streets are the same, the buildings. The town of Absinthe will spread this far then and lay itself down over Sabor-Zane and absorb it, like a towel on a spill.

Freddy starts to his feet, stumbles, shins glancing off the wheel of the chair, sets his feet more securely and begins to walk like a toddler pushing his wagon of wooden blocks, each step an act of faith.

Here is blank space, an ellipsis of hours until the story picks up again. She has tried to write it down, leaving placeholders, forgoing completeness.

She lets him—
He rests there—

Half-truths, loose swings. She is no archaeologist, does not know when she wrote what, but here are whole lines of angry zeniths in blue-brown pen, things blotted and scribbled out. Then space.

She writes *walkwalkwalkwalkwalkwalkwalkwalkwalkwalkwalk-walk* for three pages. *Walkwalkwalkwalkwalkwalkwalkwalk.* The bare mechanics of the journey, the stripping away of all aware-ness and afterthought to reveal the pure directed gesture of bod-ies moving towards their end.

Even as she deteriorated Ruth developed a range of ges-tures, hard, precise, spacious, that fixed her in outline and then brushed her in, like a Renaissance cartoon. In sleep her hands moved, conjuring a next day.

And Freddy. One of those bodies the world wore slung to its hip long after it ought to. She hasn't got his face at all, the coral of his burnt-out acne, the flat baker's nose. That's what she has of his face. His gait, half-shell belly against the wheelchair, incorporating the bar so that they made one thing, a modern centaur, man-torso wheel-feet.

He wants to get into his suit, the smart blue suit.

It's—

Suit, he says, insistent.

He is soaked through with sweat and it takes nearly half an hour to undress him and then tug the suit on. It fits exactly—this is what he wanted, she thinks, why he fasted. Buttons up, tie. Polished shoes, loafers. She finds a thumb-sized piece of mirror at the back of the theatre in the rubble that must have been the stage. Freddy is breathing very quickly, his eyes are rolled back.

Lie down, she tells him. You are in a bathtub.

A bathtub.

The water is warm, soapy. There is a game you play. You take a breath and hold your nose and lean back underwater—

Spptttt, says Freddy, getting it, gamely acting along.

But then the bulb goes out—

Yes, says Freddy. Nothing keeps me here, he says.

Lie back, says Dory.

I lie back, says Freddy.

Once—

Once.

Twice—

Twice.

Three times, says Dory and brings the pillow down.

When he is quiet she punctures the pillow and packs his open mouth with feathers. Freddy's eyes do not move but his breathing seems to stop, and he opens and closes both hands. He looks well, she thinks. Rested.

She draws a newspaper up over his face and leaves him the treasures in his pocket—gallery pamphlet, a magic egg, the program from an *Aida* with a library sticker on the back. Thomas Pitcher's perfect fingers play from the house across. In the newspaper covering his face a boy has pulled his family from a burning house, his mother and his father and his spotted dog. It was my Scout training, says the boy. In this improbable assertion, as an improbable assertion, Dory leaves Freddy Fychan; she leaves Freddy Fychan she leaves.

On her way back the trails are busy though it is still night. She must wait for others to cross before her: a cart pulled by stout horses, a man dragging a case. Four boys corner a wild dog with sticks tipped with long, threaded concrete nails—prodding and jabbing until the dog drips a thin brown liquid from its rear. She makes her way down the paths, round the rocky point, through the yew shrub. The clay soil is rippled and glazed in the heat. The few flowers droop. Everything is dense and flat. Dory sits and listens. She is cold but does not move. She is hungry but does not move.

—

Now Dory listens to cats—one cat?—screaming by the end of the yard of the house with the room she sits in. Not the aggressive commanding scream of the tomcat but something frailer, more dissenting, the last cry but one. She is due back tomorrow afternoon; her daughter will be there to collect her. Ruth's silver broad-hipped car.

What had she gained in returning? Her parents have been dead for years, Barnett first in a series of heart attacks, June soon after with a quiet form of cancer that had come, she swore, thirty years too late. They were living out west, minding their diet and exercise, taking classes at the library, honing their memories down to a few dates and places and times. They had forgotten Absinthe in the same unsurprising way they had lost the names of classmates and doctors and one-time readers of the radio news. Well, what is a place? A frame, a backdrop. Those who want place to be everything are disingenuous, Dory thinks, pandering to people's misguided belief in their own sensitivity to life's elementals: food, family, home. She is amazed at how few echoes there are for her here. The old house, extensively remodelled, the town boundaries now extending a good twenty miles. Where Sabor/Zane was bumps a street of pie and antique shops whose fronts are maybe ten years old. The lake is the focus, the whole town has been prodded and twisted to face it, uncomfortably, mandated to recognize the beauty at its feet. She has enjoyed her walks. She has eaten at the pie shop. She need never come back.

What had Tilly said? Silence. That she felt like she was delivering this baby into silence. Silence that Ruth would—what? Would not have allowed? Was that the implication? It wasn't Dory who was wanted here but Dory playing Ruth.

Come cry, come cry, Dory will make herself say. She will open up her facial features, curtain off her lower brain. Immerse herself in the hue and cry of inadvertent motherhood and say nothing about paternity or who will fund this child.

It has to do with envelope, Dory thinks. With resources. Ruth was unequalled in this. Her scope for love. Nothing fazed her; not once was she let down.

I will always want you always, she said to Dory. They were lost on old-fashioned skis. Snow to their shoulders. Between them they had left a finger of chocolate and a child-sized wheel of cheese. Terrified. Cold. Clueless. And still there was Ruth with her impossible, trenchant human focus, her muscular honing-in.

And here is Dory and where is Ruth?

Dory has cut another seven pages. Cut and burned it, and in its place three spaced stars signifying ellipsis. This is the work of memory, to let symbols stand in place of lived experience, to substitute holes for words. It is late, she is tired. All this bending of the neck and warmed-over parcel pasta. She has come to no resolution. She thinks she will leave the letter as it is now, secret passage and all. It has been too long and she has other obligations. To her daughter, yes, and to Ruth's unhappy friends, and to her own quite separate archives. This was only one project among many she has made little headway on. Why should a letter take priority over an unhedged yard or radios requiring fresh batteries or the other unmended recollections that Ruth left behind? Outside the cat has refined its cry into something lower, finer. A raindrop pivots on the window, flattens down. Dory eases the napkin from between the lid and the top of the desk. She must pack before she sleeps.

On her way to the station the next morning Dory finds that she has taken a detour. Unplanned. Is it though? She has after all given herself several hours to make a ten-minute trip. Not another second, she thinks, of the bed and breakfast, its embroidered everything, its odours of quinine and fried breaded fish. Happenstance. That's what she'll call it. She is surprised to see the building looking much as it had when she'd left it.

I'm in town for the day, she says breezily. The Fisher place, she says, but the receptionist does not know the Fisher place and barely registers Dory's name.

She is able to leave her coat and bags in the cloakroom. No one minds who she is. Old, dressed unaccountably in a smock of Ruth's mother that remains the only item of clothing she has ever paid to have altered, Dory is a seamless addition to the fabric of biddies and cleaners that makes such places run. There is the nurses' station, a brightly lit crescent of telephones and filing strategies; there is the elevator where lifers went up to the fourth floor to play penny bingo, to be wheeled reluctantly about during holiday dances, to watch pro bono conjurers palm their tie pins. She follows the painted lines down the corridor and wets her shoes obligingly on the broad pad of bactericide that thresholds the burn ward. She remembers it, but the quality of her memories is uneven, fine disconnected jots rather than narrative expanses, as though someone very skilled indeed were injecting by stages a cortical tattoo. Here the rooms are smaller and more numerous and in some the light is kept artificially red and low. One of the doors swings wing-like on its hinge, number 22, a slice of sweet air from within. The chart on the door indicates that the patient is due for transportation. Helicopter, Dory thinks. Stabilize them here, then transport to the city. There—at the end of the hall the activities cart, updated she sees, rows of films and books and music and an SKU scanner attached by umbilical. She has to tiptoe to get the thing moving and then she is at the door, a pivot, in the room. In a cup on the cart a quantity of ribbon; she takes a red one, ties it to the bed in a festive way. In the bed a man. A young man so damaged as to seem a distortion of the light. There is very little of him that has not been interfered with. This boy died, she thinks. Or very nearly. And what a blessing if he had been the young Freddy Fychan or any of a hundred people she has met since. We cannot all be Ruths, she thinks, good and stout and expeditionary. Some of us are marked for lower things.

In the only interview that was ever published twelve-year-old Dory, genuinely distressed, said she had been very fond of Freddy Fychan.

He wanted to go out walking and I did as he wished.

Dory sits down in the chair beside the bed. On the table a stack of hats with sterile liners, a machine to turn typed letters into sounds. What she can see of his face is like tree bark, curling back nearly to the bone under the breathable second-skin wrap.

Dory takes the letter from her handbag, counts her pages, checks her watch.

All that she needs is there in the beginning, in the secret passage. It is all there, all of it. She has this letter in her head and she is ready at last to be free of it. Hand it over. Pass it on.

I have—

She gets up. Walks to the door. Confirms herself. Returns to sit just where she was, a foot to the left of his head.

I have done a terrible, terrible thing, she says to the man on the bed.

The station is silent. The train will not come. But maybe. Will it come? Is it still running? Dory looks up and down and sees that it is no longer only her. There is an old man, and another. They pay her no attention. The old man reaches up for the station lamp, manipulates the wick. The other sits, unmoving, suitcase close by.

Dory looks around at the man by the lantern, at the man sitting still. She sets her bag down, buttons her coat, slips her gloves on. She spreads her arms and begins a slow wave to draw the engineer's attention. The train will come. It will come. She trusts the moment, this simple moment, to take care of itself. She closes her eyes: there it is, there she is, stepping off the train and into the city, blooming like a tiger lily into a bold new life.

THE TRAIN

The train, the two trains: the scheduled and the overload.

There will be an inquiry. Witnesses will be called, deposed. The language of numbers, from the counting of the dead and injured to the agreed-upon ratio of acceleration to brake force. Forty-odd carriages at six tons each plus two bookend engines at thirty tons requiring a force of 11 pounds of force per ton along a straight road with additional force, say 2 pounds, required to drive a train of the same weight round a curve, uninclined. Thus, the force required to drive the train from C to B stands at 2,950 pounds and the strain on the linking chains not less than one ton, 1⅕th the tension of the very best iron, per square inch. All this changes with the quality of iron. All this changes with the quality of the couplings generally. All this changes with excess steam put on by the engines. Ascending the incline of a gradient, say 1 in 80, gives a force of 40 pounds per ton on the train as a whole, though not equally on all parts of the train.

Some parts of the train are heavier than others. Some are cleverer. Some more amenable. It follows, then, that some parts of the train will tend to work against the laws, the immutable, unfixed laws that govern the movement and behaviour of trains, and that the vectors, caught out, will leave their tracks and slide into one another, and tango blankly.

Therefore the chain that broke. The chain that broke in ascending the incline must either have been of bad quality, or, as likely, was the victim of too great a pressure produced by an excess of steam, resulting in what is known technically as "back-lash."

The train. The second train. You time it beautifully, minutes to go before the cataclysm. You walk the broken line from engines to brake van, through carriages crammed with children—you do not remember them. It is easy, to pass from one train to another. To reorient yourself. Here is a reverend gentleman, his watch on a piece of linen, his scalp red and welted. Here are the boys of the Guilfoyle Chorus, one asleep with a marble in his ear. The train. Twenty-five carriages, built by William Guthrie. Those used in the excursion train are quite as good as those used in any other train and, indeed, would be used in such trains. Every carriage chain is examined and passes a series of tests.

The inquiry will establish, what? That in any really complex narrative, logic and sequence are seldom overweening. That trains aware of other trains will act differently than trains alone. That there is variability in the quality of standard iron, that human error trumps human ingenuity. That there is no such thing as an unpolluted order, no event that may be understood as fully self-contained. That the lives of these trains, their destinies, must not, cannot, be treated separately. Inevitably, uncontrollably, they intersect.

It is established that the chains connecting the engine and first six carriages to the other thirty-odd had broken. Seven times. It is established that:

the rails were wet in consequence of a fog that was breaking

the chains had broken and the carriage was held only by a
side chain
best practice requires ten minutes between trains
on this night the ten minutes became three minutes
somewhere, three minutes were lost

On the third day of the general inquiry Mr. Standish Buttons,
the company's chief engineer, agrees to make up an experimental
train in order to illuminate the events of that night. Two neatly
turned one-twelfth scale models of the company's carriages are
built and set on short lengths of track. Each matches exactly the
descriptions of the originals: number of seats, striations on
upholstery, handprints on the glass. Buttons is an artisan. He constructs the train so its roof may be removed. He inhabits the seats
and aisles with the passengers known to have been on the train
and affixes a signature ornament to each: a marble, a cameo, a red
cravat. Where identity or position are unknown Buttons places a
parchment flag. This train is weighed. It is prodded up an incline
identical in pitch to that outside the town of Moar. It is acceler-
ated and braked and the distances are noted and double-checked.

Then the second train is loaded with iron. One engine, ten
miles per hour on the incline, hind brake then applied. Train
stopped in 912 yards, 90 yards short of the point of collision on
the night of the accident; the rails were slippery. Conclusions:
had the rails been dry then the train would have stopped. Had
the train not exceeded its speed of ten miles per hour then the
train would have stopped. Had the brakes been applied as soon
as the carriages skidded then the train would have stopped. But
the brake was bent and the nut was greasy and therefore indicated that the brake was not turned on.

What does the brother of the dead brakeman remember?
The tremendous groaning as the brake was applied. Sparks from
the brake shoes trousered his brother's bare legs.

—And it was then that you noticed?

—I noticed he was dead.

They call Martin and Collier and Stanton and two different Graveses. And afterwards Hannah the head guard. No one, it seems, is responsible. No one's duties appear to have included keeping the train safe. It is not Hannah's duty to ascertain the cause as well as the fact of the breakage in all cases. It is not Hopkins's duty to inspect the locomotives. It is not Cooke's duty to check all shackles once underway. It is not the guard's duty to report breakages to Hopkins. It is no one's duty to discover the cause of breakages. On this train, there are seven breakages.

In examining a train, Hannah walks each side and stares at the wheels and the couplings. He pauses between each pair of carriages and inspects the fastenings. Then he forms an opinion as to cause of breakage and reports this to Mr. Jones. It is then Jones's task to supply fresh chains and report this to Hensley. Hannah forms one opinion, and Jones another. Sometimes, walking beside a train, Hannah sees in the forged reflections a distraught figure, an emanation of a fallen world, and he must force himself to turn away and continue.

—Are you religious, Mr. Jones?

—I believe in a mercy that is granted to men.

Jones provides a visual check. This is all that is possible. He cannot test each link by weight or by hydraulic pressure. He cannot test them by sound. On this day, he issues a verbal report to Jones. He says that there are four broken couplings and three broken side chains but that it would be difficult to repair these given the crowding of the carriages. The train, says Hannah, is perfectly safe to return. To say otherwise is not his duty.

Hannah tells a parable. He is a brisk, cantilevered man, not previously given to whimsy or too many words. But the accident has changed him—when he speaks of it, he becomes a softer and more oratorical creature.

A train wreck is something we see through a glass, says Hannah. We each have our glasses and our bit of train to see.

But we none of us see the *same* train, he says. I am sorry, very sorry, for the damage this has done.

The train—what happened on the train? It was a defective weld—the iron was not of the best quality but the cause of its giving out was the defective weld. Only a third of the eye was holding in consequence of the bad weld. It was not a weld but a wet track. The track was wet and the brakes had little purchase and thereby stuttered and the chains were snapped. It was not wetness but greasiness. Generally fog makes the rails greasy while rainwater washes grease off. On this night there was fog and this lay thick upon the rails and bonded with the grease and interfered with the braking. It was not greasiness—there was plenty of power in the brakes and strength in the welding and purchase on the rails and room to stop. It was human error, the brakemen and their fifths of brandy and their concentration on the deck of cards. And somewhere was lost three minutes and in this time anything might have happened.

Shortleigh the vicar says: I arranged this trip. I thought it advantageous for our children to see another town and to travel on a train for this purpose. We lost Drusilla Grevus, a Welton girl. I am vicar to the town of Welton. How must I appear to them now?

What connects the inventor to the girl? The girl to the suicide? Where is the injured man?

Okay, you tell them. Let's continue. Four trains, four strands, four characters, four rungs, a ladder, a spine. A spine, you say. You're building a spine.

You leave the Sunday school children at their drowsing and the brakemen at their cards. From memory you can plot the angles, of the stories, of the trains. The time is nineteen-oh-two. Seven p.m. on the seventh of September. The train is near enough to touch. You close your eyes. You cross over.

CAL

EARLIER, JAY

Cal and the Traveller are waiting for Jay. Balanced on a steep ramp, the Traveller weighs heavy against Cal's knee. Its easy-grip skin flutters and pulses; it is dreaming of contraband, of French cigarettes. He pets its twin latches, its cool dial mouth. He scans his list, checks his watch, pops the hasps on the Traveller's left flank and finds a vinyl envelope with the papers he has for Jay. Sketches, photos, a details sheet: height/weight/ eyes.

Cal meets Jay in the café where she works. It is the interval between Merle's fourth and fifth attempts, and Cal is trying, in a steady, uncomplicated way, to broaden his focus.

Hey, says Cal. Nice bones.

Jay is in town to study medical prosthetics. She has baked her first real limb and is icing it in skin. When finished this will be an arm in which the wrist will rotate 220 degrees and exert eighty pounds of pressure per square inch—sufficient to crack a walnut. She has a few images, lays them out on the table for him to admire.

It isn't finished, she says.

Well, it's very good.

Not yet it isn't. It isn't *natural*, she says.

Cal begins telling her about escaping the Giant, about meeting up with the Vampire, dressed in red denims, a tribute to the vena cava. The Vampire has smuggled out some close-ups of that miracle foot.

I got most of the angles but my flash crapped out, says the Vampire. Water in the bulb, electrical failure—*never* happens, he says. A sign? Who knows. You're looking *ruddy*, he says, speculatively.

It isn't good health; it's allspice. My father and his baking, says Cal.

This foot, it's Victorian, he tells Jay. It flexes and settles. It *learns*.

But Jay is on duty. She makes coffee in a spare, bored way, stopping to stare at an arm or a thigh or a special grade of collarbone. He thinks of her hands arranging the cups in their saucers. Every movement leaves a corresponding excision in the air.

I have a passion for the wake you leave, he tells her. I cherish your drift.

This under the hiss of the steam, of the milk.

Single or double? she asks him. Cinnocolate or carapecan?

Between orders, she draws freehand on a pad backed with jute, worrying the paper in the way of trueborn lefties, so that he can glimpse only lacing and smudge.

Perfect. Stunning.

She stares at him. It's all but erased, she says.

He's high on unrequited, doesn't leave easily. He freefalls into macchiato; double, triple. Babbles, invents. He admires her resolving power, her way with bone and cartilage. There is a magic in the lines of her new-made thumb. He has a book or two he'd love to lend her. She can keep them—he'll buy others.

Mould me, he says.

Hey—slow down, fancypants.

I mean it: make me new.

She studies him, critically. I don't think so.

A second, a spare, a used part, he says. I'm an inner-beauty person. Rebuild me.

No.

What do I have to promise?

Next time he sees her she has a surprise. A spine, rough and rubbery, barely symmetrical, the vertebrae stretched uneasily, the discs a little floppy, imperfectly attached. It is headless and less than three feet long.

Voilà—the spinal cord and the merging spinal nerves and *arteria vertabralis*, Jay says. Cast from real life. Take it, she says.

And do what?

Cuddle it. Serenade it. Use it for your hats.

It's hideous.

You wanted moulding. Here's moulding. It's yours.

It belongs to someone.

It's resin and paint.

But it belongs to someone—someone was born with this spine; *this* spine.

This spine hails from Indiana. Certified union-made.

The spine clicks and rustles. On the bus there are comments.

Your friend rides free, says the driver.

Puns on the word "bones."

With the spine he begins his collection. Installed in his office, the spine fits easily among the trappings of a make-believe medical man. His framed middling B.A., a coat and stethoscope, costume-shop grade, his collection of the Giant's brochures. During calls he leans back and just watches it. Ambition, desire, love, knowledge—all anticipated in the plan of the human spine, in its bars and discs, its precise distances and allowances, in its nerve harnesses and oxygen pads, tree-shaped and star-shaped and rough, rough, rough—like infinity with stretchmarks, a little lived in.

Around the core he adds pieces: microanatomy kidney with vessels, the diseases of the esophagus, a bronchial tree. Then an inguinal hernia, a sixty-stage model of malignant melanoma on the skin. Muscle fibre. Gallstone. A towering digestive tract he pops a tray over when company comes.

I can't eat off this, Jay says. It's so *glossy*.

A brain in copper, a glass block skull.

I've got a goitre on order. Omaha World's Fair.

Goitres, toasts Jay. Huzzah!

Jay is a live wire. She agitates on behalf of a number of fringe movements, carefully and with astonishing attention to detail. When advocating for refugee claimants, she achieves in a space of months functional fluency in three languages. When battling Big Tobacco she reads the litigation back to 1968 and hooks and quits, hooks and quits, until Cal isn't sure whether to borrow or hide his smokes. For her, all politics is unstable, atavistic, defaulting to its origins if left to itself for too long. It must be forced onwards. They argue diligently, fundamentally. He prints up a ream of cards, *I AM NOT THE ENEMY*, in 80-point Garamond. Jay is committed to fair trade and eats single-origin chocolate and wears bright breathable clothes and smells faintly of coconut and has flat, dented skin. She lost her mother young to stomach cancer and confesses to spending her school years standing on the edge of friends' photographs, pigeon-toed and floppy-haired, indiscriminately caustic. Cal finds her electric and exhausting, the way a power station views a lightning strike. She is soothed by his inconsequence, his harmlessness.

Like a quince, she says.

Once, Jay passes his place by accident. She would like to eat something/anything, she has missed her train, she is fraught in her office, her haunches ache.

I wasn't in the neighbourhood even, she says. I don't know why I'm here.

Jay. The Healer. The pastor. The deep, deep distraction, the mica in the blood. Merle dies and for months after Cal suffers cinematic migraines: a cast of thousands, flashbulb moments and structured music, violins and traffic jams, jet blades and scimitar and organelle, he lies with a bag of frozen peas against his brow and sees his whole life, leached of colour, pan and scan from the top left corner down.

There is a world outside of yourself, says Jay. In a way, that's encouraging.

Cal's biweekly meetings with the Healer are (according to the Healer) "bearing fruit."

His grief, as apostrophized by the Healer, is gushing, abandoned, prolix, absorbing. It is not a grief to understand itself.

Stop thinking, says the Healer. Just feel.

Stop *how*? Feel *what*? His grief is no longer a feeling but a substance, silt upon the heart. It is particulate, a salt, something to be shaken onto a plate of tossed pasta or a soft-boiled egg. Intricate, a product of Swiss mechanics and modern polymers, with a fold-out instruction manual and a lifetime guarantee. It is separate from any way of talking about it. The usual gambits— conversation, letter, phone call—fail uniquely when confronted with this grief.

I won't do this, Jay says. Do you not see it? You are becoming this kind of awful, circling, *homing* creature; and it's beneath you, it's de*cayed*.

Seven times, he says. The car and the pills and the bridge and the traffic and the propane and the bag and the car and the cookies. Seven times, and then I—

But not here, says Jay. Your dad isn't *here*, she says.

Are you with me? Cal asks the speakerlet.

An electrician and his tanned apprentice have come to wrangle the out-of-spec furnace, on a three-day bender and pushing 35 degrees. They will save it by means of copper wire and therapy. They will coax and bleed it. They will change its filter and pronounce it cured.

I'll get there, Cal says. We're all in a rush but there's a process, he says. Pay attention—the foot, Merle and me. Keep it all in your head at once, Cal tells her. That's how this works.

He thought he was getting through to me, Cal says. All that time. Making up, you know? Some parents fish with their kids. It was something we did together. I thought I was catching up but he was waiting on me. We had a standing appointment, Cal says. But he was losing time. A few seconds here and there, it added up. And the eighth time, I stretched it. I was late. Two, three minutes—he must have thought I wouldn't show. I *let* him.

Cal says. I let him go.

I don't know what—says 801. Falls quiet. She thinks that what is bound to happen now is something she fears. The more he talks the more she will be incorporated. Already she is too hot. Flopped on the couch, her socks off, shirt and trousers rolled. Behind her knees the forthright stain of eczema.

I went to his work, surprised him. I followed him so he would know he was being followed. I told him I planned to go travelling. I let him think his time was short.

Merle is offering a new closeness. They go to a ball game, the home show, the market, where Merle stands mesmerized by the pink, stubbled, unnervingly pig-like sides of pork.

Everything's compressing, says Merle.

They go to the children's museum. To the Heritage Village

to watch molasses taffy made. Merle has trouble walking, the injuries he's done himself. But Cal presses him on.

The fun fair? You're sure? Merle asks, anxious. It is childhood for them both.

What did I expect? Cal says, to the speakerlet. I was so fucking *angry*; it got out of hand. I pushed and pushed him, and each time he took the bait and I found him I thought—I pretended—that I was learning a little more. The truth about Merle was that he wanted to die. That was it, he says. That was it. He wasn't especially good at anything, he says. Except that. He was as fine, as concentrated a killer of himself as ever there was. And how does that augur for us? What does *that* mean? he says. The stories you wrote were sad. But Merle was optimistic; he knew he'd get it right.

Optimistic, says 801.

And *febrile*, says Cal. Inventive, always. Quick on his feet. Example: we're in some shop, some store, Cal says. And we're trying on something, a sweater, together. And he buys it but in a smaller size. In *my* size, he says. He *buys* the thing as a hand-me-down. What am I to do with that hint, with that *semaphore*? I tried. I put myself in the way, I became an obstacle. It didn't work. But I tried.

It's that phone and its predictive texting, he says to the Healer.

Every time he starts "Merle" the program suggests an alternative. Me . . . begins Cal.

Melon? suggests the program.

Me . . . writes Cal.

"Merit?" suggests the program.

It is a tug-of-war. Cal and the program. Merle becomes "Merge" and "Merganser" and finally—does the phone own a thesaurus? it seems to be boning up—"Merlot," and after what seems a weekend of this it becomes clear to Cal that the program has in its bizarre pedantic word-blind way won, and Merle can neither be suggested nor offered nor saved because Merle is no more.

I forced it, he says. I forced the fucking thing to learn "Merle" and what's more to suggest "Merle" every time I put in any combination of letters. Now whenever I type a definite article I get "Merle" and that is as it should be. I won—but where is he? I won—did I win?

And the Healer, whom Cal has paid by the hour since before there were hours it seems can say nothing.

You cannot talk grief out of itself, Cal says.

The Healer clears his throat.

Cal has cashed a savings bond, rents a cabin in the hills for a two-week air exchange, trying to dissipate this grief. But the whole time he's there he is sick with it—this grief sifts into his lymph nodes, his sweat glands, his kidney, secretes itself into his mucous membranes, urine, tear ducts, so that he can't cry or piss or blow his nose without getting this grief over everything. No amount of water drunk or cheap scotch synthesized is enough to dilute this grief. In the water and on the backcombed hills, low-lying grief he can't see till he's in it.

Cal talks and talks, the Healer is his placeholder, the talking is the process not the goal, there is no goal, no termination, and Cal says:

Entropy is a process, decay is a process, death is the longest, surest fucking process—

And the Healer produces a tear Cal is sure will appear itemized on his bill, so obviously constructed is it, shapely, light-caught, wet as a Labrador's mouth, and says:

I have no answers, no one has the answers.

And Cal wonders: When will you deliver me from this grief?

Let me tell you a story, the Healer says. We were in a supermarket in Paris and a girl came up to us, no more than six, a little ragged, jelly round the mouth. She came right up to us and said, "*J'ai des gants; ils sont rouges!*" Smiled—she was proud of them—walked off.

Red gloves, says Cal.

No, says the Healer. One was a mitten, the other was blue. We cannot be sure of *any*thing concerning ourselves. Please understand, you're in all kinds of danger. You must not must not *rack* yourself, he says.

Cal and the Traveller stand alert in Jay's house. Bamboo mat and zodiac wind-chimes.

Jay isn't happy to see him, here, at her home.

I live here, she says. *Live*. It's out of bounds.

I went by the joint—

Café.

—the café.

I'm off tonight.

I know. I was there. I asked for you. They said take this envelope, you're going her way.

He hands her the primly dressed cheque with its peepshow plastic window.

Vacation pay, she says.

He asks her. Pleads. He can't help it. It has come to this. He wants a new arm, new ribs. Build me an arm.

No.

A wrist.

No.

A hand, a finger, a single joint, the air pocket between a joint—

No, no, no, no, she says.

I wasn't always this way, he tells her. All this grief—it is *toxic*.

He thinks of superheroes, born under different stars, freakishly powerful, helplessly moral. Goodness clogs them, leaves dumpsites through their veins. Each act of rescue, of salvage, of mercy, signals the last, the thrombosis of doing the right thing.

And *I'm* toxic, he says. Infectious. Rebuild me. Please.

You talk by rote, she says. You talk and talk. You're just *list-ing*, she says. A*rranging.*

I'm not aware of that, says Cal.

You wouldn't be, she says. It's a problem, she says. Your grief your grief—what of it? she says. You creep up on people. You way*lay.*

Listen, he says. Listen: I am serious. I am calm. I am going to take myself apart, he says. I will begin with my arm. I will dismantle it. Twist, twist, twist it; counterclockwise, do you see? I will find the thread that holds it on, the ligament, and twist it off, the pulp in the middle the colour of milk. Get ready, he says. Prepare your instruments, your bindings, your glue.

Oh no you don't, she says.

He is suddenly, blindingly, conscious of her construction. The shapes and the textures and the quality of the joints.

Your scapula, he says. Trim as a fin.

It's my legs that are remarkable, she tells him. If I was found dead and dismembered, they'd think I was four inches taller than I am.

He hands her the papers: the sketches, the photos, weight and height and eyes.

I won't do this any more, she says. It's degrading and it doesn't help.

It isn't what you think, he says.

Forget it—it's Thursday.

Just look at it, he says. He tries to tell her. Eight times, he says. It's all there.

It's Thursday, she says, hands it back, shuts her door. *Thurs*day, goddamnit. I'm off.

I want you to build something, he says. It isn't for me. Just look at it, he says.

Jay opens the envelope, keeps her foot on the door.

This would take me months.

It doesn't have to be perfect, he tells her.

Fuck fuck fuck fuck fuck, Jay says. I know what this is, god-damnit. If I do this for you, she says.

Anything. Sure, yes; anything, Cal says. The thing is, it's got to be exact, *faithful*. Please. Please. It's all I've got left, he says.

It escalates, says Cal to 801. The fourth and fifth time. Merle by then is making mistakes. Some of his accounts are rescinded, handed over. Certain numbers come up time and time again in his analyses. Certain dates. Recurrence, rather than impartial assessment, themes his reports. And he seems to become conscious of taking the time to leave tracks. Previously camera-shy, he survives in three separate shots in the June/July summer issue of his firm's bimonthly newsletter: smiling at the presentation of an oversized cheque; poised by a slice of retirement cake; front row at a lecture on the power of unleashment. Cal has never thought of him like this, corporate entity, mnemonic for success, yet here is Merle agog at the novelty cheque endorsed to Feed the World; Merle licking his lips at the prospect of high-chocolate icing. The newsletter has run for twenty-eight years and Merle has never before appeared in it.

So why now?

I think—I think he was advertising, Cal says. I think he was showing off.

Merle changes his habits. He purchases a suit of body armour. He installs in his apartment sophisticated alarm systems against fire and theft. He walks on the inside edge of sidewalks and alternates between elevator and stairs. All part of the project of eliminating risk.

Safety, says 801.

No, says Cal.

Merle is hoarding chance. He is filleting the risk from all his enterprises and banking it, locking it up so it can't get in his way, and save him.

EARLIER, THE PASTOR

Here, says the pastor. Keep it.

Cal and the Traveller sit in chairs at the Church of the Elucidated Soul. And what chairs—green cloth over humpy fibreboard, boys bent for leapfrog. Affixed to each right armrest is a plastic mechanism for holding a drink. In it Cal has folded up his list.

The pastor holds a pamphlet. *The Church Disseminating.* Brought vividly to life by the Reverend Donny Blake and illustrated with Hogarthian rigour by one Jeremy C. Scott. On the page facing is a man bisected, soul issuing from within in short, hotspring puffs, unadulterated. *The Church Respiratory.*

This is the basic, the gut-level stuff, says the pastor. Obviously, there's more.

They have come here to talk after the sermon, a short affair in a rented church where two children raced round the pews and a tiny congregation sat uncomfortably close among the choir and the pastor queried his beliefs by way of affirming them over an Isley Brothers descant played by the radiators.

It is a basement mission, unpolished surfaces and wood laminate, low table, wire rack stuffed with cheaply printed publications: *Twelve Steps to Heaven; Soul Owner.*

Like this—says the pastor.

The soul was great, unbroken. Sourced from heaven, threaded into a billion lives. Pure as glass. All deeds, all desires, sacrifices and corruptions, etched upon that glass.

Like this, says the pastor, drawing his knife over his tumbler, etched, Cal can see, with countless cuts.

Cal is two-thirds water. He bobs inside his skin. He is a danger to others, wayward tides and currents. They will bend over him and sip, and fall into a whirlpool. He is tired. He is damp and his feet hurt with walking.

What do you charge for redemption?

The pastor thinks. Redemption is harder and harder to move, he says. The idea of it. Because after that, what? What's next for the redeemed? he says. We used to think of the stuff as more or less permanent, he says. Now we top it up like a drink.

The pastor does a card trick. Keep your eye on the jack, he says. Now, he says, pulls with hummingbird delicacy the card from between Cal's first and second finger.

Amazing, says Cal.

That was a trick. This is a miracle, he says, indicates the room, the universe.

Silence.

Why did he do it? the pastor asks.

Cal thinks of his list, his list. Time—there isn't time.

I wanted him to die, he says. Then I could remember him.

Cal tries to tell him but the pastor isn't listening.

Seven times, Cal says. The car and the pills and the bridge and the traffic and the propane and the bag and the car and the cookies.

Hey, slow down, cool it. Three things you need to know, says the pastor. One: there is absolutely a God. Two, He has a plan. Three, His plan includes you.

How? Cal asks. He is lost among the fractals of the pastor's dark-on-light scalp.

Weh-lll . . . says the pastor, makes profound motions with his hands. Scissors, Cal thinks. *The Church Tonsorial.* He has a story for people like Cal, a jovial and finally severe story in which the road to Damascus is suburban and serviced and spotlit by night. He says he was lost and wayward and that he had hit his nadir, struck rock bottom; there's not a scenic thing about it, he says, and he should know.

I was low, low, low, he says. Sanka?

No thanks, says Cal. He wonders: do the contented ever convert?

Failure is a bet you place on yourself, says the pastor. He drifted, drove a truck and lost the truck, ended up wearing a sandwich board advertising clearance sales, designer fashions, 70 percent off. He walked around on the half-shell, an oyster with a pitch. Two thugs grabbed him, clapped him together, lashed him to their car as a roof rack.

Clickety click, he says. The sound of my chips being cashed in.

It was there, on the roof, that he had his vision.

So we're doing sixty onto an exit ramp, he continues. I could only turn my head one way. It was an industrial estate, sheet glass, pharmaceuticals, movable hoardings. Three different ads, alternating; this is the big time, right? Your sandwich-board guys, believe me, they *fantasize* about this. So: ice-cream bar, headache pill and French sedan. But rotating. So I think: I'm dead or I'm dreaming, and it's the ice-cream bar again—revolving, right? Dark chocolate coating, creamy centre, caramel vein—and suddenly, there He is.

In a hoarding?

Ridiculous, right? says the pastor. Loony. I know.

The kids pulled into a slip road bar and forgot him on the roof. The speed had loosened the rope on the boards and he slipped out and hitchhiked into the city. First car past stopped.

That *never* happens, says Cal.

Ex*actly*, says the pastor. Happiness is not a debt God pays interest on, he says.

Cal tries to tell him. Seven times, he says. *Seven.* What do you call the man who dies and lives, dies and lives?

It isn't so bad in this world, says the pastor. But he trembles like a squall.

Merle and Cal. There is a time when it is just the two of them. Tannis is ill and they drive into the country for snow apples and they find snow apples. Even then, perhaps, Merle was oppressed by his split vision, his ability to see a shadow world a few degrees south of the one he lived in. But who knew? Merle had spare apples: in his pockets, in the glove of the car. Later, Merle had backups and backups of his suicide kits. Twenty-odd boxes and bags, neatly labelled. Nooses and bottles and surgical bands, razor blades stored in ethanol.

What was he like? Well, Cal says. I didn't see much of him. He was there all right, but I didn't see much of him. He had tremendous expectations, he says. There were problems. He had past lives he only recently knew about, Cal says. And in these lives he'd done terrible things. Terrible, he says.

Well, he will have been forgiven, your dad, the pastor says.

His hair is brushed and set flat; from time to time he reaches up to buff it at the edges. There is a towel plugging a hole in the wall and a pamphlet with emergency numbers and a set of greying liturgical cartoons.

Salvation is the original zero-sum game, he says. A soul lost is a soul saved.

These homilies are automatic, tugged from him by a string. On a table by the window is a church in cheap origami, a scale model of the "worship complex" they will build once they have paid rent and heating and bought fire insurance and a brown site and FM funding-drive airtime. A number of these churches will be built and alongside them the houses oriented towards magnetic north. A critical mass of believers will pray and a great unlimited moral putty will fill the fissures made by want and cynicism.

They're flat-packed, says the pastor. They make them down in Kansas and ship them out. Less than a month to build, he says.

I left him with a minder, Cal says. I thought with someone else he'd be ashamed.

The minder was Joe, married to Jo. And when Joe left to go full-time at the restaurant, Jo, who was perfectly well qualified, stepped in. Three times a week in the afternoons they came to visit with Merle.

Merle had no idea. These two people, just dropping in. He wondered where he'd met them. But he was very polite. He offered them snacks, which of course would just terrify them— tampered with, etc. Gateaux? he'd say, and they'd fold them into their shirts to throw away later.

After a few weeks Jo took Cal aside as she was leaving. Merle was on his balcony—chicken-wired, USB-camera-ed—with his legs like two blue wires crossed at the hip.

How was he today?

He fell a lot, Jo says.

Fell how?

How can I put it? He has no motor-memory, she says. He walks, and falls over, she says. Look at his legs: they're threads. He toddles a step and tips over. It's horrible, she says.

Jo left and Cal stayed. He watched as Merle took a step and wove and fell. He walked tilted back, legs wide waddling, arms tight to his chest, and shoulders shrugged back as though navigating a narrow passage through a door. Walked and fell. And fell.

His mind, he'd emptied it, Cal says. Kept only one out of all the maps he had ever made. He knew the way to my mother's house, he knew his way around it. Everything else had to go. You did the funeral, Cal says.

Your mother—

Won't say. I wasn't there, you'll recall.

I'm trying to remember, says the pastor, riveting his brow. It was a simple ceremony. "Bread of Heaven" was one of the hymns.

We hadn't seen one another for years. Eight years, Cal says. Eight years and eight times. Jesus. Whoops—sorry. I've told this story so many times it has become—

Stuck, suggests the pastor.

Fibrous, says Cal. There are some stories that refuse to settle, he says. You go on and on and no one is any easier. It isn't that it can't be represented, that it can't be explained, he says. Every time I tell it there is some new bit of information, some unseen perspective that threatens to snap things in place. Every time it is more compelling, he says. Exhausted. The story refuses to be exhausted but I am getting that way. It is a poison pill, he says. So he went, so I go. That is what I can offer him and the world—why not?—the world, he says.

A gift, says the pastor, winces.

Is it a gift? asks Cal.

Abraham—begins the pastor.

Abraham, says Cal. Spare me that old fraud! Abraham! What was his lot if not simple? Did he pick up a blur in his eyes from checking his phone for messages? Did he have to examine the Rocky Road for flakes of naphthalene?

He might have lost his son—

Never, Cal says. Abraham was a gambler and by God he won. Who wouldn't want to live as they were divinely commanded? he says. It's the *options* that do us in.

Merle is before him. He is naked as if for a bath. There is a brown swamp at his right foot and Cal sees that his father stands in his own wet shit.

Jesus Christ, he says, and marshals paper towels, hot water, a cleanser with bleach from the locked cupboard he has installed for Merle to contain all household poisons (though Merle has been inventive, making deadly potions after ancient recipes, baking soda and cherry pits, rendering the cupboard useless) and sloshing the floor, scooping and folding, and all the while Merle stands shivering until Cal can get him to the bath (the mat!) and into it (the water!) and there Merle is rinsed clean and speechless.

I was sleepwalking, he says.

And Cal is inclined to disbelieve him until he thinks that this expression of Merle's will is so potent, so far-reaching, that even unconscious he works towards this end, that if Merle were a plant he would be a plant bent on self-destruction; that if he were brain-dead, paralyzed, in a coma, his few remaining working cells would join forces, adapt, settle round the new purpose and fashion for him some death.

And yet he did not suffer, says the pastor.

I expect he suffered a good deal, says Cal.

No, says the pastor. He assured me of that. He was easy in his heart.

At the time Cal brushes this off as so much Godterfuge. But later he thinks that what the pastor described is perhaps the truth of consolation, that it is a form of forgiveness administered to oneself, that it is a variety of nostalgia with a retroactive power denied to all other mercies, that it cleans up as it goes.

Merle was overlaying something with nothing, Cal thinks, obscuring what he'd done and been. What he'd looked like. What he'd weighed at birth. His knowledge of sea-life. His enthusiasms. Merle had found a way to conquer memory. He had scalloped out his perfect absence, settled in to wait.

The pastor has an adult son he rarely sees now. This son lives a vortexy, indefinite life out on the west coast and works as a bartender and computes for a band and lives, generally, against all the pastor stands for. For years the pastor has made him a subject of his sermons.

But not so he'd know, says the pastor.

Colossians, chapter one, says the pastor. "He is the image of the invisible God, the firstborn over all creation. For by him all things were created: things in heaven and on earth, visible and invisible, whether thrones or powers or rulers or authorities; all things were created by him and for him. He is before all things and in him all things hold together. And he is the head of the body, the church; he is the beginning and the firstborn from among the dead, so that in everything he might have the supremacy. For God was pleased to have his fullness dwell in him, and through him to reconcile to himself all things, whether things on earth or things in heaven, by making peace through his blood, shed on the cross . . ."

My eldest, says the pastor. My eldest son.

That's something, says Cal.

The pastor allows that he wrote tricky set-pieces for his son—psalms, proverbs—in which the boy appeared as a goat, a Hebrew, a seeker after pleasure, an unrepentant farmer. These sermons became ciphers.

If he'd have been there, he'd have known, says the pastor.

Why?

Why what?

Why would he have known?

I would've looked at him, says the pastor. I would've looked right at him. I would've sort of drawn him in, a little. Fascinated him. And then I would've bricked him up.

The wallpaper in the mission is bright clovers. They intersect in threes and fives.

Let me ask you, says the pastor. He shuffles the mantelpiece clutter about. Who's responsible?

For what?

"Train a child in the way he must go and when he is old, he will not turn from it," says the pastor. Proverbs? Ephesians? I have no idea, off the top of my head, where that's from. Who's responsible? he asks.

I can't—

Forget it, says the pastor. You're here for other things.

I can't help you, Cal says.

It's hard to be a cold-weather preacher, the pastor says. That old Christian feeling just shrinks right up.

On the radio men comfort a woman who has lost her spouse to carnal fascinations her children to the government, and now her hair and sense of smell.

God's all over that, says the pastor.

He shows Cal the letters he receives, some of them with tokens, prayer cloths, coins, photocopied prophets.

I can't help you, says Cal. I can't help you, he says.

What do you make of him? asks the pastor. My son?

I can't help you, Cal says. I'm full up.

Thanks, Merle says, the first time.

He is dripping hose and smoke, listening to Sibelius on the dashboard cassette. Paint pots, catalogued by colour and age. On the ceiling the wire tracks of the remote-controlled door that emits a low-level radio frequency shared among a thousand garages and conscientious parents and out-of-town radio hams.

Thanks, Merle says, dusts his left cuff, walks terribly terribly slowly to the streetside door and into the welling noon sun.

Thanks, he says, and lets himself out.

The garage, the paint tins, the ceiling hardware. The smoking hose, the cassette tape—playing, Cal can now remember, on a loop.

The second time is pills.

They are blue and spade-shaped, strips of thirty. Merle melts them into a slimjim of cola with a lemon twist, the organdy peel and a single lemon crystal, suspended in brown. There is music from next door, time-delayed, trapped in the walls, so that the bars stack up and he hears every note, every beat, every slur twice.

right . . . right . . . now . . . now . . . carol the walls.

Merle is seated in a chair with a half-chewed fringe. His arms are folded and there is a pyramid of cashews in a square glass bowl. A magazine. Upturned loafers with coins in the toes.

The phone and the doorbell ring; it is the realty firm. The realtor at the door is offering a free valuation and the realtor on the phone would like to speak to the realtor at the front door. Each realtor calls an ambulance.

Dad took an antihistamine, and overreacted, Cal tells Tannis.

He shouldn't self-medicate, she says. Look at how he salts his food. What's happening? Tannis wants to know. I'm just in a frenzy. I get out of my lecture and they're paging me and it's you and your dad, and he's *what*?

Overreacted.

Overreacted. An allergic reaction to something designed to prevent allergic reactions. Does that make sense to you?

No, Cal says.

No, it doesn't. And I'm just, in a frenzy, because there I am in the lecture and then there's this emergency phone call, and it's your dad. Christ christ christ. I thought someone was dead.

He's fine.

Now I know that. I know he's fine. Well, I don't know that, I'm taking your word. But, when the phone call, the emergency phone call, I thought someone died.

I'm sorry—

I thought *you* had died, on that stupid thing—

Scooter.

On that stupid scooter going ninety minimum without watching the road tipsy no doubt you know how you like your wine along dead man's bloody curve.

I'm fine. Dad's fine.

He's fine. Where is he? Which room? I'm here and I'm wandering about—visiting hours are long over, by the way—and no one will say where he is.

He's fine.

Well, which floor is "fine" on? I don't know. No one will tell me.

I'm coming—

Not on that death-trap, you're not.

In a cab.

Well, visiting hours are long over. We can't see him. We don't know where he is. Fine, you say. Fine, how? How do you know? I'm just so in a *frenzy* here—

The third time is a bridge. The car is spotted near a railway traversing a sixty-foot gorge. Merle is finishing his picnic when the patroller knocks on his window.

Last supper? the cop wants to know.

It's close to an hour over a used-up road, sentried by squat fluorescent-banded stumps, sporadic service stations, bent billboard spines, storage barns and burger stands with their shutters tamped down. Cal's car, a rental, is white and wants a wash.

You drive the rental, he tells Merle. I'll take yours. Careful, he says. It's on my card.

They stop once on the way home, Merle signalling right and drifting onto the slip road to an offshoot diner signposted by crossed forks wielded with bravado by gastronomic musketeers. They order coffees, one apple dumpling to share.

Thanks, Merle says. Not bad, he says, of the apple dumpling.

Cal has the idea of driving both their cars. The one he will drive with his hands, huge hands. The other, with his huge electric mind. He will think the car in a direction and it will purr into gear. All other cars he will think off the road, the better to speed the trip home.

I'll get this one, Merle says, pays with a twenty.

Cal will think himself free of them, of Merle and Tannis, of family. On holidays he will address his cards to the ether.

Go ahead, he tells Merle, over the engine, and hand-signals. *You first.*

The fourth time Cal follows him. From the house, the shortest route to the number 11 bus stop, diagonals to Merle's office block. He sits in the lobby, an oasis of shaky, bitten-down palm trees and leatherette sofa set, nods at the security man with his

Jetsons headset, visits the washroom with its premium cream soap, declines to sign in. Which he must, to qualify for elevators.

I'm not going up.

Which he must, to meet someone.

I'm not meeting anyone.

The sign cautioning vagrants, loiterers, salespeople. Nothing to see here.

The security man is impressed by Cal's mysterious business. Periodically, he looks up from his screen and nods conspiratorially.

At four o'clock Merle magics himself into the atrium with a polystyrene coffee cup. Cal notes this in his diary. Security notes this in his diary.

Outside the city's deliberations. Skyscrapers alternately strolling and at prayer and the astonishing vague catch-all of the thousands and thousands of discrete actions carried out within. The vibrations of all those photocopied pages, all those tapped-out briefs, all those spoons stirring, loading the air like shot.

When Merle steps into traffic Cal is just behind him. There's an offset strike and a recoil. Merle's briefcase, exploded, is hinged like a bird.

The fifth time is propane. Merle paints his body with it, packs his nose with cotton, waits in the sauna he has made of his bathroom reasoning that the heat will open his pores and accelerate the reaction. A pleasant wooden room, triangular, low-ceilinged. The door is green metal, thick, with a rubber gasket and a small murky window making up its top third. Steam jets from digits placed low in the walls. Pans and gutters collect the moisture, funnel it into a dimple in the centre of the floor. Merle sits in a chair with his feet up. He is naked but for shorts. Thin shoulders rolled forward. Drawn-bow chest. It is painful to watch him breathe. Cal can see him and then Merle is a smudge in the steam and then he can see him again. Something in his hands. A book. Cal watches him, the effort of breathing, of reading. His hands run with ink, the pages stick together. Frustrated, he nonetheless is deliberate, careful, easing the page over with his pointer finger, laying it flat. Sometimes the steam plain blinds him. He waits for it to pass.

The seventh time Merle adds the plastic bag. Takes Nembutal an hour before with juice. Mixes a whisky sour, light on the seltzer, no lime. A clean, thick, transparent bag lined with a thin strip of weatherstripping. A sparkly gold twist tie. In Merle's outgoing message he is contemplative, absent. Struggles for the number and the upbeat tone.

So I'm trying out this new voice, he says. Different. *Sunn*ier.

When Cal arrives there is a play of facey images across the stretched and frosted plastic. Merle is folded in half, a thin sputum at the neck of the bag.

With each incident Cal finds himself waiting longer before wading in. Now, for instance. Lets a minute slide, then pops the door. He watches the bag over Merle's face as it is drawn in, puffed out. Reaches for his tool kit, selects a long pick. One precise thrust, one slice, and Merle is uncovered, skim-milk complexion and great shouting pupils. Cal strips the plastic from him, hits speed dial.

Cal is still in the game. But Merle is taking steps.

The sixth time—a car. Merle has lost his licence—strange quirk of common law that a car cannot be purchased for the purpose of doing harm to others or self. He haunts the sidetown dealerships where the prices fill the front windscreen, and everything has an exclamation mark, and everything refers to itself in the third person. Pays cash. Disdains insurance. Halves the tank with low-octane, gets the oil checked, tunes the radio presets.

Cal surprises him at home and finds the rubber hose.

Stay there, he says to Merle. Stay put.

He walks the house with a trash bag, collecting the pills and the rope and the string and the blades and the bleach and the butane and the hangers and the distillate and the fish-line and the slingshot and the toothpicks his Great-Uncle Melville made. He thinks about installing bars for the windows—Merle could just about manage it, jumping from the third floor. Limiters on the hot water tank—Merle could boil in his bath. Cal stands in the living room (ceiling fan blades, glass coffee table) and thinks that there is no way to Merle-proof this house or the world short of being there, always, ready to step in.

See this? This? he shouts at Merle, shows the trash bag. This is what it's come to.

Merle sits in his chair and will not look at him.

It takes Cal nearly two hours to finish his search of the house. First the lethal objects and then the benign. These—blanket, Christmas-tree holder, decorated urn—he holds up to Merle, quizzing him.

Is it safe? Does your head fit in it? How about this? This?

Merle maintains his moral placidity. He is right to be shouted at. But he is not ashamed.

The seventh time Merle makes cookies. Hermits, macaroons, olde tyme chocolate chip, icebox. He spends a day making dough and setting it in wax paper to chill overnight. Then he greases cookie sheets and lines the oven and discs the dough, dozen per sheet. He has creamed the butter and folded in brown and white sugar and sifted the dry ingredients in a separate bowl. And with a mortar and pestle brought back from a Greek island sojourn he has crushed four different kinds of pills, blister-packed in 28-tablet sets. He has baked death into cookies and he sits in the shared garden and watches the good witch do her toes on the quilted grass and eats cookies and drinks a malted milk. His downstairs neighbour, home from work, hears choking and phones it in.

The Nanaimo bars, Merle says, anxious. They'll freeze.

His pumped stomach is flat and stretched. The pills have leached the colour from his skin; he has all the haleness and presence of a watermark.

I'm going to have to live with you, and watch you, Cal says. How closely do I have to watch you? They want the rest of the dough for analysis. What do I tell them? Open your mouth. I want to make sure.

And the eighth time. The last.

He had this trick, Cal tells 801. He would lean in to you, lean right in, and go limp. Limp, he says. Like ripcord.

Enough, says the speakerlet. What do you think I am?

You're my scapegoat, says Cal. Hold on.

Funny was one of Merle's words. Funny, he says. View, he says. View. It was one of a score of words he formed with his whole arched body. *Funny. Interesting. View. Rapt*—he made *rapt* into a great soft acre of a phrase. The story of the gophers and the throttling traps. The story of the false pagoda. The trick of the numbers that add up to twelve, always, any way you stack and sort them. The sick lining of him. The skin of his hand on the soap bars. Filthy cupboards. Tubes in the sink.

This grief. This grief. What is Cal to do with this grief?

N. Lee from the ninth floor. N. and maybe R. Lee. A man with a sidesack of infopaks, coupons and contests and sample sachets. The appalling formaldehyde fabric softener.

Hello? Cal says. Hello?

The woman in 801 has put away her memo pad and reseated her chair. She sniffs her slippers, slides them on. She disciplines herself: a snack, mint tea and something crunchy. She settles in. She decides that she must not give in and make too much of this. Instead, she will enjoy it. She is already thinking of the anecdote she might fashion about this night: the phone ringing, the awkward low tones of his voice. In her version she is gentle, attentive.

I'm listening, she says.

It is a credit to her training that even as he speaks she is sorting and reallocating, overlaying his words with her own. She has put away her memo pad. She doesn't need it now.

I said he was unconscious when I got there, Cal says. I said he didn't speak. Well, he did speak, says Cal. He reminded me of daylight savings, the accuracy of atomic clocks. And then—he complimented me. "You've done very well," he said.

Hello? he says to the speakerlet. Are you there are you there are you *present*?

What will it take? says Cal. Sympathy. Outpouring. Your sin was not to get things wrong, although God knows you got enough things wrong. Your sin was to make my father *public*. What is distinctive in an outpouring? What is unique? It was your articles that finished us. I walked to work and was commiserated with and I went home and found condolences in the mail and I met friends who were sorry and had gifts from relatives who remembered and all of this fucking grief which is not real is in *no way* real, he says. And the only just, the only honest, the only available response to all this feeling is to feel nothing at all. Eight times, eight times, he says. This omnipresent fucking feeling. Where was my *niche*? he says. How many chances have we to mourn like this? And mine has been corrupted.

The woman in 801 says nothing. Her mouth is far too full.

Cal waits. He thinks that if 801 gives him an opening he will use it to jimmy open an end to all this. He thinks if this happens he will cash in his train ticket and splash out on a new watch. He thinks he has less than an hour left and he has yet to tell her what he has come here to tell her and if not this then nothing, and Merle deserves better than that. He thinks that confession is a way of refining a certain connection between some self and the world and that the self cannot possibly defeat the world at this game. The world must win and the self be humbled and this is as it should be because the world is older, bigger, stronger and less distracted. He thinks—

The super's arm appears from the super's window. Macaroon? she says.

Cal starts.

Eat—why suffer? she says. You are losing salts.

You're an angel, Cal tells her.

I am Mika, she says. It is a diversion to watch you cry.

Over the street a girl in a raincoat. A suited old man fiddling with overhead lights. Another man lathed in bandages. Cal looks at his watch. The girl looks up, at the clock, raises then lowers her hands. The old man cocks a pocket watch. Cal closes his eyes to clear them, refocuses.

The last time, he says.

Merle too begins his last day in this world with a list. He has thought everything through. He purchases a cylinder of CO_2 from a local industrial supplier and a mask and tubing from a medical shop. Shellacs the inside to prevent leaking. There is extra tubing and comfortable padding for his neck and head. The pressure in the cylinder is in excess of two thousand pounds. A single stout tap. In the corner he places the smoke-eater, bought second-hand from the restaurant trade. He tacks up the laminated notices: CO_2 DANGER—KEEP OUT! Important to seal the mask and to ensure proper gas flow over the nose (primary) and mouth (secondary). Turning the tap requires a significant exertion of the will and the wrist. Then he checks his list.

What happened, Cal says, to 801:
    What happened, he says, to Tannis:
    What happened, he says, to Jay:
    What happened, he says to the pastor:

—

What happens, finally, is this: Merle lets himself into the house he shared with Tannis and, for the first time in over twenty years, knows exactly where he is.

In the bathroom he undoes the mirrors with his pocket knife and gently opens the taps. There is hair in the drain, lime-scaled white windings. He thinks of the head the hair belongs to, gives in, picks a nosegay for later.

Then he sets the toilets (three of them) on permanent flush and travels light to light, stowing bulbs in an old Easter basket until the house is dark. He sits on a curvy swing chair he'd bought and broken and never repaired, and traces a visible mole.

He goes to the kitchen and balances the hot with the cold. Milk skinning a tartan bowl has resolved itself into a paste and a clear light serum. He removes one speaker from the radio, leaves it unwired and fragile, listens to static in mono.

He descends to the laundry where the dryer gravely wagers with the wash. He strips, clotheslines his vest and shirt and tie and trousers, pre-treats them for stains, puts them on again. Nearly there.

He turns the clocks against the wall.

Then he clicks to the timer function on his atomic travel clock, sets the countdown for ninety minutes, opens the closet door and flips on his flashlight and during the next hour he ties a series of knots, pokes paper into the keyhole, coils the bathtub hair, rough nautiluses, into his ears, cycles through eleven separate memories; and when everything is settled he shuts his eyes, breathes out as long and hard as he can, opens the tap on the cylinder, effortlessly aches.

Seven times, says Cal, to Tannis to Jay to the pastor to the speakerlet. Seven times that I know of. He called me, Cal says. He called me, and confessed. Seven times, he says.

There was no note. There was the scene and Merle who in his mask and tubing looked like a man about the reef, the dense squat friendly gas cylinder, a rushing of water through taps. The mask had ironed all expression from his face, lifted it like a wax transfer, whatever he had thought or said. The watch—he had unsnapped the watch (Tissot, silver) from his wrist and held it to his palm, though by then he could not have read it, the fumes were that thick. No note.

801 can listen no more. I'm out of room, she says. She will finish her snack and then she will be all but overflowing and she will switch him off. No matter where he is she will switch him off. Please, no more, she says. I'm full.

All that time I was chasing him—it was the other way round, he says. He wanted me to find him, he says. And it got to the point where I wouldn't. He looked at me, says Cal. We knew. That I couldn't save him. That I wouldn't any more. I think of it, he says. And my heart just roars. He's there when I open the door, wearing this contraption. And I'm exhausted, exhausted, and I've got this broken watch. I've let this watch stay broken, and even with this broken watch I'm nearly on time. Some knitting or embedding has taken place; we have become synchronized, and it is very difficult for me to show up even three minutes late. I'm looking right at him, Cal says. And we knew. He wanted us to be a family, he says. And he'd wanted to kill himself all his life. Why shouldn't I be a part of it? Why shouldn't I? he asks.

Silence. The word "full" followed by static from the speakerlet; 801 is gone.

Cal checks his watch, gets up and taps on the super's window. Your chair, he says.

Okay. You leave it, she says. Did you enjoy the macaroon?

Delicious, Cal says, I want to—

The misery has begun on television, she tells him. At ten o'clock sharp I lock my doors. The chair belongs to the building.

— 226 —

You may use it anytime you wish to weep in our lobby. The fish, the art and the floor-lamp are separately for sale.

The window slides down. He looks up the pavement. The Traveller leads by fifty feet, and growing.

Cal and the Traveller stand in the rubber slinky that connects carriages. North-northwest. There is an arrangement on this train—any passenger may depart wherever she or he wishes. Inform a conductor, choose one of thousands of mileage posts. Cal will take his place and make small talk with the service manager. He will wait for the long glide, the steep unfolding stairs. There is a coat on the floor, a rain slicker. By his side the Traveller stamps its wheels in their lubed-for-life housings, dreaming of sagebrush and Departure gates, reconciliation with the herd. Cal picks up the coat and bunches it into a shield. He will wait for the long glide. One minute. Two minutes. Three. The Traveller, that hothead, jumps. Then Cal jumps.

I

I REBEL

I'm not sure at what point I begin my insurrection. Against
order. Against clean. Spoon. The spoon I will not wash. The
spoon is my first refusal.

I have been told this week by Half-Australian that if I only
decide what it is that I want I am on my way to achieving it. Of
course, if I manage not to decide, I can remain here, ageless, forever in-between. I think of the owl and the mudfish and the
daddy longlegs, all those interstitial creatures, caught between
species, between habitats, between meals.

I would like to be handsome, I tell her.

Well—

Why not? I would like to be younger, I tell her. Smarter—I
would like to be smarter than I am. Taller, I say. Taller and with
long legs, I would like to be able to wear skinny suits and lounge
convincingly, I would like to be fair instead of dark, to double
the speed of my synapses. Blanket immunity. How about that?
I would like to blink my eyes and start a car, or a whirlwind. I
would like to be part of weather. There, I say. I've decided.

Wonderful. You see? Half-Australian says. But I know she means: You ingrate!

I think that part of what we've been doing here since I awoke is bringing me round to an appreciation of culpability. All these months, a dozen operations, the relentless disciplining of my every function, physical, cognitive, spiritual. All this in order for me to recognize that I was to blame for whatever it was that put me here. Every accident short of a meteor strike is shadowed by the suspicion that those suffering have somehow incurred it, helped to bring it about. Accidents are impure, they are messy. Wasp on a ladder, sneeze at the wheel. In my case it is more specific: I have done this to myself. Why would I not do it again?

The blood tap at the wrist. The taste of the cardboard tube, the hummingbird throat of the peak-flow meter. The kidney pan glazed with my urine. The shopping lists of the cardiologist, neurologist, physical therapist, plastic surgeon. Each divided from the others by a bit of Latin, angle of microscope, grade of glass slide. The cure is holistic; it requires that I confess.

Mea culpa, I am meant to say. I have made you do these things to me.

So it starts with the spoon and by the weekend I find that I am conducting a guerrilla war. I knife coffee grounds into the grouting between sink and countertop. I leave dishes, newspapers, napkins to rot where they lie. I let my nails grow. I wet myself, passing an exploratory dribble into my boxers, filtering into my slacks until the wet patch shows through, pale and otherworldly as an X-ray. Later I start to soil myself, carrying a warm soft saddle in my pants until bedtime or the itch drives me to wash. From Monday to Thursday I am howling, ragged, filthy, stinking. Why? Scattered as I am, I want to be able to follow something, all the way back to its source. On Fridays I wash up.

But soon I am impatient with the imperfections of my body, its leaking and mishandlings, unpleasant juxtapositions. I begin to imagine myself as shuttered, impermeable. I stretch a piece of plastic wrap around my forearm and admire its texture and smooth lines, its . . . murderousness. I want to block my pores, cap my penis, seal my anus. I want to control my body's emissions, want to know where things *are*.

I take the calendar from the wall and I have defeated time. But I miscalculate. Eni comes by on a Thursday, she brings me the newspaper and a supersweet beehive orange to fiddle with. I don't hear her knock. I am unshaven and bleeding at the nose. I have my cock out in my hands, twitching and pink and ridiculous when Eni glides in, orange balanced on her head like a crown.

What is this? I ask her. What am I to do with this?

It's your dick, she says. It's your goddamned dick.

For some time after that I am on probation. They can take away my house privileges—did I know that? They can place me in managed care. A male nurse can sit there day and night, even as I'm sleeping, and bathe and feed and void and walk me like a dog—is that what I want? Or I can sit on my own in a lightbox where the food comes on cardboard plates and the drinks in cardboard cups and twice a day the plastic potty gets slopped out—is that how I want to live? They sit there, waiting for me to answer.

No.

No what?

No, that is not how I want to live.

When later I try to explain myself to Eni she puts her hands over her ears.

Forget it. She points to my crotch and says: I don't ever want to see your friend again. And that's *ever*.

So I now have a monitor, biweekly, a companion for the afternoon. A brisk man named Donald who has a passion for summer carpentry and can quote statistics from three major sports. Donald smells of lime and oxygen. He is hearty, immune to insult, tall enough to swing from.

Steady, he says, lifts me over a puddle I was loath to cross. He is married. Two sons.

Darren and Brad, he says, as if these names were innovations first applied to his boys. Four and five. Brad is the feisty one, he says. Built like a brick whatsit.

His sons string onto every story. Where I used to work there was an Olympic-sized pool, he says. Brad used to come see me after nursery and jump right in, all his clothes on. Turn left here, he says, and we'll come to the bookshop. You're supposed to choose something, he says. Ten bucks or less. Darren likes the goofballs, he says. Eats 'em up like pie.

I'd rather—

Just choose. He waits until I am finished.

Every weekend, all summer long, it's, "Dad can we go to the beach can we go to the beach?" Little demons. But you don't mind, when they're yours.

He looks at me, wills a tricep to pulse over, gives me a pat.

Do you? You don't, when they're your own.

In the book exchange I find a Puffin, *Curiosities of Anatomy*. A bargain at 3.99.

Hey, Donald says, looks it over. Bones!

I PREPARE. I RECONSIDER.

With a little instruction I am shopping and cooking and cleaning for myself.

Duster, Hoover, J-Cloth, mop, says Polly. We dust and vacuum, we wash and we wipe. And no shortcuts, she says.

We dust the bases of bottles on the shelves and wash the inside of the refrigerator and vacuum under the beds and shift the smaller tables. We spray ammonia on the glass and squeak it away with a stripy cloth. Poll unveils her tour de force, a dusting mitt, a huge facsimile hand. With telescopic attachments we snick cobwebs from corners.

I am to view this unpaid labour as part of my rehabilitation.

We want you to focus on tasks, and from there, tasks in series, says Blood Nails. Behaviour is all about basics. Once we have those down as second nature, we can concentrate on expanding the boundaries, mixing it up a bit.

There is a danger, I think, of getting into a groove so deep I will never emerge, like the boy-men from the hospital's Matthews wing, dressed in smart shirts and wool trousers in a range of three colours, toting metal lunchboxes and listening to bits of symphony on their large unfashionable headphones, men who have learned to walk in sympathy to their injuries, to defer to their limitations, shitting on command, taking pleasure in Sundays and model cars.

Gotcha, I say. Ten-four.

I get into the habit of waking early, before the sun is up, opening the heavy blinds and watching for the moment at which day arrives for good. It can take half an hour. Trees appearing out of the dark, first their outlines, then the branches, finally the connecting sinews, the leaves. What comes last is the background— yet this is when the yard begins to make sense. Why is that? I think it has to do with incrementals, the withholding way in which the world is made available. So much light required for basic understanding, so much for what we'd call a decent grasp.

I have been a patient of one kind or another for 347 days. The initial euphoria has passed, the Team has moved on to other cases. What more can they do with me? The only animation now lies in the big push, deploying all their pneumatic resources for my catapult into the straight life of jobs and home security, marriage and drapes. I have gone to morning classes where I learn to make photocopies and speak politely into the phone. I have vouchers for automotive mechanics, should I wish to retrain in that direction, and retail management, office receptionist, maître d'. Arrangements are being made for limited home care and my relatives have received letters with the details of my syndrome, my preferences in food and drink, a sample shopping list. My landline and my mobile are programmed with the phone number of the best hospital in town. In medical circles I'm a public figure, a VIP. My passport will have my treatment files encoded in a chip beneath the photo. I can never go anywhere ever again without having been this ill.

I write to my mother and two friends. To the minister who was kind enough to ask his congregation to keep me in their prayers—keep me, and that is not a small thing, not for me now. I write: *Looking forward to receiving you in my revamped digs evening of September 7. Note: I've been fitted with attenuators so please, a heavy hand on the bell.*

I want to leave. I wonder, how will I leave?

MEMORIES AND INTERPOLATION

The house was painted, up and down, says Loon Amulet. Up and down. Lovely.

I am some age between six and eight, it is winter. The cottage is in a waistcoat of woods, trees enough to make it hard to see from the road. There is ice in my boots, we have been hours in the car getting here, the boy next to me has just vomited, tunafish reek from under a towel. The boy is my friend, his hair is almost colourless, gull quills. He has a toy car in each hand and he rams them together, sirens, looks at me to join the game.

I'm freezing, I tell the driver, this boy's father, when he asks how I'm doing.

We're there, he says, and a woman beside him, the boy's second mother, says:

We're practically there.

The boy has a harelip, or I pretend he does. For some reason, I want to make him awful, grotesque. The cottage appears at last through the headlights; the car scrapes to a halt. The boy—his skin is damp, he is breathing quickly. The doors grind open against packed snow. He pushes, steps out onto the running board into a drift. One step to disappearance, slipping out of time.

Oh, he is saying. Oh.

This place is my home and these are my parents, whom I have not met before in these stories about myself. Even now I barely recognize them, odd as they appear, foreshortened in Loon Amulet's jigsaw reminiscences. There are three lawns at the house, and trees, blue spruce and dome willows and a few tiger lilies with dropsy, bird-mutilated heads. My father is absent from the scene; he left two years ago and what is left of him is parentheses; gaps, though fewer and fewer of them, in syntax and rituals, and some of his old tools and clothing like the gloves I am wearing now, striped canvas and leather and a wadding of electrician's tape in the palm. My mother has her hair swept under a dishtowel, mud creaks upon her boots, slaps of it on her forehead where she has wiped it clean of sweat. She is up from the ravine. I have brought her something. I have been there with my friend Roger whose house is just a mile down the road, whose sister, round-faced, bright as jelly, will disgrace them. They are an unfortunate family in their children. Roger will gain a reputation for violence, tying his high school lovers to trees in public parks, leaving bite marks and cocaine dust on their throats. His sister will have two kids by sixteen.

But now he and I root about in the ravine for old soda bottles and cigarette boxes, for treasure that goes with the maps we draw, inspired by pirate islands. We are lucky today and we find something—a woman's bag, leather lozenge, black with red piping.

Not cheap, says my mother.

Next to the bag we find a man's necktie, knotted and shrunken, with the maker's label torn off. Shoes stuck like beaks into the moat around a red oak.

Goodness, says my mother. Who knows what they get up to down there?

Years ago this neighbourhood was stalked by a man with a sharpened switchblade comb. He waited on the path near the Catholic school and put the comb to young people's throats for their money and shoes. Here, it seems, is where the shoes ended up.

I'd like him to take these ones, my mother says. He'll have six years' worth of dog shit on his hands.

There are fireworks beginning, shocking rips into the night sky. Whistling and banging and bulging—Roger and I have already forgotten about the bag.

I am surprised then when I find it in the living room, hanging from the arm of a chair. At the chair's base, a pair of shoes, and a lamb coat on the back. Then I see it next to the figure my mother uses when she alters the dresses she bought as a girl in London, where good clothes never go out of style.

It's that full of mould, my uncle says, during his monthly check-in. For Christ's sake throw it away.

She doesn't, but she puts it away by night. In the day she still carries it around the house. It's all cleaned up now, wiped down with leather creme and waterproofed with mink oil. The inside has been sprayed and disinfected and the piping fixed where it had torn. She holds the bag and walks the corridor between the bathroom and the stairs and, I don't know, imagines she is murdered, in the gulley, in the loam.

Now, Eni says. Her hands are nylon, they are springy and slick. She is angry and excited—witness her chair-bound ballet.

On the count of five, she says.

I am learning the tenses. I am engaging with the future and the past.

Ready, I say.

I will go, Eni says, to get me used to it.

I will go.

I went, she says.

I went.

She thinks that to say these words is to breathe life into them; for me to say I will go is to will myself into some determinate future. She puts my hands on her upside-down ones.

I'm going to slip my hands from under yours, and try and catch them.

What for? I ask.

It's a game, she says.

She slaps me six times in a row.

So move your hands, she says.

She slaps me three more times.

The past is what we have done. What has been done to us. History is what may have happened to the Egyptians, or a girl in France. The future has yet to happen and it is what we want or fear. If we think a parcel will arrive for us, we are pleased. If we think someone is bent on slapping our hand, we are afraid.

Are you afraid?

No, I say.

Things will happen to you, she says.

My skin will sag, my head will empty. Someone I love will leave me.

I'm not afraid, I say.

The future is people who fly by pursing their lips and willing gravity.

My hair will go grey, and fall out. I'll forget things.

I'm not afraid, I say. I was not afraid. I will not be afraid. She was afraid. They were.

That's it, says Eni.

I look at Eni and see her hands where she has bruised them, bruising me. I look at her and I think that love is something that is older than it looks, that recalls the past and sees the future, and steps anyway like the mammoth into the tar pit and doesn't bother breathing.

—

I've been amusing myself by generating a profile of the person who lived here before me. Collecting objects and jotting down hearsay, impromptu interviews, looking round the apartment when I have the time. So now there are one or two things I know about him. I know he had a sense of humour. I know he wore size ten shoes. I know his taste in toothpaste and in books; he liked thrillers in paperback, not too long. I've skimmed several and they do nothing for me. I know he got a bracelet for his twenty-fifth birthday, silver-blue, that he clipped to his bed at night. I know that on the day before he disappeared he purchased work gloves, insect repellent, an emergency shovel, a single-use camera and surveyor's tape. I found the receipts in a drawer. I know he wore out the inside edge of his boots and that he took sugar with his tea—cubes, not granulated, perhaps in an effort to cut down. I know that he preferred cream cleansers to sprays and sticks to aerosols and scotch to wine even when the scotch was blended, and that he kept valuables in a dummy box of tissues by his bed. I know that on the day before he disappeared he emptied out the sugar and the tea and the coffee and the scotch and the cream cleansers in a single long spume over the sink and stretched the tissues in a single long-leaved accordion over the counter and never cleaned it up, as though he were trying to leave marks, and even under the new finish I can see them still, right down to the splashes. I know that he took to be precious things I can't understand, post-its and blueprints, an old mining brochure he kept in a book that had a block of its pages cut out to make a cavity, and I only know that because I removed and inspected every one of the books he owned. Height and depth were the axes marking what he considered precious; these things were stored higher and deeper than others, and once I discovered this I stopped bothering with anything below the top two shelves. I know that he disliked or distrusted reflective surfaces—there were none left in this place, even the drinking glasses were dull and opaque. I know that he relied on his telephone. I know he was someone who took care and I suspect that he was preparing for something, but I can't imagine what. I think that he did not expect that someone like me would come to this place and, as it were, excavate it.

I know that sometimes he had trouble breathing. I know that he wore 34 waist, 32 leg. I know that on the day before he disappeared he bought a new pen and wrote carefully his name and the date and then the words *grapple* and *terrible terrible*. I know his father's name begins with *N* or *M* and his mother's with *I* or *T*. I know he kept love letters, eight of them, in a subsection of his correspondence box under *Personal/Personal Histories*, talismans, perhaps, proof of past attractions and a gauge of things from there on. I know he kept a baby tooth. I know he had allergies to cats and dogs and grass and shellfish and that he was liable to earaches. I know that on the day before he disappeared he wrote something indistinguishable on a cereal box scrap and folded it into an airplane and flew it into a hedge where it stuck like a leaf until I found it when I finally took a shovel to the quadrant of the lawn where Manners would not stop digging. I know he was comfortable with metric. I know he never slept in. I know that on the day before he disappeared he went through his refrigerator and threw away everything except the long-life milk and then changed his mind and replaced the crisper full of vegetables with roots and legumes at the bottom and soft fruits at the top, expecting, maybe, that this would form a furred grey sludge. I know he pissed from the right side of the bowl. I know he tried and refused cable and the cable people know that too. I know that on the day he disappeared he unplugged everything in the place and sat on a chair and listened to the awesome absence of polyphonic hum and lit a match that burnt itself out in a glass. A brown glass.

I know he travelled by train. Like I did.

Like I did.

I am on a railway platform, waiting for a connecting train.

What were you like? *Thirsty*, Pink Slingbacks says. You wanted tea but there was no tea. It hadn't been delivered yet—I don't know. It was late, past midnight. You asked did I mind, could you sit down and wait until the place shut down? Sure—nothing was running any more, the coffee machine or the toasters. The bread was in its crates. The fruit came packed in Styrofoam. Could you sit down, wait there?

I'm not sure about departure times, I'm not sure about connections. Used to be when you travelled you booked everything well in advance. There were schedules. One train, one bus or one plane met up with another one on a journey factory-stitched in time. I have bought a ticket to the other end of the country but I can get off wherever I please.

I board the train in good order, as confirmed by closed-circuit footage—a six-year-old has died here and her brother was injured as they lay on the tracks, hands under them, waiting for the train to pass over them and burn them free of their sins. And there's been vandals, smashed the windows of the old Ladies' Lounge and the mirrors behind the L-shaped bar, where the glasses hung still, scrawling CUNT and FUCK over the counters and pissing up the walls. So they installed cameras and notices attesting to them. Here I am, at the tail of a month-old tape, a faded scurry in and out, up and down, then in to stay, window seat, rear-most window. And beside me—what's beside me? Only an inch or two is visible. Brusque toppled *L* of a rectangle, red plastic, apparently in furious motion, a surge across the frame.

I think I've been barking up the wrong tree. It has always seemed to me that I knew at least two or three things about him. Now I'm not sure. For instance, it was clear to me that he left after a period of preparation. Everything pointed to it. Draining the taps, unseating light bulbs, bleaching all the plants. The hangers in the closets, the receipts, the post redirected to a mailbox that's never been accessed, the shaking empty and the capping, as it were, of his home and life. These activities have always seemed to me to represent the end of something—some process, some decision, some closing. Now I think it was less a closure than an ellipsis, a spasm in time.

This has resulted in a shift in my thinking. It was clear to me that should I ever find him I would do so among the dead. Now—I don't know.

Who lived here? I ask Eni.

Eni isn't looking at me. It's my fault. I am relentless.

What's happened to you?

Who? I ask.

Who? You know who. You. You. You're supposed to be getting better. You don't know what a gift that is. To have a target, to be able to improve. Why don't you think? Or think less? Don't think. Do something! What's happened to you? Like you've been programmed, she says. Like it's a career.

Do what again?

You're a man in a room, she says flatly. A man. In a room.

And from that I'm supposed to?

"A man in a room dot dot dot." It's a beginning, she says. So begin.

Gold Medallions wants to make the most of me. Only a few sessions left and he's pulled out all the stops.

I am read scripts of things that I have told them, recent experiences, neutral, happy, angry, sad:

Getting up in the night, a bad dream
Eggs dressed up for Easter
I go berry-picking
Someone is knocking on my door

Read those back to me, I say.

It isn't part—

Please, I say.

Gold Medallions signals his assistant with the delicate nails. Ready? the assistant asks.

I will keep these scripts running and cross over from one to the other and make between them reliable bridges that I will use. It does not matter where the stories cross over, only that they cross over. I will treat these scripts as raw material, units of action and character and feeling and consequence. Sitting down. Leaving. Egg. Gloves. I will develop from the scripts a grammar of stories, a cell structure I can plug anything into; all I have to do is remember it.

Again, I say, when she is finished. Again again again.

I bite down on a set of wax lips.

Why lips?

Back of a truck, says a Sapphire Band flunky, under her breath.

I am told that I will receive a shock. I lie quietly.

Then—surprise.

We got you a little something, says Sapphire Band.

It's a gateau approximation of my brain. Little flags illustrate the regions and celebrate the neural highlights: peak temporalis, self-healing of the cingulated.

It isn't strictly accurate but it is fondant, he says. And we *are* fondant of you, he says.

General hilarity. A dimming of lights.

We rush the cake, dissecting its moist pinkness like so many sweet-toothed cannibals. I'm on seconds when Sapphire Band leans over to me.

If you don't mind, there's something—

I am jolted by the starkness of it, his feeling like a line of blood.

I can't help you, I tell him. I'm full up—

On the day I am officially discharged the sun is very bright. I sign three separate releases and agree to wear a medical bracelet. Eni escorts me home.

I'm going to drop in on you and surprise you and get up to things, she tells me.

That'll be fine, I say.

The ride is short and the door rattles. The driver's seat has a plastic barrier on which someone has scratched *narc*.

Here, says Eni, after the car has stopped.

In the garden is a chair for me to sit in. Poll has wiped it clean.

Watch out for lemon balm, it grows like the suburbs, she says, returns to a grass basket she is suspending in a birch.

I buy a set of notebooks in different colours and make an index of the stories I am told:

there was a ravine at the house I rarely played in
various hijinks
no nuts are allowed me
will my father come?
I am in a car with Andrew S., a boy who throws up when cornered
I cut out circles and distribute these to my friends. I am very young. Though I have no good explanation of these circles, my friends accept them.
I have notebook after notebook of life drawings, poorly done. Profiles, feet, hands, the backs of backs. Sometimes these include legends I cannot make out.
I run away three times. At eight, fourteen, fifteen.
I arrive at a train station. Night. I climb aboard.

I understand the value of learning these. But I'm not sure what to do with them. Nominate one incident as the beginning, perhaps, another as the end. Puff a little air into them so the sides don't stick together and presto, a sequence that can pass for a story. A man in a room. Rote. I will do it by rote. Like making pastry: roll it over enough times and the edges don't show. We have an idea that there is an infinite divide between lived experience and storytelling and that within this divide is something like the soul. But perhaps this divide isn't unbridgeable after all. Repetition. I will repeat these stories about myself over and over and eventually I will construct a life; a way of being, not seeming.

Open it, says Eni. She hands me a hatbox in an expensive wrapper.

I form my fingers, shovel bluntly at the soft paper until it is a mess of rips and peaks and I have access to its contents: blue, felty, round, one or two folds and a bobble.

It's one of those . . . a beret.

It isn't a beret. It's a hat from Spain.

Well, *gracias*, I say.

The last things I know about him are a mishmash. I know that on the day before he disappeared he shaved all his body but his head and brows in the doorway between his room and the hall, and left a mountain of tricolour hair and applied rubbing alcohol to the irritated skin and spilled most of it on the floor. I know that he stripped the shower head of its silver mail and tied its tubes so no amount of pressure, anywhere in the house, would produce water. It was come as you are. I know the last numbers he dialled. I think there were still options open to him, he may well have waited there, all pinpoint blood and goosebumps, for salvation to arrive in a knock at the door. I know that he stacked soap in oval bricks and tucked it into a box containing candles, shoe polish and Hallowe'en teeth. I know he considered leaving a note. I know his shoes had no laces and he had taken the trouble to spray them with a waterproofer and arranged them neatly in the closet, toes out.

I know that he worked downtown, in a building tall enough to have turret lights for the safety of airplanes. I know he wore his watch on his right hand, and suddenly, on the day he left, on the left. I don't know why he switched. I know that on the day before he disappeared he used a pin soaked in alcohol to let some blood from a finger onto a slide in a schoolboy microscope set that he kept in a wooden chest. And, finally, I know where he went to.

He came here.

THE NEW WORLD

The last time I see Eni I tell her what I know.

Eni is troubled. Fatigue is through her like a steam. Long hours, little relief. Her sister, delivered two months ago of a baby girl round and brief as a decimal point, has grown nervous in her motherhood, comes by incessantly for advice on odd behaviours, raised rashes and effluvia, and in return cooks absent-mindedly for Eni, covered dishes of chicken legs and hammered veal afloat in timid cream sauces.

My composter smells like a banquet hall, Eni says. So it's a nice place, this apartment, she says. Do you like it?

I think: she is trying to leave, she wants to leave. She owes me nothing, fair enough.

There are one or two things I know about him, I say. The man who was here before me.

What does it matter? Of all the things, she says.

I want a record of the way I was: skinwise, nervewise, bonewise. Speechwise. Witwise. Everywise she'll let me have. I want a story to attach to each slick or ragged jarring of the flesh. Each weird growth and aftershock. A story of all of the layers of scar.

I reach for the pad, attach the glasses to the hooks in my skull.

Even if it seems small to you, I say. Even if it seems unimportant. Even if you aren't sure. I know some things, I say. I know one or two things already.

It isn't helpful, she says. This picking at things.

I am not picking, I say. I am . . . *grappling*. Please, I say.

I'm not qualified, she says. Do you know why I came here? In what capacity? As your friend, she says. Your friend.

This should comfort me, matter to me. It will. But right now I am relentless.

Who found me?

Who cares?

I want to know.

What does it matter?

Who found me?

Found you? No one, Eni says. Who do you *think* would find you? Who would take the time? It isn't fair, she says. All of these resources—you'd be ashamed, she says. If you could, you'd be ashamed. Why did we effing *bother*? she says. You're like this excavation, she says. This dig site. You can walk fine, now. You can manage. Why don't you manage? she says.

Here, I say. I open the wardrobe, drag the thing out. What is *this*?

A suitcase, hard-shelled, filthy, red. And inside—

Don't, Eni says.

What was I *doing* with it?

You brought this on yourself; you *courted* it, says Eni. And here we are, she says.

I didn't get to the suitcase for a couple of weeks. It took me most of that night. I had only my spoons and an edger Poll kept for weeds. There were roots to shift, and stones. The thing was deep enough that I mightn't have found it on my own. How had it got there? Fell like a meteor, why not? I found the handle and with more edging and hauling the thing came free. I had no luck with the combo lock, had to take a chisel to it. Strike, strike, and with a tremendous great whinny the lips parted.

Inside the suitcase four layers separated by grey closed-cell foam. Vinyl bones and organs. A spine, a skull, a kidney, an esophagus, a bronchial tree. A hernia, a small intestine, a massive goitre, brown with age, a cancer I will have to look up. A bunch of papers tied with jute tree twine, everywhere bent, stained, torn, burnt, hollowed, the lines cut out, struck through, written over. There is very little of it that has not been interfered with. *It is autumn, September. It is evening. The girl waits*—That is all that is left of the page.

Beneath these curiosities, meticulously reproduced in paint and resin, the body of a man. Seventy inches, fifty-nine years old. Cause of death: suffocation.

A deltoid. A gallstone. A healthy pelvis (male). A wall-hanging nervous system, a scuffed copper brain. And there, at the bottom, still rough and unfinished and on a scale totally different from the rest of the body, the most gorgeous, brittle foot.

I am invited to address a varied group of doctors and explain myself. I am given a chair and a bolted-down table with a tankard of water on it. In this jolly atmosphere I am to answer a few questions.

It is theatrical. Road magic. I oblige. I tell two stories I have memorized in the order I have been taught by Medallions, that impresario of the flash card.

I say: Once there was a man named Reg. Reg's friend had been having a very hard time. Reg thought he might surprise him after work. Reg asked his manager: could he leave early? Unfortunately, he said no. Ask me tomorrow, he said. The next day Reg realized that his aunt's birthday was just around the corner. He'd better get her a present! This time he could go early. When he left work he went to the shops. He found something there he knew his aunt would like. What was it? A small appliance.

Well, that's just remarkable, says someone and my audience severally applaud.

I manage to curl my hands around the glass of water, sputter for a while. There is the usual moment where they must decide whether to endure this spectacle or come to my rescue.

Sometimes I wake and catch my hand at my throat, I tell them. This anarchic hand. Then, a short struggle ensues—the grappling hand and my other, good one. I experience ellipses in which I am several people, several agents, out of time. Vacations from myself. What is it like? I can't tell you what it's like, I say.

I tell the joke about the amnesiac and the record player that took me weeks to get right, and they smile briefly, some of them.

I have another story, I tell them. It's little more complicated. It can go on and on.

For this one, close your eyes, I instruct them. Picture it—

PICTURE IT

I jump from a train. I am on my way to a town in the woods and I guess I can't resist it. There is an elastic quality about the morning, a great trampolining from one moment to the next. I have my red suitcase and inside it my father's bones, his body, that foot. The steward and I discuss the colours of the forest we hurtle through.

I notice trains, all of them. This track, beside us, behind, opposing, carriage after carriage, hands and faces, eyes. I have the impression I have done this before. I mean to throw the suitcase but the suitcase jumps. Then I jump.

I am thinking of this day, this first day, as I stand bored in a station, waiting for a train. The seventh train I'll take today, crisscrossing back and forth my own journey, fretting the path.

The town I am staying in has a memorial to the dead, a length of track in a glass envelope. The track under glass is the actual track, curved like script, wrinkled from the extraordinary heat, huge bolts like popped stems. On a plaque are the names of the dead. Where there are no names a silhouette indicates child, adult, woman, man. Ames to Zane. There is nothing more to see.

THE TRAIN

Seconds away. You check your watch. Brace yourself—now. Where are you? Between carriages, perhaps. Safe in a nick of panelling. The brakes hiss. The iron hinges, heavy and brittle, shear apart. Shocking change of state, iron pulled like taffy. Terror, the terror. Screaming and crying, panic, but also quietness and sighing and staying put—is it resignation? An ascent to grace? The carriages twist and split. Passengers tumble to the back of the car and are ejected or ground up. The rear door springs open, wobbles briefly on its hinge. You step away from it. You walk.

They come from the town, they come with blankets and tools and any working torches—the lights are out at the station's north end, gas valves stopped with creosote or cocoons; fearful, awoken by the vicious noise.

What has happened? cries a woman from her window. What has happened now?

What happens is that at 18:18 the switchman has his hands on the iron lever pulled to break one track arc and create a new one, forcing the slowing train to change direction. The fit between segments must be perfect. The train must slow down for the switching signal. But tonight the switchman, pacing up and down the platform to stay warm in his new boots, is late signalling, has to rush to his position, skinning his right arm on the sharp stone incline. The commuter train speeding from the north, the excursion special groaning along from the west. The brakemen. The inferior iron. Gesticulating vicars, drowsy clerks.

His feet, hot and swollen in these bastard boots, don't support him like they ought. So when he gives in to the sneeze that has been hours in coming, it fells him, topples him right off his feet. Without his weight, the lever wanders back to upright and the tracks break their fragile handshake. The train, slow to decelerate, leans hard to the left; its wheels find the gap between sections of track and it twists like a spring, like a double-helix, engine first, live coals spilling into first class, onto flammable Reid collars, doubling in temperature before leaking into older carriages with windows locked on the outside, tinderwood dividers, feeding on collars, newspapers and decks of oily cards and anything else.

They walk the line and make guesses. In places bodies form a rough mash with the earth. There are fine shoes and filthy bonnets. There is glass in a Bible. One of the chaperones is turned inside out. Even now the final carriage smokes and palls, still too hot to enter.

They come from the town and its outskirts. They wait for the wreck to cool before picking it over with whatever comes to hand, pokers and pitchforks and surveyors' stakes and pointed, elfin shovels. They wade in and pick, delicately, as though it is lobster meat.

It is a play. The train tracks ripped from the stone beds, the posed and covered bodies. The real from the imagined, the living from the dead.

The train, the train. We began with the train, and the condition of the train, the facts of it. Which are: the 16:10 from Cavern to Birkenhead to arrive at 19:04. And then. And then.

The third train, out of service since midnight, September 7, carries mail and a grand piano from a town in the northwest. There is a girl at the station who has been there since last evening, and though he shouldn't the driver lets her on for free. He's got fourteen carriages from coach to first class, a sleeper, an observation car, every one of them clean as a whistle and bare.

My gloves are red, she says.

He thinks about it. Well then, he says. Hop on.

The last train travels between forests, lawn-like pine stands, a broken mouth of birches rotting along their trunks, second-growth shrubbery surrounding. The train slows for the corner, a door opens, a suitcase and then a man. His fall is unpractised, disjointed, his legs and arms come loose and for a moment he is undone, and then his head hits the oily gravel and he slides behind in a long, slow burn. The suitcase, hingeless, opens its mouth, and roars—

Three years have passed and things are different. You are better now. You have other considerations, a whole life to run, with its priorities and incidentals, its loose bits and joints. You get up, walk swiftly through the train you have made and walked through, a hundred times before. Collars and Sunday schools, gamblers and clerks. Engineers dismounting. A door forced open in the middle of the world.

Wait—

And wait. You hear it—the rumbling—the rumbling and the shudder and the iron links that, any second now, will break. The arcing engine, the mis-thrown switch, the pent-up sneeze, the stoker's sideways leap—the train switched off at midnight, the suitcase and the leaping man—these are all still seconds away, and all around you the bodies are blinking, in and out of time. You pass between a mouth and a teacup, a sentence and a full stop. You see the long forward cheeks of the engine, the reflected opposing blaze.

For a moment the trains run side by side, in harness. You have just that long to glance, sideways, into another life.

And then. And then. You leave.

Though even now, you will surprise yourself. In the middle of something you will pause, drop your pencil, rub your chin.

Something's come over me, you'll say, a fleet, darting apology, an upside-down smile—isn't that you all over, a little bit rueful and a little bit scared.

No, you'll say. It's gone—

ACKNOWLEDGMENTS

This book benefitted greatly from the kindness and patience of many who read and commented on its several drafts. Bethany Gibson and Greg Hollingshead spotted and helped solve some early structural problems, while Kelly Dignan and George Toles through notes and conversation provided crucial guidance down the home stretch. Dr Vanessa Warne and Richard Newell, F.R.C.S., lent their expertise concerning medical history and prosthetics. Adam and Emily Muller made all things possible from their Sherburn Street HQ. Special thanks are due my editor, Martha Kanya-Forstner, for her extraordinary insight and patience, and my agent, Anne McDermid, for her grace under all sorts of pressure. Many friends and colleagues supported the writing of this book in ways too numerous to mention here, and I am very grateful to them for the time they took, and for never inquiring too closely. Finally, I would like to thank my family, particularly my wife Victoria, for her great patience, perspicacity and unflagging support, and new arrivals Madoc and Oscar, who will get some of those hours back.

The Canada Council for the Arts provided much-needed time to write in the form of two grants and the Banff Centre's Leighton Studios proved the perfect place to write in. This novel includes found text from a number of sources, most importantly Walker's *Handy Book of Object Lessons* in its revised British version and Greg Hollingshead's "The Roaring Girl," the last line of which appears with variations.

A NOTE ABOUT THE AUTHOR

Struan Sinclair is the author of the acclaimed short story collection *Everything Breathed*. He lives in Winnipeg. *Automatic World* is his first novel.

A NOTE ABOUT THE TYPE

The body of *Automatic World* has been set in Monotype Garamond, a modern font family based on roman types cut by Jean Jannon in 1615. Jannon followed the designs of Claude Garamond, cut a century earlier. Garamond's types were in turn based on the work of Francesco Griffo in the late 15th century. Monotype Garamond's italics are derived from types designed in France circa 1557 by Robert Granjon.